ν

Hayner Public Library District - Alton

W9-BKQ-277

RECEIVED

OCT 1 5 2008

By _____

No Longer the Property of
Hayner Public Library District

HAYNER PUBLIC LIBRARY DISTRICT
ALTON, ILLINOIS

OVERDUES .10 PER DAY. MAXIMUM FINE
COST OF BOOKS. LOST OR DAMAGED BOOKS
ADDITIONAL $5.00 SERVICE CHARGE.

BRANCH

Belle

IN THE

Big Apple

A Novel with Recipes

BROOKE PARKHURST

Scribner

NEW YORK   LONDON   TORONTO   SYDNEY

SCRIBNER
A Division of Simon & Schuster, Inc.
1230 Avenue of the Americas
New York, NY 10020

This book is a work of fiction. Names, characters, places,
and incidents either are products of the author's imagination or
are used fictitiously. Any resemblance to actual events or locales
or persons, living or dead, is entirely coincidental.

Copyright © 2008 by Brooke Parkhurst

All rights reserved, including the right to reproduce this book or
portions thereof in any form whatsoever. For information, address
Scribner Subsidiary Rights Department, 1230 Avenue of the Americas,
New York, NY 10020.

First Scribner hardcover edition September 2008

SCRIBNER and design are registered trademarks of
The Gale Group, Inc., used under license
by Simon & Schuster, Inc., the publisher of this work.

For information about special discounts for bulk purchases,
please contact Simon & Schuster Special Sales:
1-800-456-6798 or business@simonandschuster.com

Designed by Kyoko Watanabe
Text set in Bembo

Manufactured in the United States of America

1   3   5   7   9   10   8   6   4   2

Library of Congress Control Number: 2008026101

ISBN-13: 978-0-7432-9696-0
ISBN-10: 0-7432-9696-6

F
PAR

b18321537

For my mother, my *everything*

And for Jamie.
You cooked for me and then you changed my life.

Belle
IN THE
Big Apple

PROLOGUE

"IS THAT ALL?"

It was an acorn.

If Mamma had ever found herself in such a situation (though I swear on Grandmother's opera pearls she never had the displeasure of such an off-color moment), she would have mitigated the unease, clapped her petite hands together in awe and exclaimed, "A Chinaman! It's a verah, verah smawl Chinaman!"

Yep, an impotent Chinaman, his cap firmly in place.

But it was his pecker. Lord. I sat there on the silk coverlet, heels tucked beneath my ample bottom, staring at the smallest, most flaccid pecker on the planet.

Dear God of all things great and <u>small</u>—how did I get myself here?

Just moments ago Fritz and I had been standing on Sullivan Street, outside <u>my</u> apartment building, <u>my</u> keys firmly in <u>my</u> hand. I knew what I wanted and it wasn't him. But for some reason, I slid in the small jagged key (not the big, smooth one that I loved to run across my cheek) and pressed on the door. Why? I don't know why. I didn't want it to give. We crossed the threshold anyway.

My first Manhattan boyfriend. These are the things you are supposed to do, I tell myself, looking down at the hairs on my thigh, white as birch bark, standing at attention like toy soldiers from the static electricity. I moved my gaze up to his eyes, squeezed shut like a child's, trying to disappear into their own blackness and shame. Suddenly, I wanted to take back the words, dinners (so many dinners), forkfuls, mouthfuls, spoonfuls. . . .

1

I was a twenty-five-year-old commodity who had to face facts: sex with a man his age would be fast, bland, uninspired—I would always be the fresh catch of the day that had been flash-fried instead of slow-roasted. He reminded me of a fisherman out in the Gulf, fighting ten-foot swells and the merciless Florida sun to catch one prize snapper. It's finally on his hook, his aging cronies congratulate him—a gleam of envy in their eyes—he can almost taste the sweet, clean flesh. Problem is, by then, his forty-eight-year-old body is exhausted and just a touch resentful of the damn thing.

Mamma told me twenty-five was the best year of her life, I think, sitting naked on the bed, watching Fritz's body slowly relax after his defeat, his eyelids fluttering open.

"I'm gonna reload and then we'll try again in fifteen, hmmm?" he asked, staring up at me from his pillow with the reverence usually reserved for clergymen and neurosurgeons. His arm reached up for the comfort of my breast. "Three hundred and sixty-five days of glamorous livin'," I liked to tell myself. Since I was a girl, birthday candles served only two purposes—as vehicles for licking Mamma's chocolate buttercream frosting and as a means to subtract from that magic age looming in the future. Twenty-five, twenty-five . . . there was something that made it the year of singular beauty and opportunity. It was supposed to be the time when my profession, my sentiments and my social circle formed a flawless sphere—a shape as perfect as a hen's egg.

I deserved more.

"You know what?" I said, easing myself away from him and off the bed. "I'm hungry." I slipped into the silk kimono he had brought me back from one of his finance trips to Bangkok.

"Hungry? We just had dinner. My God, your appetites, Belle—you always want more!"

He was right—I was never satisfied. New York City had taught me well.

Mamma's Chocolate Buttercream Icing

Sweetness . . . with an edge. Mamma's icing started it all.

ICES A 9-INCH TWO-LAYER CAKE OR 18 CUPCAKES.

2 sticks butter, room temperature
1 large egg yolk, room temperature
6 oz. semisweet chocolate, melted and cooled
1 Tbsp. espresso or instant coffee
1 tsp. vanilla
1¼ c. confectioners' sugar
1 tsp. cinnamon

With a handheld mixer, cream butter and then add egg yolk. Continue by adding melted chocolate and beat well. Add espresso and pour in vanilla, gradually beating in confectioners' sugar until mixture is creamy. Finish by adding cinnamon to frosting and blend.

1

I DIDN'T LIKE not being able to buy strawberries. Blackberries were, of course, totally out of the question. Avocados, peaches and blueberries—never. I supposed that I could no longer afford to eat anything with seeds: the strangeness of it all, in New York City. The roofs somehow grew trees. Husbands and wives sat up there, in the sky, on their chaise longues and patio chairs, reading the daily papers and yellin' into their phones. Lower Fifth Avenue was the best place to gaze upon these rooftop dramas. The old brown-bricked buildings reached up to the sky like aging men trying to capture the importance they once possessed. Distinguished columns, arches and gargoyles garnished the ninth and fifteenth floors. I imagined that the building's inhabitants, like its gargoyles, had sloped foreheads and pointed ears. They must be the ones who could afford to buy iced pomegranate kernels at the corner deli. I certainly couldn't.

I wish I could say that my family had run me out of town or, better yet, that I had run away from something, someone—a miserable engagement, a shrewish mother. That would be delicious and tragic. Who wouldn't want to whisper about that over a finger of whiskey? But the truth is, I moved from Alabama to New York City with notions of a journalism career and an appetite for downtown French bistros and charming, angular men. (Also, I refused to accept the path of least resistance for a well-bred Southern girl halfway into the third decade of her life: marriage and babies.)

I gave myself a deadline of one year. I would have New York City paying me for my personality on paper in twelve months' time. I'd be a star journalist of the above-the-fold, left-hand-column variety. I pictured myself as a hard-hitting (though more right-wing-leaning) Maureen Dowd, delivering bon mots, society news *and* the political beat to America. And if that didn't happen, I mused, I would leave when my Bounty drier sheets ran out. My dream of big-city life and a journalism career would be forgotten and I'd move back home and do something sensible—join the Junior League, start a ladies tennis quadrant. Quite an exit strategy, don't you think? I rationalized that without the drier sheets, there'd be nothing left to soften the hard edges of my clothing, the seams of the city.

Southern families, along with private, Southern universities of the $35,000-a-year variety, don't exactly foster such flair and professional aspirations—quite the opposite. They encourage excellence but only within the environs of our native soil, as my thesis advisor, Dr. Gibson, and our favorite Dixie scribe, Willie Morris, would say. Dr. Gibson saw me as a good, slow-livin' girl although I so terribly wanted to be fast. The Manhattan media whirl beckoned like the tinkling of a carousel's tune and I was enraptured by its sweet song.

At first, I forced myself to turn down the volume. I had to. Everyone was so dedicated to the idea of me and Mobile; I was pledged to the tales of Alabama. A lovely childhood was my promise ring and I had to return to my beau and its quiet heat so I could write about what I knew: the personalities, the routines, life on the Gulf Coast. I resigned myself to stepping into Mamma's well-worn Ferragamo pumps and writing for the only paper in town—the *Mobile Constitution.* For a spell I enjoyed local fame. Doctors, shrimpers, cotillion chaperones—they all loved the easy reading over their morning coffee. My "Eat the Tail, Suck the Head" feature was one of the paper's most popular pieces (mind you, the Interstate Crawdad Festival is big news in those parts). And let's not forget my travel article on the rustic, coastal beauties of Apalachicola. The oyster bed owners were so grateful for my coverage, they anointed me "Queen Bivalve, 2006." I'm not going to lie, small-town celebrity agreed with me. But, damn, I had my sights set on so much more.

Question: Why can't I write like Margaret Mitchell and lead the life of Katherine Mansfield? I, too, wanted to be a great Southern personality who wrote about the big things like love and death, all the while going to the most splendid balls in the most glamorous city in the world.

But no one—including me—had an answer, so I kept my pretenses and ambition tucked away while I continued writing about the little things. Small-town journalism was my birthright, I conceded. Anyway, holiday dinners would have been so difficult if I hadn't taken the job. Granddaddy owned everything in town—including the newspaper.

And then, at age twenty-five, I shocked 'em all. Right when the *Constitution* offered me the position of columnist—and a desk next to Mamma's with my own landline and everything—I made up my mind to head North. Oh, they tried to keep me, all right—they even flew in a man from Atlanta to draw up one of those *Wall Street Journal* pointillism-like sketches to accompany my byline. His rendition of my photo might have been the toughest thing to give up (after all, everyone below the Mason-Dixon line knows that for Southern women, self-love trumps good common sense). In the sketch, I resembled a Dixie Grace Kelly (plus a pound or twenty), what with my blond hair pinned back in a loose chignon, perhaps a bit too much blusher and my smile eager and accommodating. Dead Aunt Maybel's big sapphires sparkled on my earlobes. One moment with my editor, however, and I forgot the vanity project.

"What *are* you doing?" he asked, looking defeated, taking long, slow drags off his Newport Menthol. He stood just inside the paper's back shop, the door frame seeming to sag with his mood and the heat off the printing presses. "There's more to journalism than city council meetings and bottom feeder festivals. Get outta here. Go cover the *real* news."

I took the cigarette from his hand, raised it to my lips and took a good long pull. The mint tickled my throat. I'd heard his lines before but this time they stuck. That was it. Has something like that ever happened to you? A fleeting remark or repeated moment just happens to be the one that finally convinces you to follow your dreams. One pull off a Newport Menthol cigarette and I had made up my mind. New York City: it held more mystery than promise, but that was enough. A faceless foe always excites me more than an intimate friend—that's just the way I am.

So, this is the story of how I—a Southern girl from the Gulf Coast of nowhere—set out to become part of it all, an elegant, colorful piece of the Manhattan media puzzle. How I tried to prove Granddaddy, Mamma and their newspaper wrong, make New York City my city, even if nothing was all good or bad or nearly as lovely and depressed as Joan Didion's essays told me it was going to be. Things would work themselves out, I thought. Life always seemed to have a generous way with me.

2

MOVING DAY AND the morning lay heavy on my skin. I slid my hands into the back pockets of my khaki shorts (remnants of North Carolina college life), threw my shoulders back (practicing good posture for Mamma's sake) and looked out at the new expanse I'd call home. From the front stoop, Sullivan Street stretched before me, a string of redbrick buildings, brightly colored awnings and small ginkgo trees. Ladders and fire escapes on the building's facades crossed and ran together like overgrown honeysuckle vines on a garden trellis. The space was compact, clean—like nothing I had ever seen before.

"You're a new face," the woman said, surprising me with her strange vowels, the sudden jerk and clatter of her metal gate. She expertly raised the rusted links that protected her boutique with one hand while balancing an oversized cup of coffee with the other. As I tried to think of something memorable to say, I felt pearls of sweat slide down my bosoms and finally plummet into the two-pronged front closure of my bra. Large breasts—all that flesh of mine men seemed to love so much—weren't fun in the least, I decided. The weather, however, suited me just fine. With all of New York's anticipated eccentricities, at least the climate was familiar. Being from the Gulf Coast of Alabama, I knew how a slight wind could feel more like damp linen than a refreshing breeze. I had made my peace with sticky sunshine.

"Movin' day," I said brightly, pressing the white cotton T-shirt against my skin, trying to absorb the sweaty mess in my décolleté. We eyed each other and she roundly declared victory. She was devastatingly chic. I had never seen that kind of sophistication off the pages of *Town & Country*. She was a citified goddess meant for the magazines or a white-carpeted salon, champagne flute in hand. Fudging the lines of politesse and decorum, I stared a good sixty seconds at her thick, auburn hair pulled into an elegant bun. The simple hairdo sharply contrasted with the complexities of her linen ensemble, its series of knots, twists and ties confounding me at eight o'clock in the morning. The mannequins in the store window were dressed just like her. A wooden sign embossed with gold letters hung on the cast-iron arm above us. TWISTED, it said, the sign presumably addressing the style of clothing and not the owner.

She busied herself with keys and padlocks while I silently promised away my firstborn if only the moving men would show up before morning rush hour. I desperately wanted to be comfortable and settled in my new surroundings. Shop Lady smelled my foreignness. I do believe if I had looked closely enough, I could have seen her nostrils twitching. She wasn't unkind, mind you, but I could tell that she had put me on the shelf until a later date. She decided not to pick me, but to leave me hanging on the tree until I was a ripe little fig, bursting with city experiences and heartbreak. *Then* we would be friends.

"My name is Lisa," she said with a nod of her head and a pronounced British accent. "And would they be yours?" she asked, casting a glance across Sullivan.

Even in the hushed humidity of the early morning, I hadn't heard the movers, their clunky shoes falling silent on the asphalt. The two twenty-somethings stumbled my way from across the street, looking more like overgrown adolescents than the burly moving men that I had expected. They were a lesson in opposites: one was tall, wiry, and hesitant in his gait while the other was short, proudly led by a big, soft belly. I tried to remember their ad on craigslist:

Need Fast Cash
No Job Too Small, Too Large
Anything South of 14th St, North of Canal

Beer money, date money—hell, I didn't know. I was just cutting the guys a check to drive a van to a place called Port Authority, pick up the outsized, oak-wood farmhouse furniture that Granddaddy had shipped up and unload it into my apartment.

"Morning, uh . . ." The tall one lifted the bill of his cap to get a better look at the tattered piece of paper he held in his palm. ". . . uh, Bellelee?" he said, merging my first and last name in a slur of consonants, pronouncing them without their familiar molasses coating. His pale, lean face, deep-set eyes and wiry frame made me think of a childhood spent on cement playgrounds, syringes poppin' out of public trash cans. He was young and just short of being a tragedy. "I'm Bryan and this is my buddy Shreve and, uh, yeah, so we're your movers." He kicked the pavement with his scuffed sneakers like a five-year-old boy, embarrassed by the dozen or so words he had strung together. "Gonna get in the van with us and head uptown to pick up your stuff or you stayin' here?"

"Save yourself—he's a bastard behind the wheel," Shreve said, chuckling, fumbling around in the side pockets of his jeans. Everything about him was round except for his smile; it was a thin line beneath a pug, ruddy nose. Jet black hair poked out from beneath his baseball hat. I suspected his daddy hadn't cut that hair in the kitchen sink for a good, long while.

"I thought y'all already *had* the furniture," I said, feeling my temper rise with the August heat.

"Nope, we just got up—"

"No worries," Shreve said, looking at me and then staring down his friend. "You just hang out, crank the AC on high and we'll be back in about an hour or so." He finally pulled a crumpled cigarette from his jeans pocket, looking at it proudly—his piece of urban lost treasure.

These were the guys that I was entrusting with the family antiques? I panicked and then called to mind every Southern man's weakness, hoping that their Yankee counterparts could be as easily bribed.

"I'll make sure to have lunch waitin' whenever y'all get back. Either one of you ever tried a Virginia ham?" Zeola, our maid, had stuffed my carry-on luggage with what seemed to be a side of a Virginia smoked hog. A few sliced ham sandwiches and sweetened iced tea and the boys would be putty in my hands.

"I'm from L.A., he's from the Bronx," Shreve said through tensed lips, trying to draw out the first drag of nicotine. "We don't see—or taste—much of anything from down there."

Damn it to hell. I had honed my swine and sweetened water act since puberty. What next? Would they think blond hair and lipstick were vulgar? I was tempted to tell him not to be so indignant, that the tobacco he was suckin' on came from the fields of R. J. Reynolds in North Carolina. But I held my tongue and smiled and waved them off with a packing slip and the promise of a good meal.

"We're gonna make you easy on the eyes," I said, walking into the new apartment. I had spent the previous day, my first in the city, mixing paint, trying to replicate the soft brown color of a New Orleans chicory café au lait. I wasn't too far off—after two coats, the walls were finally beginning to look this side of mocha. The southeast-facing kitchen windows saved it all from looking too dark. Light poured in, gold and ivory hues skipping across the polished hardwood floor.

Craigslist (my Wal-Mart of the Web) claimed that my little nook was a cross between a studio and a railroad flat because of its width and the size of the kitchenette, set to the back, overlooking my private garden (a "garden" on the island of Manhattan apparently meaning two trees, a crumbling redbrick ledge and a tumble of ivy). To the side of the bathroom was a small alcove meant to be a workspace though I couldn't see myself doing much of anything in there because it was so dark. The kitchen, with its windows and warmth, would be my center, just like back home.

It was all real sweet but I still couldn't believe that Granddaddy was paying $1,700 a month for me to live in a room the size of his toolshed. He kept fish food, standing lawn mowers, a tractor and the cousins' hunting rifles in his space, while I was going to carry out a life—eat, sleep, love, write, entertain—in mine. Yep, it was uncivil but I had to have it.

Lord, the heat . . . Temperatures like that always played a steady buzzing tune in my ear. It was an intoxicating mix—the rising mercury, shellacked floors smelling of astringent and pine, paint fumes, moving day jitters—that held me still in the middle of the apartment. I knew that I needed to walk over to the window unit and turn the air on high, just like the city movin' boys had told me to do, but I couldn't. If that motor got going, air pouring out, I'd get a drip in the back of my throat and neither Mamma nor Granddaddy would be there to mix me up a nighttime toddy of cognac and fresh lemon juice to make it go away.

Note: Mamma playin' doctor meant a swan dive into the liquor cabinet. She liked feeling helpful and I liked getting warm and tipsy. Fallin' ill was something to look forward to in our household. Unfortunately, the hangover usually proved more intense than the initial malady.

Right then I sunk down on the old mattress that some dirty soul had left behind. On the floor, things were better, my ears quieted down. I forgot about the big ham sweating in my purse and the hot neighborhood just outside. All I thought about was Granddaddy.

"Belle's the only one with any sense in this goddamned family!" Granddaddy bellowed to no one in particular. A turtle's head popped up from the freshwater shallows of the lake, heavy, concentric circles marking its appearance. "Come and sit over here by your old granddaddy," he said, motioning to the empty space next to him on the deck swing. I picked up the ridged Folgers coffee canister of fish food and sat down slowly, careful not to spill the brown pellets.

"You're doin' real well down at the newspaper, darlin.' Good thing because there isn't another goddamned thing that you're qualified to do, no suh. . . ." His voice trailed off and he took a sip of scotch. He extended the glass in my direction, but I wasn't thirsty. With me, Granddaddy was frank: he treated me like a man. "I think you should keep on, show these bastards how it's done. Keep pluggin' away and in another ten, fifteen years I'll make you editor-in-chief. How would you like that?"

I didn't look at him. We faced the lake and I drifted upward into the moist, twilight air and—just for a moment—I suspended disbelief and worries and everyday life. Then I came back down, the balls of my feet touching the wooden deck. I wanted to push back up, I wanted to push both of us back up.

"I want you to spell 'parallel' for me," he said, a smooth palm now resting on my forearm.

"Granddaddy, I know how to spell and I know that I could keep on writing for you but I'm moving. I've made up my mind." I looked over and his eyes were fixed on nothing and I pushed us back up because he was too old and too distracted to do the practical things anymore.

"I said, spell the word 'parallel.'"

"P-a-r-a-l-l-e-l."

"You're goin' to be the youngest editor that joint has ever seen." He grinned, genuinely pleased, punching the air with his index finger. "They all misspell 'parallel'—my reporters, editors, the boys in the back shop—"

"I'm moving to New York City," I said flatly.

Granddaddy stopped the swing. The oak tree and its curtain of moss above us stopped moving. I felt dizzy.

"Let me tell you a little something about this place you're so anxious to leave," he began, pacing his speech and temper. "We're twelve hundred miles south of Park Avenue for a reason. I decided to establish my family in this town because your granddaddy likes being the boss, likes doing as he pleases.

"I see you at the paper and you're the same way. I've always given you what you wanted, when you wanted it. Maybe your ol' granddaddy's a patsy, I don't know. But, I can't keep on. If you go up there and leave me and the paper, things are going to get real hard, darlin.' I won't be able to help you."

"Don't treat me like a girl," I said.

"Damn it, Belle, you can't just pick up and move away!"

He had a way of presenting the modern-day American South as if it were nineteenth-century Gallic society—albeit a bastardized version. For Granddaddy, it wasn't just the pace of life or the rhythm of speech, but the social structure. Money wasn't so much earned as it was inherited. Down there, wealth wasn't acquired through brilliant ideas—it was maintained in estates and property. Staying in his good graces would be far more lucrative than chasing a dream up North.

And maybe he was right. If I were outside this skin, I might have realized that a Southern girl in my position was loony for looking toward New York City and ways so foreign. Trusting—never testing—myself and the demigods of the South had yielded returns as great as any. Live? Try? Fail? Nah. Life as I had known it was one gloriously long second act filled with promise. Granddaddy and the ushers (important men firmly tucked in his back pocket) had always assured me that the audience would clear out before the third act, right before this girl blessed with a touch of attitude and cursed with an ego far surpassing her accomplishments actually had to prove herself. Limitless potential makes for easy livin'.

"Belle, goddamnit, what are you going to do? How are you going to get a job, earn a living?" Granddaddy said, this time his voice betraying more concern than anger. "I'd try to give you a name or two but they all died on me, all my contacts are dead. That's what happens when you get to be my age."

"I'm sure I'll find something," I said, trying to reassure both Granddaddy and myself. He went on, not paying me any attention.

"There's only one but, no suh . . . he's all about the buck, nothin' about the news," he said to no one, taking a long, slow sip from his glass. I gave him his first job—Christopher Randolph was the youngest beat reporter I ever hired—and now he's up at American News Channel, right-hand fool to Robert Cleveland, the big news director."

I liked when Granddaddy said "fool"; he made the word long and lingering so you really understood.

"I'm not quite sure how Chris came up in the ranks—from editorial page of the Grey Lady to CNN, somethin' like that. Flip-floppin' from a good ol' Southern Democrat to a bleedin' heart liberal, finishing off as a crazed conservative at the American News Channel. Can you imagine, in good conscience, livin' like that?"

"The sun's leavin' us," I said, knowing better than to press the subject.

"What are these boys after, the immoral bottom dollar?"

"Why don't we feed your fish before it's too late?" I put the canister to the side of the swing and stood in front of Granddaddy, giving him my hands and forearms for balance. Our arms twisted together as only the young and old can manage to do and he pulled himself up to a standing position. I looked into those eyes, so full of quiet, blue secrets, and recognized that he was everything.

He surveyed the water. "Now, I want you to look out for Nathan. He comes runnin' when he knows there's food. Yep, there he is—oldest, fattest bass in my lake. Greedy bastard, isn't he? You know, I named him after that bloodsuckin' lawyer uncle of mine. . . . Comes around at feedin' time." Pappy scattered the fish food, wrist bent, fingers pointed in: for a moment, he was the King of Mardi Gras tossing chocolate and gold-foiled coins to the crowd.

"You'll always be here, won't you, Nathan? No place for you to go, no one else to tend to you. . . ." Pappy said softly. He tossed the ridged, metal canister into the grass and then reached for my hand. Together, we watched the last of the bass swim from the clear shallows into the deep green of the distant lake water.

The sound of rubber-soled work boots echoed in the hallway, jolting me out of my dreams and back into the godforsaken heat. Voices bounced off the linoleum floor and into my apartment. "What's going on out there?" I asked, brushing myself off, and like any sane Southern girl, instinctively reached for a tube of lipstick.

"Come and see for yourself," Shreve yelled.

When I got outside, I saw her lying there naked on the dirty sidewalk—she was pitiful. Without box springs, mattress or sheets, Grandmother's sleigh bed sat there exposed before the entire neighborhood. I wanted to throw a blanket around the legs and underbelly but everything was packed away in boxes. She was so big and inappropriate. She wouldn't fit through the front door.

"Wrong stuff?" Shreve said breathlessly, palms resting on his lower back. I thought that the posture made him look like a decaying, resentful old woman. "None of this is going to fit into a studio apartment, I can tell you that," he said, shaking his head from side to side.

I stared down at the cement and tasted salt. "Take her apart," I said, trying for a mild and steady tone, wiping away the tears.

"If something happens—"

"Just do like I say. Break her up into parts and bring the pieces into my apartment. I'll put her back together when I find the time," I said quickly. "And keep on with the rest of the furniture. Looks like we're gonna get crowded here come noontime," I said, eyeing the delivery trucks pouring onto Sullivan.

Before I walked back inside, I forced myself to look up and out at the place I'd call home. There was a church, butcher shop, bakery, furniture store, French restaurant, Laundromat and store dedicated to mozzarella balls and nothing else. I could wake up, buy a cup of coffee, furnish my apartment, eat fancy French food, get married and die and still not venture beyond my block. A Billy Joel tune fought its way into my head.

> *Sergeant O'Leary is walking the beat,*
> *At night he becomes a bartender.*

I knew the song mentioned something about him working at Mr. Cacciatore's on Sullivan Street by the medical center. And one day I'd find that restaurant and take Mamma there for dinner. She'd begin to understand why I had moved. We'd have spaghetti and casks of red wine and I would put down a piece of plastic when the bill arrived. "No, Mamma—I insist. This is my city and I'm treating," I'd say. She'd love that my street was in a song by Christie Brinkley's ex-husband. Christie's exercise tapes were her favorites.

"Looks like we got ourselves an audience," Bryan said.

A young man stood several yards away watching the scenario unfold. Town cars with tinted windows and sports cars with important drivers formed a line down the block as a kitchen table and settee were transported, assembly-line style, across the street. The sound of car horns bounded from building to building and shot back to me like a boomerang, the noise returning to its rightful owner. The man didn't say a word. Lisa stood in her store window, staring, coffee mug in hand. Several floors above me a window slammed. No one spoke to me.

I didn't understand the paradox of city living. The coexistence of intimacy and anonymity was something I had never experienced. Homes rested atop businesses while coffee shops and liquor stores flanked either side of St. Anthony's Church. Life and all its motions were condensed to such a compact area that anonymity was a gift from your neighbors. They had to look the other way—feign ignorance or otherwise—and you would be expected to do the same. Back home everyone knew my business, but only because we frequented the same tea and coffee hour after the ten-thirty Episcopal service. We repented our own sins only to turn and promptly discuss the sins of others. When two lakes and a hunting camp separate you from your nearest neighbors, casual run-ins aren't possible.

Damn us! Mamma and I were stubborn broads. She should have been there to help me. She could tell me exactly what to do and how to think and, for once, I would listen. Egos and bylines could be left down at the paper and it'd just be us again. But she had refused to come to the city. She claimed she had to help Zeola prepare a luncheon for her Pentecostal church. Really, though, I knew she was scared—frightened of the city and what it implied and how it would change her simple girl.

"This is Zeola," a rich, sad voice greeted me as I clutched the phone, wondering why I had acted on my impulse to call.

"It's Belle. Is Mamma around?" I said, trying not to sound too amused by the proprietary phone greeting. Zeola could never bring herself to announce it was someone else's household. Really, I didn't blame her—she ran the joint. Mamma was always investigating some political fiasco in Montgomery for her Sunday op-ed or running off to shoot a spot on *Scarborough Country* and Daddy . . . well, Daddy liked the high seas, open fields and bottles of anything dark and expensive. And he liked his phone answered formally. I was glad he hadn't called and heard her.

"Miss Belle? Is that *really* you?" I could just see the whites of her eyes growing bigger. "The connection's so good I'd think you're right here at the stove with us," she continued.

"I'm in New York City!" I shouted, unaccustomed to the dimensions of the tiny cell phone. Technology-wise, the family and I were stuck somewhere between aforementioned ridged Folgers cans connected by string and a town switchboard. Only after Mamma read about the "Preppy Murder" and watched *American Psycho* on TBS did she realize that Osama was not the only evil force at large in the city; she quickly purchased me a cell phone. "I just wanted to check up on y'all while the movers unload my furniture. New York, can you believe it?" I realized I was trying desperately to fit "New York" into every sentence—I had to remind everyone, including myself, of my whereabouts.

"I didn't think your granddaddy would ever let go of you," Zeola said, her accent slow buttermilk coating every word. She lowered her voice. "What are you doing up there with all those son-of-a-bitch, city-slickin' Yankees?"

"Oh, Zeola . . ."

The guys began stacking boxes of clothes, linens and books against the far right wall. I grew nervous thinking about the china and silverware that had yet to be unpacked.

"Listen, I promise to call back and talk all about it but can I just speak to Mamma for one minute?"

"Lands above, we worry about you!" Zeola had adopted the urgent, strained tone that adults use when chastising loud children inside the local cineplex. "I'm telling you all this now because Miss Nelda can't hear me but I just *know* she cries herself to sleep at night thinkin' of you up there."

Such phone conversations with Zeola and Mamma warranted full days of beauty and booze at Elizabeth Arden—rubdown, scalp massage, Jack Daniel's in lieu of green tea in one of those Oriental clay pots.

"Why'd you go and do something like that? You might as well be in Chinee instead of living in New York Ci—"

"Zeola, for Lord's sake, put Mother on the phone."

"Well, I don't know if your mamma can make it to the phone on account of the bacon grease that's popping in the skillet but, being the good Christian that I am, and seeing that I need myself another grape soda, I'll just go on back in the kitchen and see."

Zeola was angry. I was angry. Mamma would soon be angry. Marvelous how even long distance, we could all get worked up in a matter of minutes.

"It's Belle you've been talking to for all that time?" Mamma called out in the distance. "Lord, look who's running up my phone bill—hand me that!"

Frying bacon for charity always put her in a bad mood.

"Belle, is that you?"

"Hi there, Mamma. I just wanted to see how everyone was getting along down there." I could see that now was not the time to talk about fresh mozzarella or the landscape of the neighborhood.

"Are you all right? You haven't been mugged yet? What about the Arabs? There aren't any stockbrokers in your apartment, are there? Were those gunshots?"

"Those are the movers, Mamma. Remember? Today is moving day." She was still fighting to believe that I'd be home any moment, that the move had been a foolish whim and I would soon admit defeat. "Anyway, how are *you* doing?" The little discretion that I possessed encouraged me to make small talk instead of speaking my mind. Mamma, I'm *your* blood, I wanted to say. But *my* guts made me move and pursue a dream. Now can't you just help me navigate this thing that is uniquely and completely my own?

"Oh, darlin,' we're fine, just fine. I'm settlin' in to fry about five pounds of bacon for the seven-layer salad I'm makin'. Zeola says her church will just love it. I've already whipped the mayonnaise, done the lettuce, grated the cheese . . ."

As she listed the different ingredients, I stopped paying attention. I'd always preferred to watch Mamma, to see her delicate fingers and long, naked fingernails move over a tabletop, run in and out of her short blond hair, smooth down the bedcovers, hold a pencil—all of it extraordinary. Right then, I imagined those fingers readjusting her shower cap as she stood over the stove. Mamma only fried bacon when she had a noontime appointment to get her hair foiled and an afternoon meeting with the executive editor. Even still she wore a shower cap to protect her hair. She claimed that the grease just sat on her follicles otherwise.

Mamma kept on so I turned to face the movers. Aside from the bed, Granddaddy had shipped up a kitchen table and chairs, damask settee and leather ottoman. Everything was too wide, clumsy, proud. The pieces were gorgeous but awkward.

"Nothing fits," I muttered.

"What, darlin'?" she asked sweetly, cutting short her laundry list of artery-clogging ingredients.

"I'm just lookin' at all this stuff—"

"Lawd!" she shouted into the phone. "Zeola, you mean to tell me that you think that hunk of pig is done? You mean to tell me that all of the germs have been cooked out, there are no more trichinosis running around—you would serve that to one of your grandbabies?"

"Mamma, please. You're shouting in *my* ear, not Zeola's."

Growing up, her greatest fear was that my sister, Virginia, and I would die of either trichinosis or asphyxiation.

"I have to run. Wish that you were here to help . . . and, maybe," I hesitated, "give me a little bit of advice." Mamma had been the only working woman in the Mobile Country Club set. She had done it all, conquering small-town living like I wanted to rule New York City. And now I was starting out with nothing. I would have given anything for her guidance.

"Letting you go was my sacrifice—"

I clicked off.

Butter her up and then cut her off—I was becoming a card-carrying New Yorker already.

Seven-Layer Salad

Once her shower cap is firmly in place, Mamma is a bacon-fryin' fool. After hearing her at the stove, making this salad with Zeola, I ran right out and bought all the ingredients at the corner deli. See? From the get-go I was different from the city girls—my oven did not double as a shoe-rack and I believed in full, proper meals. And with the rest of the Pyrex pan I tried to make friends, leaving paper plates mounded high with the salad on my neighbors' doorsteps. I explained that I was the new girl, Garden Apartment.

SERVES 8, GENEROUSLY.

- 1 head iceberg lettuce, chopped
- ⅓ c. green pepper, diced
- ⅓ c. green onion, green and white part, diced
- ⅓ c. frozen peas
- ½ c. mayonnaise
- 1 Tbsp. sugar
- 1 c. sharp Cheddar cheese, grated
- 7 pieces bacon, fried until crisp, crumbled

In a 13x9x2-inch pan, evenly spread iceberg. Top with the green pepper, follow with green onion and then the frozen peas. Top with mayo, spreading it with a knife in a thin layer over the frozen peas. Sprinkle with sugar. Follow by adding the sharp Cheddar cheese and then, the pièce de résistance, the bacon.

Cover and refrigerate for at least one hour.

3

BY NIGHTFALL, the movers had left me. I had nothing to do but watch the summer storm rage on in the gray, city night lit by apartment buildings and streetlights. I supposed I would never again gaze on a peaceful, black sky. All those people, their energy, that noise, just kept on regardless of the hour. I sat Indian-style on the hardwood floor, propped up by table legs, cushions, bed linens, and rummaged through all the boxes. I didn't unpack, mind you, I rummaged. Within a half hour's time, I'd made myself a fine mess. But, in that chaos—in the muddle of furniture parts and pieces of my life—I found it.

The leather journal bore my initials—*BGL*—like all the ridiculous debutante gifts before it. I ran my fingers over the cover, pressing down on the gold-leaf letters. A thin, red silk ribbon marked my last entry. Months had passed since I had written about the simple things. But I knew that my New York City story had to begin somewhere and that I might as well be good and earnest from the start.

Heat lightning flashed outside, trying to explain the skyline to me. But it failed or I failed and all that seemed to exist out there were the burglar bars on the window. I didn't know whether I felt safe or sad cowering behind them, whether I had become a prized parakeet or a redneck pawnshop owner, what with the thick, cast-iron bars obstructing my view of the outside world. And so I sat there and wrote about my first solitary summer evening in the city, about my old world—the South and its pieces—that had been thrown away so I could fit into a new life, about the family antiques wasting away out in front of the building—the rain slipping down the red bricks, sliding off the windowpanes, soaking the curb. My pen glided across the page recording what had taken place and what I hoped was to come.

Was I just navel-gazing? I hoped not. It felt too damn good. It felt important. Writing about my life for its own sake, instead of for Granddaddy and his newspaper, filled me up, it completed my day. My life transcribed on paper began to satisfy the void that a good glass of whiskey or a deep kiss couldn't. And thank God I didn't yet know about those adult toy stores on Sixth Avenue and Mercer; I'd soon learn that masturbation was the next best thing to writing a good, honest paragraph. Oh, but I can't go saying things like that—the first thirty pages of my life on paper shouldn't be so sexy. An extraordinary climax takes time.

So I'll just sit down and write . . .

4

FRIDAY MORNING, 8:03 A.M., I found evidence of Mamma on my front stoop. I'd been in the city a mere fourteen days and there sat her mighty will, stacked in a neat pile outside the building's front door: the *Wall Street Journal, New York Sun* and *New York Post*. A thick rubber band girded the bundle of right-wing rag sheets. Without telling me, she had signed me up for home delivery of the only papers that embraced her rabid conservative views and Bible Belt ideology. The *Post* subscription, with its bold, seventy-two-point declarations of Hollywood fornication and government corruption, could be interpreted as Mamma's belated admission that I had become an adult. It was like the time she called me on a whim at college and shouted into the receiver, "Use foam and a rubber!" and promptly hung up. Before that we had never discussed the possibility of premarital sex—much less the various forms of contraception—for an altar girl from the rural South.

Too many thoughts too early—I needed to get back inside and have myself a cup of coffee. And, yes, *I* would be making it. I couldn't get into the whole Starbucks phenomenon. A girl has to save her money and spend it on the important things. Diamonds, for instance. With the price tag of Brazilian eco-beans and fancy whipped toppings, it was no wonder that the Yankee women wore little more than tiny gold hoops and colored chips for jewelry. Those fancy drinks would be the end of their bank accounts *and* their femininity.

"Brew the best beans you can find. Fill cup with three-fourths coffee, one-fourth cream, two teaspoons raw sugar; the ratio of bitter to cream to sweet is very important," I recited quietly, listening out for Zeola's feet shuffling behind me. I wanted another morning with her in that big, darkened kitchen. She fashioned slippers with her size 13 feet—pink, cracked heels squashing the back ends of shoes. When it was just the two of us—Mamma locked away, bangin' on her typewriter, the rest still asleep—she didn't lift those heels, she shuffled. I knew her dance. I missed those god-awful big feet.

But the apartment was silent and I was alone, making my own coffee and stepping out to collect the morning papers. I supposed that I would also have to fasten my own pearl necklace and zip up my dress, elbows flailing, neck twisted toward the mirror. How was it that I felt independent and pitiful all at once? Both sentiments were absurd: I wasn't paying the rent, therefore I wasn't self-sufficient, yet, I had just fulfilled one of my greatest dreams by moving here despite my family's disapproval. If New York was a city of immigrants (I believe F. Scott Fitzgerald said that no one is *really* from here), did everyone new to Manhattan feel this way?

I settled back down onto the floor covered with black and white newsprint and grabbed a handful of headlines. Presidential candidates and movie stars; economists and artists; society ladies and Wall Street wizards, they all stared up at me. I should be interviewing those people; I should be telling their stories. And for the first time, a woman was running for president. I was achin' to tell her story. But how? If I couldn't find a way to fasten my own dress, how could I land a journalism gig in the most competitive media market in the world?

Remnants of my desperate two-week quest to define myself as something in New York City were scattered about. I had faxed and hand-delivered résumé packages to just about every legitimate magazine and newspaper in town. Unfortunately, my life transcribed on paper boasted nothing more than internships, trips abroad and my writing gig at the family paper (and, yes, ma'am, even I knew that the latter shouted nothing more than nepotism with a dash of talent).

Pride laced with panic, that's what I felt.

I picked up one of the classified ads and laid it across my upturned palms like I would a Bible. With my eyes tightly shut, I pressed my nose and lips to the almost translucent, gray slip of paper. The scent of the newsprint thrilled me just as it had when I was a girl, hoisted on Granddaddy's hip, taking a tour of the back shop while Mamma finished her day's column.

Young men, old men, black men, white men, self-proclaimed Gulf Coast crackers worked side by side in that hangar space of flickering orange light and deafening noise. They hunched over the monstrous printing presses, smeared in ink, sweat dropping from the tips of their noses. Limp cigarettes dangled from thin, colorless lips. As we walked around the periphery of the machines, he mouthed to me, "No rules," wagging his index finger in my face like a Broadway stage actor. My five-year-old perceptions of his words made that cavernous expanse of cement a sort of Willie Wonka Chocolate Factory of whimsy and possibility. I thought Granddaddy rolled out cotton candy machines during the midnight shift while Mamma dealt the deck for a rousing game of Go Fish. Chocolate milk spurted from water fountains. The association of newspapers with fantasy and otherworldliness is a strange one because we all know there isn't another profession so grounded in the day-to-day. Yet somehow the visions held fast. The fantasy remained.

The news business had always been a type of sustenance for me, a steady supply of nourishment and fulfillment. I didn't just like it—I *had* to have it. Destiny: maybe that was the word I couldn't quite get my tongue around. I smelled the newsprint and swallowed.

5

MY LIFE WENT and fixed itself on the subway. Of course, this was only *after* I assembled my Underground Beauty Survival Kit. The plasticized makeup bag festooned with pink powder puffs and rosebuds held a carefully edited selection of grooming products. Murray's Hair-Glo Pomade, mini Colgate, velcro rollers, Purell, and industrial-strength tweezers would ensure that I look and feel presentable after any sustained length of time on public transportation (fly-aways, midmorning coffee breath and ingrown hairs on my bottom just wouldn't do).

The job predicament I've been yammering about went from having bloodshot eyes and fangs to being as digestible as a weevil on a flake of Kellogg's ("Go on, now—eat it. Nuthin' wrong with a lil' extrh protein," Zeola used to scold me, hands on hips, hovering over my cereal bowl).

I'll explain.

Earlier in the day, the heat had broken suddenly and unexpectedly, the cool morning begging me to slip into Mamma's vintage tea-length Burberry coat and cream-colored kitten heels. I had it in me to take on Sixth Avenue one last time, résumé in hand. And so I went and I nodded and I smiled at security guards and polyester secretaries, entrusting them with my life-in-a-manila-envelope as if my task were an easy and thoroughly enjoyable one. But wearing heels and a smile all day for strangers was hard.

All those factoids and bullet points that would determine my future,

I deposited like a warm bundle of tea cakes, something that would delight and please them and "Oh, it's just sugar, flour and buttermilk— take one!" But the office drones were otherwise occupied. I was not nearly as important as their keyboards, cell phones and Lee Press On Nails stained with last night's supper. No one so much as winked in my direction. Not even the clipping of my exclusive interview with the right-wing Baptist minister—the holy roller held his congregation hostage until they tithed—elicited a laugh or an intercom buzz into the upper floors. I do believe many of the envelopes (my life!) went straight into the trash. Naturally, I got to fantasizin' of ways to teach them a lesson. . . .

Soon enough, important and wearing some serious St. John on my way to have luncheon with Cindy Adams, I'd deliver them a surprise. Special delivery, Ms. Secretary and Mr. Rent-a-Cop—flaming poop! They'd sit up and take notice then, wouldn't they? As long as I could manage a hundred-yard dash in Ferragamo heels out of the building and into the sidewalk milieu, I was game. Daddy would support my symbolic gesture. He claimed that all Yankees were nothing more than a bunch of turds and as a graduate of Sewanee University—a fraternity with lecture halls high up in the Tennessee Mountains—he knew a thing or two about practical jokes. This fantasy of mine was wholly appropriate.

So cruel on the avenue. Ten o'clock, that Neverland of Midtown Manhattan morning when anything seems possible: efficient janitors and busboys hose down their patch of sidewalk; short-order cooks yell eggs every which way; taxi exhaust mingles with Aqua Net, garbage and the scent of the woodsy cologne of the rich. Life seemed extraordinary—for everyone but me. The sun showered New York City with rays of opportunity and hope, which burrowed deep in between the coarse blond hairs on my scalp and made me itch. The midmorning bounce escaped me at the precise moment everyone else felt the caffeine kicking in or saw their bank accounts swell from big-city capitalism. I hated my moments on the sidewalk with all the busy people. Avenue of the Americas, Times Square, Grand Central and their mess of delis and coffee shops emitted a din of purpose that mocked me.

You have to be in a mode, I quickly learned, armed with something that will get you through another day in Manhattan. The commuters that rushed by me had something of consequence in hand: a ringing cell phone, a crying baby, a shiny leather bag stuffed to bursting with documents that just might change the world. My ego needed me to have these things . . . and more than all the rest.

Time for my debut voyage on the subway.

Hsssss. Stepping down onto the Grand Central platform, I watched as the shiny doors opened and disgorged passengers into the dank, subterranean air. It was as if a steel artery had burst and the lifeblood of the city were rushing toward me, surrounding me in a hot, red pool of angst and excitement. Until that point, I had abstained from taking underground transit as a means to appease Mamma. Sure, I could have lied but she had extrasensory perception and I knew that she'd catch me taking the number 6 train while she was standing at the stove. The hot oil would be shimmering in the skillet and Mamma could just make out my figure being pickpocketed by a corrupt youth. She was all-knowing.

"*This* is New York," I said aloud, blinking my eyes at the feverish bodies, their purpose, our collective sneeze-inducing dirt. Total disclosure. Mamma, you watching and listening? Because I want to touch it: the blue suits leaping up the exit steps two at a time, a mariachi band strumming guitars and extending sombreros for quarters and crisp, green gringo bills, strollers being hoisted up in the air—the tiny babies maharajas of the number 6 train exodus. I saw head wraps, tight sweaters, garbage bags carried over shoulders like Santa Claus's Christmas booty, black boys selling bags of M&M's, folds of fat squeezed into tight blue jeans. We walked past each other, tragedies brushing against tragedies, each of us going our separate ways never to meet again.

"This is a Bronx-bound local six train," a woman's husky voice announced as I stepped into the subway car. It sounded as if city officials had mechanized Kathleen Turner's voice and in a moment of propriety, stifled the throaty seduction with one of those FBI witness protection voice synthesizers. This all fascinated me. I wanted to know more and hear more and maybe, just maybe I'd take the train all the way around the island just so I could listen to her announcements. "Next stop, Fifty-first Street."

Suddenly, the artery sealed and I was thrown onto a blue plastic bench seat as we lurched forward into the black belly of Manhattan.

Breathe.

Right hand: make sign of cross as we trundle into Hades.

Left hand: clutch brown bakery bag filled with résumés.

Pray last night's lemon square crumbs are not affixed to today's curriculum vitae.

Bite inside of cheek and *do not* cry.

Remember luxury of scooting around town in Grandmother's convertible Caddy.

Happy, Mamma?

Avoid eye conta . . . Wait a minute. What—*who*—was that? Just as I had sworn off kindness of spirit and goodwill toward men (all in an attempt to become Manhattan's most popular media personality; brilliant, huh?), I looked across the aisle. A pair of hand-tooled, brown cowboy boots and dark, denim legs were directly in front of me, spread as wide as the backend of a set of pliers. I could see a thick crop of dirty blond hair while the rest of his face was hidden by the morning newspaper.

"I wonder if the view from the Top of the Rock can beat that," I said, trying not to look between his legs.

Had I just said that out loud? Dagblastit! No, no, *no,* Belle. Horny editorializing will get you nowhere.

Journalism 101: Find the facts, make the material relevant, create a fine lead, select a pull quote (or pickup line . . .), build a solid story.

A sentence above the cowboy's left shoulder, courtesy of the Metropolitan Transit Authority, caught my eye.

IF YOU SEE SOMETHING, SAY SOMETHING.

"Excuse me," I said, nervously rubbing the back of my neck, "excuse me, sir." I pressed deep into my spine and that expanse of skin between head and shoulders that is meant to be a no-man's-land for kisses and sweetness. The neck rubbing was a nervous habit that the family shared. It was something we did when we knew we were going to lose. If only y'all could have seen everyone's hands going to town during the Clinton/Bush Sr. presidential debate of '94.

"Ma'am?" His paper lowered an inch to reveal honey brown eyes. They were wide and just young enough so that I recognized them as my own.

"You're wearing some mighty fine boots," I said, not quite able to believe that I was employing the basics of journalism beneath fluorescent lighting, *beneath a city,* as a means to flirt with a handsome man. But then again he was—from the parts I could see—the best-looking thing on the subway. Furthermore, I had read that all of New York, even the mayor, took underground transit, this factoid potentially making the cowboy one of the most handsome male specimens on the island. Searching for a sample group, I looked down the row of seats to have my senses quickly assaulted by a handful of bald, wide businessmen fiddling with big watches and reviewing documents while farther down a threesome of Asian men—collectively half the size of my right thigh—giggled and played Tetris on their cell phones (I recognized the resounding *pingpingpinnnnng*).

"After reading that sign right there," I said, pointing to the MTA poster and its aggressive maxim emblazoned on a bulging, black duffel bag surely stuffed to capacity with AK-47's, bombs and various contraband, "I thought I'd say something. And then of course I got to thinkin' that maybe those boots could direct me on how to get back South of Houston." I held my breath and smiled, finally adding for good measure, "You see, I'm new to the city and don't know my way around very well."

His paper descended, slowly, slowly, to reveal a golden, stubbled *Thelma & Louise* of a cowboy. The prospect of one caress from his left pinky would have inspired the ladies to pull themselves out of their crashed car, hastily apply blusher and scramble back up the side of the canyon.

"For starters, you're headed in the wrong direction. This here train is northbound. Didn't you hear the announcement? The next stop is

Fifty-first Street and we've just come from Grand Central. You need to get off first chance you get."

"Oh," I uttered in a voice that was my approximation of baby powder (didn't men love that sort of thing?) even though I was a musk kind of girl. I hoped to further convey my profound disappointment with his recommendation of deboarding—alone—by casting my eyes downward at the greasy, yellow linoleum floor of the subway car. On my way down, of course, I made a quick pit stop in the recesses of his denim, just in time to witness my cowboy adjusting his necessary parts.

"Once you learn a coupla lines, you'll get to movin' around the city like a pro. Me? I've been to every subway stop on the island. I think that means I've seen it all." A satisfied smile overcame his eyes, creasing his smooth, tanned skin for a split second. Finally, he lay down the paper and crossed his arms across his chest. "If you ain't from up here, where you from?"

"You can't tell from my accent?"

"I'm from East Texas, which means my ear is just about dead. I've heard Mexican, Tex-Mex, hick, Cajun, cracker and now Yankee. You'd think that'd fine-tune me but it's just made me deaf to it all."

"Well, I'm from Mobile, Alabama. Just moved up here, as a matter of fact." For a moment, I took him for one of Granddaddy's wild turkeys—extraordinary plumage, miniscule brain.

"What for?" He cocked his chin in such a way that made him look both curious and insolent.

"I'm beginning to ask myself the same question," I said, laughing at the thought of my current predicament. I was so shocked by the noise that had escaped my lips, I looked out into the middle distance, searching for the notes I had created. "I've been looking for a job for weeks but no one's biting. I'm starting to wonder how many times I'm going to have to cast my line. Anyway, that's why I'm all gussied up."

"Let me guess. From the looks of that coat and your eyes all done up and how you sit real tall and proper, I bet you want to be on television or in the mornin' paper, somehow making news. You have your designs on being a *somebody*, don't you?"

Hmmm . . . maybe the cowboy *did* understand people. . . .

"Next stop, Fifty-ninth Street."

He cocked an eyebrow my way as the subway halted and stuttered to a stop. But I wasn't about to get off the train. I just happened to be in the midst of something real. "Can you read everyone like that or am I just easy?"

"I'll let you in on a secret, honey," he said, leaning forward, resting his elbows on his knees, "the costume and the makeup changes but the reasoning stays the same. That's why we're all up here. You, me— everyone on this train. Hell, I'm beginning to think that even the babies up here come out with a business plan."

Walking down West Broadway I *had* noticed that the Tribeca babies wore expressions as intense as traders on the floor of the stock exchange.

"Your turn," he said, sitting up straight. "If you had to take a wild guess, what do you suppose I do all the way up here in New York City?"

Who needs labels? I thought. All I know is, after locking up Grandmother's silver I'd invite you inside, take you to bed and then baby you in the morning. Lots of cream in your coffee. Oh, Lord, it was becoming obvious, wasn't it? Three hundred and twenty-eight hours of Lifetime Television set to the tune of sirens and sexed-up neighbors was seriously beginning to inform my sensibilities.

"You're a raconteur, that's for certain. But, just looking at you— now don't take this the wrong way, you hear?" I hoped not to offend the gorgeous, strange creature in front of me. Who knew when I'd come across such scenery again? "Well, I'd say you were a tourist who didn't do much of anything besides ride the subway and memorize Mets scores. You don't seem to know too much about city living."

"Hot damn! Really?" he said, slapping his knee. "That's faaantastic." His tongue leapt out of his mouth, quickly wetting his lips in the moment of excitement. I stared at his bottom lip. It was curled and too sensuous to belong to a man. "That's just what I want to look like. I mean, I'd rather be an exotic stranger," he said, pronouncing the word "exotic" in three extraordinarily long syllables, "but looking like a tourist is gettin' me there."

I opened my mouth to speak but quickly clamped it shut as he raised his leg.

"Look at these boots," he said, cutting me off. "What do they do?"

"Get you from point A to point B?"

"These make me different," he continued without a nod to my smart-aleck comment. "And, you! You got all that blond hair and those red lips and, and, what else?"

I twisted around on the bench, trying to study my reflection in the subway window but couldn't make out much more than the afore-mentioned pile of hair and a set of dark circles under my eyes.

"I can't say that—"

"Yes, you can. Come on now, sugar, *think.*"

He was right. If I considered my Southern-ness—or my other-ness—to be my trump card, I had to be able to define it in clear terms.

"Well," I began, "let's see . . . I'm a Southerner in the city, an aging debutante, a small-town girl cursed with big-city aspirations." A pull quote! I tried to keep on, hoping that something else mildly original would come out. "If you got to talkin' to my granddaddy, he'd tell you that I'm on the cusp of feminine failure. I'm as old as a bottle of prime Tennessee whiskey, single, jobless and livin' north of the Mason-Dixon. He'd say I need to get on home and marry a doctor or an insurance salesman. Of course, at this, I dig in my heels and see how far a smile and a way with a pen can take me."

"Sounds like your move north of the Mason-Dixon is an A1, above-the-fold feature story. You got the assignment. Now what are you going to do with it?" He sat back, content with his assessment, folding his hands behind his head.

Who *was* this man?

"Ah one, ah two, ah one, two, three, four . . ." A quartet of black men glided into the subway car, interrupting us with snapping fingers and smiling faces, grins as wide as if they'd just won the Alabama state lottery. Humming, they quickly moved into their deep tobacco melody.

"Always and forever
Each moment with you"

"I left my heart in San Francisco and my soul in L.A.," I said, reading aloud the logo on the men's T-shirts as they walked past me, down the length of the car with a jingling cup, humming and hustling into the next.

"Nah. Their hearts belong to the hope that some record company bigwig will notice them on his way to work high above Times Square. They *belong* to that act. They want it so bad they'll do anything."

"Sixty-eighth Street, Hunter College."

A surge of students pushed into the car, creating a commotion of backpacks and fat fannies and loud music. I could barely see the cowboy.

"But I *do* want it," I said, springing up from my seat, forgetting everything else around me. If I convinced the cowboy of my dedication, it would be true, I told myself. I would be absolved of my lack of accomplishment because I had tried. "As long as you give it your best . . ." both Daddy and Granddaddy had always told me. I grabbed the metal pole for support. "And I've done *everything*."

"You sure about that?"

I reconsidered. "Granddaddy. I haven't gone to Granddaddy for help finding a job. He knows someone real important up here who can help me out. But these two arms and these two legs work just fine. Besides, I got too much pride. I can't ask him for more than he's already given me."

"If you want it, if you *really* want it, you'll do anything. Besides, if you succeed, it won't be on his account. It'll be elbow grease, midnight oil—all that," he said with a wave of his hand and, for the first time, a slightly annoyed look. "This is Manhattan, sugar, you gotta hustle everyone—even family, *especially* family."

With that, the cowboy stood up, brushed past me and slithered through the closing subway doors.

No good-bye?

No money or keys, either. My purse was gone.

Debutante Tea Cakes

*After years of attending debutante balls and charity teas, every South-
ern girl has her preferred recipe for tea cakes; mine happens to produce
something more akin to a sugar cookie than a cake. Come to think of
it, I should have accompanied my résumé with a bundle of these beauties. At least then the media execs in that big conference room in the sky
would have known that I was good at something. And if the cowboy
had a choice between a bag of cakes or my handbag, I do believe he
would have chosen the golden, lemony rounds.*

MAKES 4–5 DOZEN (depending on the thickness
of the cookie; I like mine a touch thick).

½ c. (1 stick) unsalted butter
1½ c. granulated sugar
2 eggs
½ c. buttermilk★
1 tsp. lemon zest, finely grated
1½ tsp. lemon juice
4½ c. all-purpose flour
4 tsp. baking powder
1½ tsp. salt
Parchment paper (or the inside of
    a paper grocery bag)

Preheat oven to 400 degrees.

★If you live among Yankees like I do, and buttermilk is scarce, substitute ½ Tbsp. white
vinegar and enough whole milk to make it ½ cup. All dairy ingredients should be
room temperature.

In a large mixing bowl, mix butter and sugar with an electric mixer. When blended, add the eggs, beating well after each addition, and then add buttermilk, lemon zest and lemon juice. In a medium-sized bowl, sift together flour, baking powder and salt. Gradually add dry mixture to the liquid ingredients in the large bowl, mixing thoroughly with an electric mixer after each addition. If the dough becomes too thick for the electric mixer, mix the last bit with your hands.

Divide dough into 3 balls, flatten into discs and wrap in plastic wrap. Refrigerate for 20 minutes. Remove dough and roll out to desired thickness, approximately one-quarter of an inch thick (I like mine thicker than most to achieve a more "cakey" consistency). Use a cookie cutter or cup to cut out dough into 3-inch rounds. Place on parchment paper with sufficient space between cookies. Sprinkle tops of cookies with a touch of granulated sugar.

Bake for 11 minutes (and not a minute over—tea cakes are fickle suckers, like Southern debs!) or until the edges turn slightly golden. Remove from the parchment and allow to cool on a rack. Cookies keep for the better part of a week.

6

MAMMA WOULD have died.

I'm not talking about the subway robbery. And I especially don't mean to bring up my subsequent nervous breakdown on the number 6 train platform. I'm speaking of my next-door neighbor, Shop Lady Lisa, and her Spode.

Your china pattern is the window to your soul.

Every lady from the Gulf Coast of Florida to the Mississippi Delta knows that your soul is on your table and most especially in the colors and figures on your plate. I sat at the teak-wood table set to the back of Lisa's store, fumbling with my chopsticks, watching her pluck a piece of browned tofu from the blue and white dinner plate resting between us. That was Mamma's pattern. One day it would be mine. And while it usually made an appearance on our table for Mardi Gras luncheons of Bibb lettuce and pickled Pensacola Bay shrimp, or at cocktail hour carrying oysters crowned with cream and bacon, I was thrilled to see it so far away, piled high with her strange, square food.

The Yankee had my china; I could be *friends* with this woman.

"Take this money and forget about it." She reached into an old cigar box and extracted five $100 bills, casually placing them by my wineglass. "That locksmith cleaned you out and you probably can't afford next week's supper," she said in her charming British accent by way of Bayonne, New Jersey. The crisp consonants that finished her

words—a bite of apple every few seconds—delighted me. "When you have a job, you'll pay me back."

Lisa continued nibbling on the tofu, its corners pursed from the heat like a mad old lady's lips, and then raised her wineglass in my direction. Slowly, with great assurance, she downed her third glass of dark, buttery liquid in one swallow. For me, it was a sign of utter sophistication—like exhaling cigarette smoke through your nostrils. I couldn't do either.

"Moments like this keep me sane," she said, surveying her store.

With the waves of dark fabric and shelves neatly stacked with velvet and cashmere, the black and white marble checkerboard floor, I felt like Lisa and I had escaped to Mamma's closet. At the end of the day, we had snuck inside with her fine china and a bottle of booze and were happy to be rid of the world outside. Dresses and sweaters and wine swaddled us, our unease.

"*You* keep me sane." I threw back my head and gulped down the last of it. I felt little rubies bead on my lower lip and then snake down my chin. Lisa was teaching me the foremost lesson of Manhattan working girls—*how to drink your dinner and forget your day.*

"I'll have a job soon enough. Don't you worry about me. . . ." No, just *I* had to worry about me. A cool, freshly cut set of keys pressed into my palm as the cowboy ran around the city with the old ones. I pushed back my chair and stood up; I felt warm and heavy. The reality that I was jobless and rudderless hit me again. The store's picture window framed a twilight and a world that seemed as if it could never be mine.

"You know what's out there?" I said, walking toward the window.

"Life, liars and thieves." She let out a little grunt as she uncorked the second bottle of wine, pouring little streams of truth into our glasses.

"An urban bazaar. White-collar Manhattan is an overly sanitized urban bazaar, Lisa, and I'm just a country girl used to the smells of the county fair. They all seem to be buying or selling something—MBA-laced résumés, straight noses, Ivy League educations, trash—and yet never deliver a damn thing. Their personalities and daily pitches can be distilled down to a push, a cry, a scream. There's a crush to get ahead

in their world and I feel like I'm not ready. I could call my granddaddy tonight and all this would be resolved. I would become one of *them*. Did you know that? I'd have a job lickety-split and *work friends,* whatever those are. I'd give you back your five hundred dollars and still have some pocket money. But would I be ready? Is that—are *they*—what I want?

"Though, I'll tell you, there are certain people that I pass every day and like. They line up on Washington Square Park, University Place and Union Square. They're Afghan, Senegalese and from other strange parts I've never been to. The fellas and I talk about life, the weather, doing business on the black, August asphalt in the spray of a fountain. I want them to be the successful ones. That'd give me hope. They're straightforward and sell peanuts, discounted men's suits, peeled mangoes cut into the shape of a rose sprinkled with paprika. *I want a slow life in a fast city.* To sit under the shade of a Washington Park oak tree and sell scuppernongs . . . wouldn't that be nice?"

"For a day, maybe a week. Then what? And you're not here to sell bloody fruit! You're here to make a name for yourself!" Lisa was officially pickled from the wine—and she was right.

I said good-bye and went back to my apartment to the only man that mattered.

"And to what do I owe the honor of speaking to my New York City granddaughter this evening? How is everything up in those parts?" Granddaddy's voice sounded especially kind so far away.

"I'm getting by . . . I'm sorry I haven't called sooner. It's just that I wanted to call with some sort of good news—" I stopped myself for a second, trying to hear the tinkling ice cubes in his crystal tumbler of whiskey, wanting to hear him and his familiar sounds.

Breathe, Granddaddy, breathe.

Let me hear you and the lingering evening play your tune. Just one more time I gotta listen to day turning into night, no one much noticing, all the porch fans set on "3," stirring just enough breeze to keep mosquitoes from flushed cheeks and bare ankles.

"And now? Can I finally tell the boys down at the paper that my granddaughter is gainfully employed?"

Stop. Please. Let me live in the sweet shallows and depths of your voice.

"No, Granddaddy. I'm calling for help."

Silence and a sip.

"What kind of help?"

"I need you to call Christopher Randolph for me."

"Belle—"

"Just listen to me, *please*. I can't begin to tell you all that I've done and the people I've seen, but no one wants me. No one wants me," I said again, this time whispering the words to myself. "And the thing is, I can do it. After learning the news business from you and Mamma, I could be at any paper or news station up here. I just need a leg up. All I want is a phone call and an interview. That's it. The rest is up to me."

"Are you finished?"

"Yes, sir."

"All right then . . ."

Who's the boss? You are, Granddaddy.

"I'll call Christopher tomorrow. Now tell me somethin' inerestin' about livin' with the strange, brilliant folk up there! How are they treatin' you? How's that neighborhood? You eatin' well? Zeola keeps settin' out plates of crowder peas and pickled shrimp thinkin' you'll smell 'em and come flyin' home."

And like that, Granddaddy had put the matter to rest. He would help me. He would always help me. I was a small town girl livin' way out of my league but I was lucky. Granddaddy would help me accomplish the unimaginable—I would become my own woman.

Pickled Pensacola Shrimp

A girl cannot function on tofu and over-oaked red wine alone. These coral-colored gems are delicious enough to serve on Spode china and down-home enough to pack for your next picnic. Puckery perfection.

SERVES 4, GENEROUSLY.

2½ lbs. shrimp
½ c. celery tops
3½ tsp. salt
¼ c. mixed pickling spices
1 large onion, thinly sliced into rounds
1¼ c. vegetable oil
¾ c. white vinegar
1½ tsp. salt
2½ tsp. celery salt
2½ Tbsp. capers and juice
Several dashes of Tabasco

Boil shrimp, celery tops, salt and pickling spices for 5 minutes. Drain the shrimp in a colander. Layer shrimp and onions.

In a small metal bowl, whisk together oil, vinegar, salts, capers and their juice, and Tabasco. Pour the vinaigrette over shrimp.

Chill the shrimp salad for one day, allowing the flavors to do their dance.

Good-Enough-for-Your-Spode Oysters & Cream

You think the perfect oyster is a naked oyster? Then you're not Southern and you haven't tried them topped with bacon and cream. Serve these baby bivalves with a good Sancerre or Chablis.

SERVES 8 AS AN APPETIZER.

24 Apalachicola oysters (or choose your
   favorite that is in season, with good salinity)
1 small, firm tomato
2 large shallots, minced
1 bunch chives, chopped
2 Tbsp. white wine vinegar
¾ c. heavy cream
3 strips bacon, fried crisp

Open the oysters, reserving the nice, briny juice from the shells. Finely dice the tomato and the shallots and chop the chives. Combine white wine vinegar, heavy cream, tomato, shallots, chives and oyster juice in a small bowl and mix.

Drizzle a tsp. of the cream mixture onto each oyster and crumble fried bacon on top.

7

AN EXCHANGE over long, gray telephone wires between two men—one whom I loved, the other I didn't know—made a city materialize. Magic. Suddenly I had a purpose and a dinner date. The loony bin along the shoals of the Mississippi would have to wait. The white rooms of Chattahoochee couldn't compare to the bright lights of West Broadway, I decided, slipping into my heels. The city was alive and waiting for me.

Granddaddy had made the promised call and so I had dinner tonight with Christopher Randolph and a 9 A.M. interview tomorrow with Gina Shaw, vice president of American News Channel. This was all proof that I was approaching some kind of city normalcy . . . right?

The only snag in the out-of-control top panty hose that was my life: I owned one proper suit—a navy blue jacquard Chloé number that I bought at a secondhand store in Birmingham (the color conservative, the cut liberal—I was giving nonpartisanship a go). It would have to stretch over two epic days of important people, red wine, liquid foundation and countless lipstick reapplications. A serious challenge.

Rushing out of my building, glancing in the hallway mirror, final thought: What if my suit whispers the crass of Deborah Norville instead of the class of Diane Sawyer? Priorities, Belle! You're ten minutes late and a touch of tawdry is good—now run!

I teetered down the block and onto Prince Street in my red peep-toe heels, the jacquard fabric of the slacks rubbing the insides of my thighs raw, making them a garish shade of scarlet. I could no longer afford matching shoes and handbags but I'd be damned if my thighs and feet wouldn't sport the same color! I looked across the street to Raoul's, the proudest restaurant on the block. The black-and-white-striped awning and bright Ballantine's French liquor sign hanging in the window made it look haughty and desirable, like a fifty-year-old woman in a skirt slit up to *there* announcing she was still the best-looking broad in town. Even though I had walked past the restaurant any number of times and perused the menu, I had never allowed myself to slip inside. I was in the terrible habit of making all the good things off-limits.

"It's *the* neighborhood bistro," Lisa told me yesterday over a brunch of Prosecco and shirred eggs. "Fanelli's, Jerry's and Raoul's were the first Soho boîtes to feed the intellectual elite back, back," she paused to upturn her flute, "when you weren't even a twinkle in your pappa's eye. Scorsese shoots his films in the front bar and De Niro fetes his mistresses in the back garden. But a work meeting at Raoul's, darling? *That's* sexy." A long, slow pour of Zardetto and not one but two raised eyebrows meant that she was intrigued.

"Christopher Randolph hasn't seen me since I was five years old. He probably remembers me runnin' around the newspaper, wrappin' phone cords around Mamma's ankles at the City Desk. If anything, I was a pain. Trust me, he feels like he owes Granddaddy an evening and an interview. That's it." But I wondered about him all the same. What would this Mobile export look like, talk like, act like, now that he had shrugged his Southern skin and been accepted by the media titans?

The long zinc bar lured me in. If it hadn't been for its silvery finger and the promise of a meal that I didn't have to make with my own two hands, I might have stood outside the restaurant's black curtains all night. For a moment, it seemed like the brave girl was gone. But then I remembered my very daring blouse and my mission and so I pushed my way inside. Slowly, I tried to adjust, not quite ready for the darkness. Red velvet armchairs, nude oil paintings, pressed tin ceiling. The space damned you until it charmed you—an Atlanta brothel with a French accent, circa Rhett Butler.

"Martini, straight up, three olives," I said, easing my way onto a stool. The line was borrowed from some movie and the type of drink from Happy Hour Girl—one of the many young, freshly independent things I spied at the bars in Manhattan at six o'clock with her head tilted back, spine arched, chest lifted, laughter and liquor playing the back of her throat. I saw her right here, outside on the pristine sidewalk, or on Seventh Avenue South at Caliente Cantina. Frivolous, glamorous—I wanted to be just like her. And for an instant, I was.

I sucked in my tummy and scanned the length of the bar. Two women, one Mexican busboy, belly up—wait, who was at the end? I narrowed my eyes and looked down the bar. There was a man, waiting, glass half empty. That couldn't be him, could it? He was too young and disheveled and handsome.

The cocktail.

Just one sip.

Burn.

Make me loose.

"You know how to make your martinis good and strong," I said, raising my glass to the bartender. He blinked and returned to polishing glasses.

Another sip.

Why not?

And saunter.

"Hello, Mr. Randolph." I stood right up next to the man in question, close, so he wouldn't be able to forget, or wash off, my smell. Hair spray and perfume mark territory more efficiently than does the bladder of a hunting dog.

"I'm sorry?" he said, running his fingers through his longish hair, squinting at me through tortoise-shell frames.

"I'm Belle," I said, shifting the martini and my lizard-skin clutch to my left hand, extending my right. I prayed that my French-manicured fingernails would convey my true classy nature, even if the *Gentlemen Prefer Blondes* setup was making me a touch brassy at present. "And I suppose you're the flip-flopper, the good ol' Southern Democrat that's turned into a fancy cable news conservative. That's what Granddaddy tells me, anyway. How do you do?" I sipped (because a Southern lady never swallows) half my martini and smiled. Nerves.

"*You're* Brandon's granddaughter?" he said, slowly making his way to his feet.

"Yes, sir, afraid so."

"Well, I'll be. . . . He's the last of a dying breed. The gentleman publisher." Christopher searched my face, looking perplexed. His brown, unkempt hair had a way of accentuating his nose and chin. Neither pronounced nor proud, instead his chin was delicate and handsome, the nose straight and serene. The thin tortoise frames slipped down that nose as he considered my granddaddy, an aging man who lived twelve hundred miles away, and me, the impertinent kin who had moved north. I imagined myself lifting his glasses and pressing the warm of my lips against his tired lids, whispering that counties and cities and states separated him and Granddaddy but I was standing right there. Here.

Instead, of course, I exclaimed, "Ta da!" and did a little jig. *"C'est moi, la belle."*

"I'd keep you to a one-drink limit," he said, glancing at my near empty glass, "but I'm too intrigued by the prospect of what might happen next," he added under his breath. With a faint smile, he motioned for the bartender. "Please, call me Chris." He pulled at the lapels of his cutaway summer jacket and everything shifted forward. I saw him in profile and could suddenly smell pine trees and his grit. According to Granddaddy, he was ten years Mamma's junior. That put him at about forty-five years old. The modest, boyish energy shaved off a decade. The broad shoulders didn't hurt his case either.

"So you decided to move to the center of it all," he said, angling his stool, moving it closer.

"Something like that. Mobile began to feel too small, the family too large. . . ." I continued to talk, I'm sure of it, because he kept staring at me, but I can't remember a thing that I said. I do recall the bartender polishing our zinc with his rag, folding two starched, white napkins into generous triangles. A silver shadow of flatware was whisked from beneath the bar while glasses appeared and were positioned amid elegant talk of wine and earth. French was spoken, sounding quite lovely; I liked words whose meanings I didn't know.

"This is a superb white," the bartender said, hurrying the bottle past me, presenting it to Christopher, "a particularly *exceptionelle* Burgundy, a Chambertin-Clos de Beze Grand Cru. I think you'll find it muscular with a refreshing, light finish and perfumed edge. You like the Côte d'Or, yes?" he stated, with that wonderful frog inflection, question marks everywhere for no reason.

"The coat door? Oh, I don't need the coat check, thank you. I'm enjoying the free air-conditioning and I didn't bring anything else to cover me up," I said, sneaking a peek past my lapels, down to my silk blouse and décolletage. Perhaps I shouldn't have undone that last button.

He served the wine with a flourish. We even got our own silver pail filled with ice. Virginia would just *die* if she could see me now, I thought. As a sister, she'd be both jealous and proud. Though she might take issue with the stingy pour, barely a dribble in my glass. He told me I had to wait until the wine took some breaths and felt rested. For Lord's sake, what has the bottle been doing all day? I mused. I'm the one who's been beating the pavement, lookin' for gainful employment. But I didn't have time to complain. Warm French bread and a pale square of chilled butter quickly appeared alongside what looked like an enormous flower, a green magnolia that was more bud than bloom.

I stared at it and, for once in my life, kept quiet, sipping the wine that had been put before me. Copying Christopher's moves, I closed my eyes and let the wine loll on my tongue and against the sides of my mouth. The bartender was right—if a liquid could taste like an image, then our wine was a bicep holding up a bouquet of peonies. I opened my eyes to look over and find Christopher studying his plate and the mysterious bloom. Working quickly, he removed a dozen or so of the outside petals, finally choosing one to his liking.

"*Artichot.* Look, like this," he said, breaking off a petal, dipping it into a yellow sauce. For a moment, the tips of his fingers and the delicate green flake disappeared into his mouth. Finally, he slid it out, scraping off the petal's flesh with one motion. "What do you think about that, Ms. Alabama?"

Pluck.

Dip.

Slide.

I was a beauty queen feasting on a flower. Well, for the moment anyway. And I wanted to keep Christopher's quiet confidence, package it and slip it inside the silk-lined pocket of my suit. I needed it at tomorrow's interview.

"I hope that I'm doing the right thing, switching from print to television. I don't have a clue about the twenty-four-hour cable news business."

"Neither does anyone down in the newsroom. You'll be fine," he said with a wave of his hand. "Besides, we can't have a pretty face like yours hiding behind the typeset of the *Times,* now can we?"

It wasn't a question. It was a statement, a very flattering one that made me fix my eyes on his left earlobe. I had no choice. His gaze was intimate and distracting, like gliding your legs over smooth, cotton sheets.

"Your grandfather's a brilliant son of a bitch." His words casually ran together, reminding me that we came from the same place. That, and an occasional lazy vowel, divulged his past. But that was it. "I bet he's still keeping everyone on their toes. He could easily do my job running ANC. A man like him would get a kick out of being a pain in the Establishment's ass," he said, reaching for the drink he had called a Manhattan. A metropolis in a martini glass?

What looked to be a mighty handsome knee pressed against the fine linen of his trousers, my leg just an inch away. "I believe that's the only reason I stay at my job, come to think of it. It's reassuring to know that Katie Couric hates my guts. I think even Brian Williams would drop-kick me into the middle of the Afghan desert if his producers would let him."

Hmmmm . . . like most women, I enjoyed being difficult, causing a stir. Maybe this television thing would suit me just fine.

"The new kid in town, the underdog . . . we're all that. Excuse me, Paul," he called out to the bartender, "bring us the escargot and the turbot. This is an evening of firsts for the girl from Alabama." He turned back to me so I was forced to return to his left earlobe. "We also have a sweetheart tax deal with the current administration—that doesn't hurt things either. We can afford to be the little guy *and* the bully whilst raking in hundreds of millions, creeping into the number one slot in cable news land," he said, shaking his head. "And mark my words, Keaton and Cleveland are going to maintain our favored status. The little thing called the presidential election in a few months?" he asked, pausing to polish off his cocktail and rearrange his silverware. "Watch and learn, Belle, watch and learn. Our brash little channel will determine the winner. A basement of egos deciding the leader of the free world. Amazing, isn't it?"

Pluck.

Dip.

Slide.

I couldn't tell if Christopher was proud or ashamed of his job. And why was he going on and on about the elections? Did it matter? I was thrilled! Suddenly, I was like a garish pink-and-green Lily Pulitzer stretched across a garden club member's fat fanny. I clung for dear life to the idea of me and telejournalism. Hundreds of millions! Number one! If I were part of their news team I'd certainly get a piece of that pie. And a smaller newsroom meant that we would be brothers in arms, friends in combat, I would be promoted within the ranks as swiftly as . . . hold the phone—where would I actually begin in the newsroom, considering I had zero experience?

"You're really set on being a journalist, aren't you? Look at you, you're glowing." Christopher smiled and continued staring at me, hard. I recrossed my legs.

"I already *am* a journalist," I corrected him, "just not the kind that's used to teleprompters and shoulder pads. And don't I need a reel or something? Me standing in front of a burning building, reporting from the eye of a hurricane?"

Wait! Forget about the Brenda Starr bit—had he said that I was pretty? It must be the jacket, the clever way it nips in at the waist and hides my ass.

"I'll level with you—we're starved for talent. Ever since we started in ninety-six the producers are terrified to dig up their own stories, venture beyond the Reuters feeds—Christ, what a bunch of incompetents," he muttered. "Listen. I could get in trouble for saying this, but just use . . . use Keaton and Cleveland and their populist news machine like they're going to use you. Get American News Channel on your résumé and move on. You might start off as an associate producer or production assistant but you'll move up. Put in a good, long year and then transfer to a *real* news operation. But, first, you've got to cut your teeth on our bullshit. Just promise me," he said, fingering the stem of his wineglass, "that you won't let them get to you. Fight tooth and nail to stay like this, like the woman you are right now. Then, you've got 'em beat. You've got them in the palm of your hand."

"Bartender," I nodded, "I'll have what he's having. Manhattan."

Manhattan

Everything burned and tingled after my metropolis in a martini glass.
I was energized, inspired . . . and maybe just a little bit in love. Now
I just had to figure out if it was Christopher or the cocktail that made
me feel so good.

SERVES 1.

Ice
2 oz. bourbon (Maker's Mark, Knob Creek)
2 tsp. sweet vermouth
Several dashes of Angostura bitters
1 orange twist

Fill a pint glass three-fourths full of ice. Pour in the bourbon, sweet
vermouth and bitters and stir briskly, allowing the liquids to mix well
and chill. Strain into a chilled martini glass and garnish with orange
twist.

Cucumber Martini

Once I could handle the novelty of a drink named after an island, I decided to experiment with the classic martini. My first priority was something cool for the godawful August heat. The cucumber water, lime and tartness of the Cointreau were just what this wannabe newshound needed.

SERVES 2.

> Ice
> 4 oz. (very good) gin
> 2 oz. Cointreau
> 3.5 oz. cucumber water*
> 1 oz. freshly squeezed lime juice
> 2 cucumber rounds

Fill a cocktail shaker with ice. Pour in all of the ingredients, save the cucumber rounds, and shake well. Strain into a martini glass and garnish with cucumber rounds.

---

*To make cucumber water: *Place a coffee filter over a strainer and place both over a bowl. Using the coarse side of a box grater, grate seedless cucumber into the strainer. When done, squeeze filter so as to extract all possible juice from grated cucumber. Use cucumber water immediately or save for up to two days.*

Christopher Randolph Crostini (Artichoke and Chèvre Crostini)

If I ever had the chance to invite Christopher into my garden for the taste of a flower, I'd gussy things up a bit, add some of my favorite flavors, like sweet, bright basil and creamy, tart French goat cheese, chèvre. For a moment, I'd be Ms. Alabama <u>and</u> Ms. Julia Child.

MAKES ENOUGH SPREAD FOR 24 CROSTINI.

1 baguette
¼ c. + 2 Tbsp. extra virgin olive oil
1 12-oz. bottle of marinated artichoke hearts
½ tsp. Dijon mustard
¼ tsp. kosher salt
Freshly ground black pepper
4 oz. chèvre
3 Tbsp. fresh basil, chiffonade (finely sliced)
1 Tbsp. chives, finely chopped
2 tsp. fresh lemon juice

Set oven to 250 degrees. Thinly slice baguette on the diagonal and drizzle with 2 Tbsp. olive oil. Place bread on baking sheet and bake until golden and very crisp.

Drain artichokes in a strainer and then move to a cutting board. Place a little over half the artichokes (about 8 oz.) in a food processor and add mustard, salt and freshly ground black pepper. Blend on low speed and stream in approx ¼ c. olive oil—or enough to emulsify—into mixture. Taste. Season accordingly with freshly ground black pepper.

Pour blended mixture into a medium-sized bowl. With a wooden spoon, mix chèvre with artichoke mixture until a creamy consistency is attained. Add basil, chives and lemon juice and continue stirring.

Spread approximately 1 Tbsp. artichoke-chèvre mixture on toasted baguette slices, warm or cool, and serve.

(Artichoke spread is best served the next day, after the flavors have done their dance for at least 24 hours.)

8

"THIS IS WHAT you want," I whispered, taking a seat on a self-conscious island of benches outside the American News Channel's main entrance. Twelve twenty-one Avenue of the Americas was a monolith—a severe rectangle of white stone and skinny windows extending some sixty floors high. There were no gleaming surfaces, no polished angles of brass, copper or steel: just hard rock with the occasional glimmer of sunshine reflecting off Rockefeller Center across the street. I had to look between the wings of pigeons, five stories up in the sky, to read the electronic ticker tape as it scrolled across the building and slipped into an adjacent Broadway marquee. It seemed unnatural to place words so high, like reporting the latest tragedies and triumphs on God's typewriter. Beneath the moving headlines was the chosen messenger, a pretty, frozen-faced blonde, playing in Technicolor across three enormous television screens. She looked at me, her over-glossed lips seductive, taunting. The eyes of T. J. Eckleberg in the new millennium.

My teeth chattered despite the morning summer sun. One hour: too much time to sit and wrestle with fate, stare up at the woman whose job I was supposed to covet. Midtown Manhattan appeared to me, right then, as either an emotional wasteland or an adult playground, a few dozen blocks where the big kids compete, show off their toys, Daddy's money, Mamma's breeding.

I had indulged after dinner at Raoul's. And I'm here to tell you, my lovelies, it wasn't a good thing. When you live alone, dabble in choco-late *not* the Internet before bedtime. I say this though I'd always con-sidered my *Mobile Constitution*–issued Lexus Nexus account to be as comforting as a bedtime story, allowing me to dig up dirt on everyone and everything (it's the latent gossip columnist *and* Episcopalian in me that propels these searches) and fall into an informed, blissful slumber. The free account was one of the major perks—if not the only perk—of being a reporter. But, lying in bed, tucked beneath my silk coverlet and feather comforter, I decided that instead of perusing the DUI's and expired fishing licenses of ex-boyfriends, I would research the Amer-ican News Channel and its executives. Christopher had given me an earful but I wanted back stories, biographies, the low-down and dirty that only some enraged liberal journalist up in Vermont or out in L.A. would dig up to sell to one of the big papers.

Curiosity is *not* good for the *visage,* y'all. A wrinkle instantly formed in the center of my forehead despite a generous application of my Chanel Precision Age Delay Nuit cream.

The majority shareholder and chairman of the board of American News Channel was Dax Keaton, a reclusive Canadian billionaire with major television, satellite, movie, newspaper, magazine, book and Internet holdings around the globe. He was a media mogul and tyrant, whose holdings and hubris far surpassed those of William Randolph Hearst and William Paley. His most lucrative ventures were a major Hollywood studio and tabloids in New York and London. Coming in last in the financials was the American News Channel—but not for long. According to multiple sources, the president, the House and Sen-ate majority leaders and many of the most influential politicians in the world depended on Keaton and his staunchly conservative station to blend seemingly innocuous news reports with right-wing partiality. The Republican presidential hopeful, Senator Hewitt from Texas, had multiple business ties with Keaton, their relationship only becoming stronger and more complicated the better Hewitt performed in the polls. He was running a successful (albeit dirty) campaign that looked to pummel the Democratic candidate, Jessica Clayton, come Novem-ber. Keaton landed votes—and sometimes even book deals—for

Hewitt and his cronies and they gave him pork. The money would come. (This reminded me of a piece I'd done on corrupt Southern politics. During the interview, I do believe I inspired the governor of Louisiana to give me one of the best pull quotes of all time: "In theory, moral rectitude and politics are coupled like mustard slaw and pulled pork on a bun, only after you sink your teeth into the business do you realize it's all a pile of horseshit.")

Robert Cleveland was the president and news director of the American News Channel, a constant presence, ever involved in the day-to-day minutiae of story selection, talent scouting and fluffing the Republican agenda. A former top party advisor, he was a master strategist, pit bull *and* schmoozer. He not only took down the competition at any cost, he was also famous for *cutting* costs, paying his vast pool of employees the lowest wages in the industry.

My crush and the contender for hometown honey, Christopher Randolph, was Cleveland's wingman. Whenever Cleveland needed a set of eyes and ears on location, in a war zone or in a board meeting, he'd send Christopher to do damage control, spy, inspect. What had I been for Christopher—business or pleasure?

I didn't know how to properly file away the critiques of my potential new employer. The *New York Times, New York Observer, Chicago Tribune* and *Los Angeles Times* seemed to think that ANC was a complete shit show (just paraphrasing—I *do* hate being vulgar), the Keaton-Cleveland method being to entertain and blitz the viewer with technological innovations and propaganda while broadcasting the (carefully edited) news. The station was viewed by many (okay, the majority) as a journalistic joke. One reporter went so far as to call it "a narcotic for the average American out in fly-over territory."

But, I sat there in my one proper navy blue suit, outside the gates, anxious to be a part of it all, to be a part of *something*. The American News Channel was Keaton and Cleveland's baby, the fat kid of the industry that everyone picked on. I was Granddaddy's lamb. I smoothed down my trousers, walked toward the revolving doors and wondered if we young things could get along.

"I have a nine o'clock appointment with Gina Shaw," I told one of the pinched-lookin' ladies behind the front desk. Her skin was just clamoring for fresh air. (Didn't these people know that polyester is an agent of dermatological death?) Clocks from every continent ticked in unison on the lustrous black marble wall that dominated the corporate foyer. There was a perfect, one-to-one clock-to-secretary ratio, I noted, making it appear as if the world was under the watchful eye of the American News Channel. The ANC crest emblazoned on the woman's blazer along with the hushed, refined air of the space reminded me of one of the glitzy, nouveau riche Birmingham country clubs.

"Photo ID," she commanded. An embarrassing golf handicap and a subpar chicken salad sandwich in the Alabama clay hills were looking better and better—that and a glass of cheap Chardonnay.

I quickly fished out my driver's license, the little white card that heralded, "State of Alabama." I was ashamed and felt stupid for *being* ashamed. An immigrant story like any other, I suppose. An older, black security guard saw my hesitation and quickly moved from behind the string of receptionists to my side. He nodded toward the escalator. "Swing to your left and take the escalator all the way down to the basement. Once you're there, you can't miss it. Newsroom and its studios take up the whole floor." He tipped his cap in my direction and smiled. "Good luck, now." I heard Georgia in his vowels. He had seen Alabama written across my face like cheap lettering on a wooden roadside sign (HOMEGROWN! FRESH OFF THE FARM!). We had both committed the cultural crime of moving north; the persistence of our big-city dreams and a mask of a smile were the only way to do right by our impertinence and our sins.

"Thank you, sir," I said, eyeing the escalator, hoping that he wasn't the last friendly face I'd see all day.

The transition between the two floors was swift and obvious. The lobby's grand elevator banks adorned with more gold than a televangelist's wife, coupled with the boudoir lighting, created an atmosphere of absurd wealth and privilege; the walls whispered of a secret, comfortable club of which I was most certainly not a member. But, walking down the silver stairs, plunging below the polish and flash, I realized that if the basement was the machine's anonymous engine, I'd be one of its drones. I touched my chignon and its tangle of bobby pins at the nape of my neck for confidence (Deborah Norville, Diane Sawyer? Deborah Norville, Diane Sawyer?). One final swipe of Shanghai Nights (my lucky charm of a red lipstick) and I was there, on the subterranean level—beneath Manhattan and polite society—standing in a completely different world.

The overly air-conditioned, pure white halls of the basement were completely silent; a series of unmarked, closed doors punctuated the otherwise sterile corridor where the escalator had deposited me and my fears. The lonely sound of my heels tapping down the slippery linoleum almost convinced me that I was in the wrong place. The cold air whistled through my chest and out my nose: there was nothing else to listen to. I turned left. Squinting, I made out two frosted glass panels emblazoned with THE NATION'S #1 NEWS CHANNEL, sliding open and closed, emitting a steady stream of frantic-looking workers at the end of the hallway. Each time the doors reopened, a chatter of voices and a din of wire feeds—sounding like a mix of AM radio and electronic typewriters—momentarily filled the otherwise empty air. The mosh pit of the newsroom was nearly a quarter of a mile away. I picked up the pace as best as my heels would allow.

"Enter at your own risk," a twenty-something guy said, walking toward me, balancing dozens of cassettes between his chin and outstretched arms. He was my height with hair too beautiful, dark and curled to be on the head of a man. The eyes were mischievous and green. Trouble.

"The busier, the better—that's why I'm here," I replied, flushed by the confusion and his clavicle.

Belle fetishes: clavicles, long fingers, skinny knees, big ears, warm hands.

Lord, how was I going to focus on breaking news with a gorgeous soul like him floating around the basement? I bet his knees could take my breath away.

"I'm Jake. I'd shake your hand, but . . ." He shrugged, his chin motioning toward the stack of cassettes.

"Pleasure. I'm Belle. I've got a nine o'clock interview with Gina

Shaw. If all goes well, we might be seeing more of each other." I was blushing like a fool. Some things even a debutante can't control. (Okay, fine, there are *a lot* of things this debutante couldn't control.)

"Fingers crossed, knock on wood—all that. Now get in there," he said, backing down the hallway, "Shaw can't stand to be kept waiting."

Beep. "Guy, where are my scripts? Get the fucking scripts up to Studio A, *now*!" *Beep.* The overhead intercom screamed at the exact moment I stepped inside the newsroom. Nervous hands adjusted my starched shirt collar. A lone secretary, seated at a cheap metal desk to the right of the sliding glass doors, frantically tried to field dozens of incoming calls from disgruntled viewers.

"News Channel. What? You're going to have to slow down, sir, I can't understand you," she said into the headset. The cordless contraption could barely fit over her mop of thick, orange frizz. "No, we didn't claim our results came from a Gallup poll. A highly specialized ANC panel determined that—"

Beep. "You're going to fuck me over in front of all of America, Guy. Bring me the scripts for the fucking C block." *Beep.*

Voices—mechanical or otherwise—competed for air time and attention. Young guys, about my age, ran past me with scripts in one hand and cassettes in the other. They muttered to themselves about voice-overs and live shots, satellite feeds and when they could take their next cigarette break. Computers, television screens and maps of the Middle East crowded every work surface. At least eight phones were ringing but only two of them were being answered. I would soon learn that Reuters news feeds and prime-time anchors were the gods of this world—everything else could wait. A mile of madness stretched before me, one slender path cutting through its core. The racket was deafening. Overturned chairs obstructed the aisle; candy bar wrappers, empty cans and takeout containers skirted the computer stations. Primary-colored desktops and chairs lent the room an elementary school air.

Embarrassed for their mess and anxious for my interview, I stood there like a fool, straightening and restraightening my collar, trying to remember the name of the Republican senator from Wisconsin.

"Belle Lee?" a whippet thin, dark-haired woman asked, approaching me. It looked as if nothing could have parted her skinny, maroon lips into a smile.

"Yes, ma'am, I'm Belle."

"For God's sake, don't say 'ma'am' around me—I feel old enough as it is. I'm Gina Shaw," she announced, a bony hand shooting in my direction, "manager of this mess you're looking at. Follow me back to my office." I moved from her black, close-set eyes down to a nose with nostrils so pitched, a tip so lifted, it looked as if she were kin of the Gloved One. Before turning on her sensibly outfitted heel, she wiped the crimson that had bled from her lips and traveled north to the wrinkles beneath her plasticized nose.

Oh, dear Lord, what have I gotten myself into? I thought, closing my eyes a beat too long.

Gina could never have made it down South. Below the Mason-Dixon, it takes five seconds and a limp handshake to determine a stranger's potential status. As I walked behind her through the newsroom, I couldn't shake the feeling that Gina was a scrawny, high-strung, second-string high school football player—tiny ass, oversized shoulder pads, helmet hair—masquerading as a starting quarterback. She was tense, charmless, overbearing. Conversations stopped and production tasks were quickly invented as she and her attitude charged past the plastic cubicles with me, the water girl, in tow.

The underwhelming newsroom decor continued into her miniscule office—a repository of cheap drywalling, plaques, certificates and crystal obelisks; dozens of trophies attempted to justify her six-figure salary.

"Christopher Randolph tells me that you come from a news family," Gina said once we were situated in our equally uncomfortable chairs, hers tucked behind an unassuming desk laden with memos and news briefs. She spoke with equal parts condescension and amusement. She held my résumé at arm's length, up to the light, as if she were looking for stains (chewing tobacco spittle, barbecue sauce?). "Your grandfather's paper is quite influential down there, down, uh . . . where is that you're from, again?" Gina sounded thoroughly bored and

I didn't know what to make of her accent—Brooklyn by way of Beverly Hills? She was the most affected woman I had ever met.

"Alabama—Mobile to be precise."

"Yes, of course. . . . So what brings you up here? What can our station do for you? It looks as if you had a very comfortable place for yourself down . . . *there.*" She intoned the word "there" as if she were speaking of my nether regions. Harlot.

I reviewed in my head all the taboos, the ever-changing roster of Bush cabinet members, the lines I had rehearsed. . . .

"I want to be the anchor of the six o'clock news. I suppose you can't do that working at a newspaper," I said quickly, perhaps too quickly.

"Well, well, aren't we ambitious?" Gina said, arching an overpenciled eyebrow. "Just a minute," she said, pointing at me with an acrylic, mauve-colored fingernail, and picked up the ringing phone receiver. "What now, Guy? Didn't you hear what Cleveland said today in the quarterly? For fuck's sake! It doesn't matter if CNN is running it at the top of the hour. If drugs are involved we *don't run it.*"

"I'll step out," I mouthed to Gina, pointing to a swivel chair out in the hurricane of the newsroom.

She cupped the receiver. "No, I'll be off in a minute. Stay where you are." A quick swivel in her chair and she was back in character. "Bush! Does the last name Bush mean a goddamned thing to you? I know that Noelle was arrested at the Walgreens drive-through trying to buy prescription drugs. And so does the rest of America because the goddamned liberals are wallpapering their broadcasts with her mug shot! Get another fucking lead story, Guy, and call me back!" She slammed the phone down.

"Now back to anchoring the six o'clock news," she began, running a finger along her upper lip, wiping away the beginnings of a sweat mustache.

"That's where I want to be in ten years," I lied. Hell, until three days ago I had never seriously considered a job in television. I had been weaned on newspapers, not sound bites. But a faraway granddaddy whispered in my ear, "When can I tell people that my granddaughter is gainfully employed?" I had to keep up my end of the deal. "Quite frankly, Ms. Shaw, American News Channel is setting the standard. I want to be part of a news organization that represents the majority of Americans. The Republican party has a lock on the presidency, the House and the Senate for a reason—our country is fed up." Gina leaned further and further over her desk, nodding in agreement as if I were a child about to utter my first precious word. It was almost too easy, I thought.

"And?" she asked, pressing for more, perhaps hoping that I would validate the headaches, ringing telephones and cheap drywalling that defined the newsroom and her life.

"All I'm asking for is a chance—" I began, interrupted by the phone.

"What? Yeah, well, I'm sorry the prime-time talent had a problem with our coverage. Tell her to go fuck herself and then come talk to me." She slammed down the phone. Again.

"Belle," she said, switching back into interview mode, touching an errant hair that had dared to escape from the carefully constructed brown mass, "I like what I hear. You're exactly the kind of person we need down here in the newsroom. Your solid morals and Republican background, your experience, your point of view—that's what management and I are looking for." A look of intense satisfaction spread across her face as she sized me up, her freshly scored piece of red-state meat. "When can you start?"

"Tomorrow?" I volunteered, shocked that the entire transaction had been brokered so quickly. Gina hadn't even checked my references.

"Tomorrow it is. We'll throw you into prime time and then usher you on to the overnight come the weekend. Great way to gain experience, learn your way around the talent and the newsroom. Welcome to the News Channel. Now, get out of my office."

Pork Roulade with Herbed, Spiced Pears

I had pork on the brain after my interview at the News Channel. Can you blame me? And like Keaton and Cleveland, I wanted all my pork (political or otherwise) but none of the guilt. Lean scaloppine from my Sullivan Street butcher paired with fresh ingredients that could be found on the cheap at my corner deli—pears, thyme and cinnamon—made for a yummy celebratory meal. I could officially declare myself a working girl.

SERVES 4.

¼ c. raisins
½ c. fruity white wine, preferably Gewürztraminer
1 firm Anjou pear, cored, peeled and cut
    into ½-inch cubes
½ small yellow onion
½ celery rib, finely chopped (about 2 Tbsp.)
1 clove of garlic, peeled
1 Tbsp. fresh thyme, roughly chopped
4 Tbsp. olive oil
¼ tsp. kosher salt
Pepper to taste
⅛ tsp. cinnamon
4 pork tenderloin cutlets, pounded thinly into
    "scaloppine" or thin slices

Soak the raisins in the wine. Chop the pear, onion and celery. Press the garlic with the back of a large kitchen knife, flattening it enough to release a garlicky perfume. Pour 1½ Tbsp. of oil in a large, heavy-bottomed skillet (preferably cast iron) over medium-low heat. Add the pressed garlic clove, allowing it to slightly color and then remove (we want it to just lightly flavor the oil). Add the onions and lightly brown. Add the celery. Continue by adding the chopped pear to the mixture and season with ¼ tsp. kosher salt and pepper to taste. Cook everything until brown and tender. Drain the raisins (reserving the wine for later use) and place them in the skillet. Quickly incorporate the cinnamon and thyme and then remove skillet from heat and place pear mixture in a bowl.

Season both sides of pork cutlet with kosher salt and pepper to taste. Place a little over 1 Tbsp. of pear filling on one end of cutlet and firmly roll. Secure with 2–3 toothpicks. (Don't be tempted to overstuff—your roulade will be ugly, not "hearty"!) Repeat process with the remaining 3 cutlets.

Put remaining 2½ Tbsp. oil in skillet over medium heat. Add cutlets and cook for approximately 4 minutes, rolling the sides as they brown. Pour wine in skillet, let bubble for 30 seconds and then cover (I use a dinner plate). Let simmer for 2 minutes. Remove from heat. Remove toothpicks. Serve pork immediately.

9

DINNERTIME. A MAD dash and a skid across the dangerously buffed hallways of the basement, a flash of my security pass and into the yawning underground of the Sixth Avenue mall—a carnival of junk food, shoe shiners, speed manicures and ethnic take-out that was alien to these provincial eyes (ten-minute beauty procedures and *tikka masala* just aren't *done* down South). Guy, Gina's punching bag and the midlevel producer assigned to train me, had given me fifteen minutes to grab something fried and caffeinated. And that, my lovelies, was a luxury.

My brow had been furrowed for the past thirty-six hours and I couldn't smooth it out. Everything felt like a challenge, a test—even if the mission was as mundane as buying supper and inhaling it before the seven o'clock news. "Pardon me. Oh, was that your right kidney? Excuse me, sir. Ma'am, can you and your bosoms kindly shift to the left so I can grab a fork?" I maintained a one-sided inner monologue with strangers as I elbowed my way through the crowded food court. Fear and determination focused my energies as effectively as a sample sale at Saks Fifth Avenue.

"It's you and your big ol' bones and nothing else," I said aloud, handing over my credit card to pay an hour's worth of wages for a Southwestern chicken adobe something-or-other and a cup of caffeine. I needed more coffee. I couldn't ease up on the gas.

Y'all know why? After moving to New York City, you can't just return home—you have to sneak back. Eyes low, morale lower, you explain away your shot at the big time, how Manhattan failed you. "The Yankees are rude. The traffic is hell. Fifteen dollars for a cocktail, think I'm lyin'? People piled one atop the other in those high-rise buildings. Madness." But, of course, the mighty and the beautiful have rejected you. Everyone knows it. I couldn't return home. I was twenty-five, an age that made me too old to keep trading on the family name.

Rush-hour Manhattan, midbite, confronted me as I neared ANC's underground entry hall. Another armed man stood sentry, his expression vacillating between indulgence and cynicism depending on the presence or absence of a company-issued security badge. His hard face—not a crease of kindness in the cheeks—made my chest ache.

I stepped out of the stream and pressed against the sloped, tiled wall, remembering Granddaddy at the Mobile airport. He had wrapped his arms around me—Granddaddy was all about clean-smelling soap and soft cowboy shirts—and whispered, "Financial independence is the only independence." This, of course, was a very strange thing to hear from a man that bankrolled the entire family. My sister, Virginia, distracted as usual, gazed out the picture window to the tarmac and the twin-engine puddle jumper that would fly me to Atlanta, where I would board a jet to New York. "Find a husband while you're still pretty, have babies while you're still sane. . . ." she murmured in her perpetually exhausted tone. Her voice warranted a moist, cool washcloth be affixed to her forehead at all times. She liked saying such things because they paved the way for other clichéd thoughts and phrases that she was so fond of in regard to my reproductive future ("As for gettin' pregnant, you're a day late and a dollar short." "You're missin' the boat").

I shuddered and forced my way back into the newsroom, reminding myself to ignore Virginia and make money instead of babies. Among other things, it would give me a damn fine excuse to feel mildly superior to the rest of my family.

"We have a hot feed coming in from the Middle East—back at it, Dixie Dorothy!" Guy ran past me and into the Intake Room as best as his low-slung, baggy jeans and Gene Simmons T-shirt would allow

him. Dixie Dorothy was the charming yet confusing moniker he and
the other boys had given me. Was I to have a Christian name *and* a
work name? Did that put me on par with my kindergarten best-
friend-cum-adult-entertainer, Beatrice, who currently went by the
name of Jezebel at the Pensacola Pussycat Lounge? I'll be straight, I *did*
stick out like a peacock from the South's backwoods with my hair-
sprayed plumage, brightly colored dresses, juliette-sleeved blouses and
tight cotton twin sets with mother-of-pearl buttons. I just assumed we
were all supposed to make ourselves up like the entertainment reporter
on the six o'clock news. Was that so wrong?

Maybe I should have taken my style cues from Guy. It seemed as if
he had flawlessly adapted his look and attitude to the environs, remaining somewhere between the untucked shirttails of late-adolescent
Georgetown frat parties and the intensity of his early twenties, number-
crunching days over at the *Wall Street Journal*. He was my first stress
junkie, a man that explained away his previous life in digits and foreign
markets as being too relaxed. "Fuck the religion of Wall Street. Politics
and twenty-four-hour news is the messiah of the twenty-first century.
It's visionary, gutsy and takes a real set of—" He grabbed his denim,
zipped crotch with such force (and this was our first conversation—
ever—mind you) that I thought he would rupture a piece of his man-
hood. Turned out this bold move was the right one. "Livin' on the
edge," as Mamma would say—perhaps even living on the edge of sanity and good taste—suited him. He fit in perfectly.

But, I do confess to feeling sorry for the anxious thing; his job of
showing me the ropes couldn't have been easy. I wasn't a genius with
the technical stuff.

"Feeds, SOT's, VOSOT's, packages and teases are your lifeblood,"
he called over his shoulder as I followed him to Intake, slurping the last
of my coffee. The space—narrow as a closet and pitch black save the
dancing light cast by miniature television monitors—was a marvel,
boasting more dials, switches and buttons than Mission Control. In
that sliver of a room (I swear we would have felt less claustrophobic in
a submarine) the greenest of the News Channel drones monitored and
recorded news feeds from around the world.

"And if—*if*—you ever work your way up, don't think your office space gets any more luxurious. Our producing booths are the exact same size." I watched as anchors from New Delhi to Capetown played in real-time across the television screens, reporting on everything from drought to guerrilla warfare. "No, no, no, no," he said in monotone. Presumably, shots of an impoverished Indian child begging for change in a Mumbai marketplace wasn't the footage we needed to rake in the middle class and affluent conservatives south of Washington, D.C., and east of New Mexico, which, as I had just been told, was our target audience. "Flies. Disgusting," Guy spat. (And I do mean he spat—hocking lugies into distant trash cans was something he did with alarming frequency and accuracy.) Several of the screens went black and then rebooted, this time, with funny symbols decorating the bottom.

"Arabic," he said, seeming to read my mind.

I swallowed, hard, panic-stricken by the prospect of the day I would have to pull that maneuver on my own. Would I also have to read and speak those symbols? "Packages and teases?" I mused, lifting an eyebrow. In my experience, naughty jokes have a lovely way of mitigating incompetence.

He ignored me and continued twisting knobs and furrowing his brow until five cassette tapes, like the tongues of rotten little children, spit out from the wall. I quickly reached into my purse, still slung over my shoulder from the fifteen-minute dinner jaunt, and pulled out a steno pad and pen. Busy hands were a preventative measure.

"'Al Jazeera,'" he said, thrusting a tape in my face, "is the new Reuters of the News Channel, Al-Qaeda the international mob. Nowadays, it's all Middle East, all the time."

I noted in my steno pad: *Al-Qaeda terrorist threats—GOOD. Bush family shenanigans, humanitarian footage—BAD.*

"The only deviation will be the presidential elections. We've gotta get our man in office. Please tell me you know who the station is endorsing."

"Trick question?"

He shook his head in disgust. "Sen—"

"Senator Hewitt from Texas," I interrupted. He couldn't hide his

surprise, or annoyance, that I had done my homework. He quickly turned back to the machines.

Note: Can wear clothes of choosing, bright makeup and unnecessarily elongate vowels so long as know senators, red-state policy, latest suicide bombing in Baghdad.

Yet I still wasn't sure how all of this was preparing me to become an anchor. And, what *was* my exact job title? Two shifts trailing Guy, and I was more confused than ever. Not to mention that Sandra from Human Resources had passed me twice in the hallway and mumbled something about blusher "like racing stripes" and "trout lips." I hoped that she and the other ladies up in Human Resources hadn't filed me away as the new makeup artist for the anchors.

"So tell me, do all the anchors—"

"*Talent,*" he enunciated, stopping to lean against the door frame. He bowed his head and scratched what was left of his tangled brown nest of hair. The years had not been good to his hairline. "The *anchors,* as you call them, are referred to as on-air *talent.* That's the industry term and that's what Samantha, your other producer, and I will expect to hear from you. They stopped using that word 'anchor' when Ed Murrow left CBS News in the sixties. I'd strongly suggest memorizing the vocabulary list I gave you yesterday. Otherwise you'll just sound . . . *pedestrian.*"

Granddaddy was right. We're all snobs about *something*—even Guy. "All right then, does the *talent* always start off this way? It makes sense, learning from the ground up and all. But when do we move past the technical mumbo-jumbo to things like elocution, delivery, story selection?" I tried out my first smile of the day, attempting to squeeze out a dimple.

"We don't," he said, very matter-of-fact. He tossed me two cassettes and made off across the newsroom floor. Water blisters be damned! I ran after him in my kid leather, four-inch heels, determined to figure out my job title.

"But I told Gina I wanted to be the anchor of the six o'clock news," I shouted, ten steps behind, over the clatter of keystrokes and the garbled PA system.

"You did *what*?" He stopped midstride, whipped around and stared at me with tired brown eyes. A U-shaped configuration of desks (a "pod," as my vocabulary sheet would soon explain to me) occupied by producers, writers and PA's decided to stop dead in their tracks during our moment of action. Fingers hovered above keyboards, fannies directed swivel chairs in our direction.

"I told her the truth—"

"Strike one. Honesty. Continue."

I loathed Guy's one-word sentences. From that moment forward, I vowed to call him Ashley Wilkes—the one *true* gentleman in *Gone With the Wind*—on account of his utter and complete lack of gentility and charm. It'd be my stab at irony, sarcasm, whatever. New Yorkers were weaned on verbal poison from day one—there was no reason I couldn't participate. "I said to Gina that I was from a news family and that while Granddaddy wasn't too pleased about me leavin' home and the *Mobile Constitution,* he finally came around and phoned up Christopher Randolph, who said that I shouldn't be hidin' my young face behind the typeset of any newspaper, so I'll have you know that he called down to Gina and she deemed my red-state values to be very attractive." As you can see, anger has a way of twisting my nerves and affecting my mouth in such a manner that I become a blubbering caricature of myself—we'll call it the Scarlett Effect.

"Strike two. Sentimental twist to a professional discourse."

This was *not* how I had planned to spend my second day on the job. I was making enemies faster than the burning of Atlanta (I *do* love Margaret Mitchell). And my legs were a continuing horror. The inside of my thighs were raw from careening down hallways in a pencil skirt, lunging toward directors named Big Moe with the anchor's cues and copy just seconds before airtime. Hours of confusion trailing an aged frat boy, trying to decipher his frenzied comings and goings with news feeds and editing machines didn't help matters. I was so agitated, in fact, my peripheral vision had ceased to function.

"Look, Dorothy, you're just a PA—"

"—I'm going to be on the other side of that camera, Guy, whether you train me, I train myself or the good Lord plucks me from obscurity and sets me behind that anchor desk himself," I erupted, causing a handful of bobby pins to dislodge from my chignon. Christopher Randolph had said I was meant to be an anchor, not an entry-level piece of trash—a twenty-five-year-old Snickers bar wrapper floating on the floor of the newsroom, kicked around by the polished heels of higher-ups—like the rest.

If I had never seriously considered working in television news, I was coming around real fast. Investigative journalism coupled with a professional hair and makeup team guaranteed a life of gravitas and good skin. Come Christmastime, when I was home for holiday, toting a trunk full of designer clothes paid for with my incredibly inflated anchor salary, I would reclaim the right side—the favored side—next to Granddaddy on the swing, look out over the lake and the geese, and all would be right in my world. Working hard (and resembling a lithe Diane Sawyer of the early seventies) would be a kind of exorcism of two decades of Southern idleness and pork fat.

I fingered the short strand of pearls that laced itself around my neck and dipped into my clavicle and moved one step closer to Guy (nice jewelry always gives me confidence), "Gina wouldn't have hired me if she didn't see what I saw every day in the mirror—potential," I said loudly.

"Strike thr—"

"Not to *mention* decent bone structure," I added, with no small amount of pride.

"We've got a firecracker on our hands, don't we? Kids, put a note in my Outlook reminding me to check her voting record and party affiliation before I give her my *full* stamp of approval." Jack Wallace, the infamous cohost of the channel's most popular magazine program, slowly rose from his chair to his full five-foot-nine-inch grandeur and buttoned his blazer in a gesture of mock formality, a grin spreading across his long, fleshy face. Jowls swelled from his weak jawline like the gills of a preying shark. He had been tucked away to the right of Guy and, presumably, had heard our entire exchange.

A god or a gasbag—if you worked at 1221 Avenue of the Americas, you had to choose sides because he was everywhere. His poster-sized face, encased in cheap metal frames, passed as decor in the ANC stairwells, green rooms and bathroom stalls. I tended to my business in the ladies' powder room under his watchful gaze. My irritable bowel syndrome was beginning to make more sense.

I stood there paralyzed as his eyebrows, arched into haughty French circumflexes, and eyes took in the expanse of my body, painfully moving from my now swollen feet encased in Nine West instruments of torture to the hemline of my magenta skirt, over my gaseous belly, finally to the sleeveless cowl-neck sweater that had an unfortunate tendency of giving me the upper arms of a pro wrestler. My extremities tingled. I stared straight ahead into his navy blue lapels, trying to figure out what horrific synthetic blend his wife, mistress and producers allowed him to wear in front of millions of Americans. I wagered a viscose/poly/cotton blend.

"Excuse us, Mr. Wallace. I hope that we didn't interrupt your staff meeting," Guy said, looking down at his sneakers like a court jester refusing to make eye contact with the king. "I'm training a PA here . . . we all know how that goes." He rolled his eyes and grinned, as if he, the veteran staffer, had seen it all.

"Jack Wallace," he said, nodding, extending his hand in my direction. "Gina told me about you and your family. I think you're going to be a real asset to us down here in the trenches, fighting our war against the liberal degenerates."

"I bet you call her Ellen Degenerate too, don't you?" I asked, wide-eyed, referring to the daytime-television talk show host Ellen DeGeneres. "That's what my cousins call her. They think she's as corrupt as Clinton." No need to mention that I had gotten in the habit of watching her show every morning while reading the *New York Times*. "And I'm Belle. It's a pleasure, sir." I released his hand and considered that I had just touched a conservative treasure, an instrument of über-right-wing rhetoric, a means of prime-time castigation. He had called to task Hillary Clinton, George Clooney and untold others.

"Please, we're not at the Tiffany Network, drop the 'sir.' Call me Jack."

I had no idea what he meant by the "Tiffany" bit but I enjoyed a

momentary mental reprieve, fleeting visions of diamonds and crois-
sants and café au lait at eight o'clock in the morning. Hepburn in
Givenchy on the corner of Fifty-seventh and Fifth sure beat my
monochromatic separates and a hand-me-down coat swigging cold
coffee on the N/R subway platform.

"You've joined the News Channel at a seminal moment in our
nation's history. Do you realize that, Belle?" He ran his fingers through
what was left of his brown hair. "The elections are only a few short
months away and then *everything* is going to be different. . . ."

"We'll let you get back to your staff meeting, Mr. Wallace. Once
again, very sorry for the disturbance." Guy turned and motioned for
me to follow him, the bugged-out eyes demanding a hasty retreat. I
wagered that a forced immigration to the Communist News Network
was imminent if I didn't scurry after him.

*Acronyms for city survival: CNN—Communist News Network, BNT—
Bridge and Tunnel, VPCB—Viscose/Poly/Cotton Blend (denotes classless
man or woman).*

"What are your shows?" Wallace asked, turning his back to Guy, a
move that was both rude and heartening.

Guy wanted to drown my first unborn son in a well out back and
I didn't care. When you have the eye of the Corleones, you perform—
even if you're putting on a show for the syphilis-riddled uncle that
lives outside the palazzo gates. I wasn't about to miss my chance.

"For *now,* I'm a production assistant for breaking-news cut-ins and
overnights," I said, knowing that this put me on the lowest rung of the
news ladder, sandwiched somewhere between the cleaning ladies and
the NYU interns.

Swallow your pride and stick out your bosoms.

I cleared my throat. "The production side is eye-opening, Jack, but
I'm anxious for the day when I can be on the other side of the camera, communicating with America, delivering powerful sound bites,
shaping public opinion."

Oh, look at that, the big boy was smiling. Could I eek out a little
bit more? Would my gut allow any more generous exaggerations of
the truth? Sure—I was a debutante!

"One day, I hope to capture the hearts of America, just like you." There. I had said it and yet I hadn't. I could never outright lie and say I wanted to *be* him, I just wanted my own show, editorial control, a faithful audience . . . unlimited access to the corporate limo service. Perhaps a clothing allowance.

"Ambition like yours got me out of small-town Iowa and into the homes of eight million Americans. I like it. I like you," he said, his jowls wobbling. "I'm going to take it upon myself to *personally* watch over your progress."

"That'd make," I hesitated, choosing my words carefully, "for an utterly unforgettable experience."

I smiled and turned away, a wave of both disgust and relief overcoming me as I realized that I was on familiar ground. The system with the city giants was exactly the same as it was with the Southern politicos and lackeys. I'd covered the legislative beat in Montgomery for too long not to know my way around aging, coddled horn dogs.

I knew to walk three steps.

Swish hips side to side (channel heavy curtains in lethargic Alabama breeze).

Stop. Rotate three-quarters. Show off generous curves to best advantage.

"And I wouldn't mind a little controversy either," I said, placing the big, red cherry on top of our exchange.

Wallace, like all the rest, was a man led by his pointer, not his better judgment or brain. From then on, I realized that I'd be dealing with the currency of ego and expectation.

Oh, and on further reflection I do believe Sandra from Human Resources considered me a tart.

Sweet & Sour Cherry Clafouti

One of my favorite sweet things to throw in the cast-iron skillet is cherry clafouti. It's just about as easy to make as it is to convince horny egotists like Wallace that you want to lie down with the devil. This is my deceptively simple dessert for girls who know what they want, for girls who understand that life demands we be sweet and, sometimes, a little tart.

SERVES 6 GENEROUSLY.

1¼ c. fresh Bing cherries, pitted
¾ c. fresh sour cherries, pitted
1¼ c. all-purpose flour
1¾ c. whole milk
½ c. heavy cream
¼ c. granulated sugar
Pinch salt
4 eggs
1½ tsp. vanilla extract
¼ tsp. cinnamon
¼ tsp. nutmeg
1 Tbsp. unsalted butter, cut into cubes
Confectioners' sugar for garnish

Heat oven to 400 degrees. Butter the bottom and sides of 12-inch cast-iron skillet. Evenly distribute the pitted cherries in bottom of skillet. In a blender (or in a large bowl, using an electric mixer), blend for one minute (or mix on high speed) flour, milk, cream, sugar, salt, eggs, vanilla, cinnamon and nutmeg. Pour the batter over cherries and drop bits of butter all over the clafouti batter.

Bake skillet in oven until clafouti is golden, the batter is springy to the touch yet set, 25–30 minutes. Dust clafouti with powdered sugar and serve directly from the skillet.

10

"TAKE ME HOME," I said, easing myself into a taxi, "the long way." I sunk down onto the black leather bench seat. It was warm and sticky and made me think of the other hot bodies that had previously pressed against it. Trying to ignore its touch, I leaned my head back and closed my eyes.

"Home? Where's home?"

I opened my eyes and looked ahead to find a turbaned cabdriver. The white cloth of his head wrap brushed against the sloped beige cotton lining that hung from the roof. Pilled fabric circled his head like a halo.

"Mobile, Alabama," I said, reclosing them. Excitement and exhaustion kept me from saying exactly what I wanted. Of course I didn't mean for us to return to Mobile but I also didn't want to face an empty apartment. A loop around Central Park might be lovely. Anyway, it was Granddaddy and Grandmother's money—not mine. And, as always, Mamma's advice loomed large.

> B,
>
> This isn't for party dresses or French martinis. If you come home with a trunk full of new clothes, Granddaddy, Grandmother and I will be on to you. Spend this money on taxicabs and nothing else, you hear me? Do not set foot in that

*subway. And Grandmother wants you to promise you won't
ride with Arabs or coloreds.*

> *Love,*
> *Mamma*

"That would be quite a trip, Ms." I heard "Meez," no *s*'s. "Your
money might be better spent on an airplane ticket."

His name, Mandeep, was printed on a certificate and his voice, on
certain words, hit the marvelous bass notes of a Low Country Louisi-
anan. The sweet highs were all his own. Grandmother might be disappointed by the fact that I enjoyed his song of a voice, but I did. I
watched him as he signaled and carefully pulled away from the News
Channel building and onto Sixth Avenue. The street's broad lanes and
congestion added up to nothing more than a tunnel of fluorescent
light jammed full of Yankee neuroses. But, somehow, the quiet darkness of Central Park saved the commercial mess of Midtown Manhattan. It was the lack of light at the end of *that* tunnel delivering us all
from madness.

I considered spending Granddaddy and Grandmother's money on
one single cab ride with Mandeep. Four days under my belt, a pat on
the back from Wallace and it was early evening, that time when the
Manhattan day crosses into night and vibrant hues turn a deep shade
of amethyst, the work week fades to black. I felt like I needed an
extravagant spin around town.

"What about takin' us the long way back to Soho? I've never been
to Central Park. Can you take me up there so I can see where all the
rich people live?"

"I'll take you wherever you want to go, Ms." He looked at me in
the rearview mirror, hesitated and smiled.

"Spyin' on the other half amuses me," I murmured.

It was nothing like my favorite HBO program, *Taxicab Confessions*.
Mandeep was so polite and hadn't once asked about my sex life (which,
of course, was a good thing because I didn't have one). He was being
respectful so I sat up good and straight and looked out the window

as we turned right at Fifty-eighth Street and zipped onto Madison Avenue. The flash and polish of Yves Saint Laurent, Hermès and Armani came and went quickly. Gold-leaf signs tickled my ambition. At times like that, I planned out my material life, imagining the smooth Italian cashmeres, perfectly creased pant legs, wrists of cool diamonds, air-conditioned town cars and thick dinner party invitations. The New York of my mind felt much more real than the city blocks beneath my feet.

"At Eighty-sixth Street I turn onto Fifth Avenue and go back down, Ms.?" He didn't wait for my approval but, instead, continued planning my grand tour. "This way, we pass the Metropolitan Museum, enjoy the green park and chi-chi hotels and then maybe we find you a nice place to go so you won't be lonely. You meet someone. Yes, we must think of a good place to take you." His measured attempts at matchmaking took a page from Mamma's book.

"Well, sir, all right," I said, nodding.

"I unroll windows a bit for breeze. Lovely time of night." All four windows lowered, ever so slowly, allowing in the ripe smells of August skin and baking asphalt. I set aside the fat manila envelope, stuffed to bursting with my official American News Channel Employee Handbook, Guy's vocabulary list and memo, and filled my lungs. I exhaled. We passed the Metropolitan Museum and I breathed in again. This time, Egyptian artifacts and Picasso's paint hung in the air. Yep, I could even smell antiquity and genius (What can I say? It's the cook in me; I pick up notes in everything). As I watched the big leaves sway on their fat, tired branches, I slid across the bench seat to the park side because at the moment, the leaves impressed me more than the buildings.

"How do you think it feels to be Fifth Avenue rich, Mandeep?"

"I imagine," he began cautiously, "it is nice."

"I can't help but think that things would be better—life in Technicolor." Like the blonde reciting the news on the big television screens up in the sky, I thought. My eyes moved quickly, possessed by each passing rock in the park's gray stone ledge, the shadow of a blue bird, the silver finger of a pond tucked away for another day and a walk.

At Sixty-first Street and 7 P.M., I had the Pierre hotel to my left and the vanishing beauty of the park to my right. Back and forth, back and forth so that my head hurt, I twisted from the opulent to the real. Finally, red brake lights disappeared and we continued on and I could see that the green would be ending soon.

"But, to be honest, Ms., I don't spend much time thinking about those things. I have food and family. These make me happy. . . ."

We slowed again, the taxi idling at Fifty-eighth and Fifth. Right there, on the avenue, at the base of Central Park—within arm's reach of the gargoyles of the Plaza Hotel—was the place to be rich, I decided. I had to have it: a ride in a hansom cab, a taste of truffle to be prepared by a four-star chef at an elegant East-side restaurant. I wanted to be able to step inside stores perfumed with retail extravagance and buy. A watch paved in rubies, was there anything as beautiful?

My two distinct New York emotions: avarice and loneliness. Greed had a silk-stockinged leg up on my lonely heart.

"I think I'm taking myself to the Plaza, Mandeep."

"By the Plaza you mean the Oak Room, yes? You want a drink and conversation—"

"—And men in nice pinstriped suits."

All of the sudden, I felt like a vaguely competent Holly Golightly going to meet the right man at the right bar with just the right amount of red lipstick on. Maybe I'd meet someone who would want to buy me all those pretty things in the window displays. A ruby watch on a bed of midnight blue velvet just expecting my wrist, waiting for my fresh skin. I caught a glimpse of myself in the rearview mirror; the face staring back was expectant and very, very young. I touched my wrist.

"I leave you at the gates," Mandeep announced, nodding toward the Plaza as the meter clicked, clicked, clicked and spit out a fare receipt of $28. I turned and looked at the doors of the hotel dressed in gold and extravagance, in constant motion, like a picture in one of Mamma's *Royalty* magazines—Princess Di off to her next gala. A sharp intake of breath lasted me a full forty-two seconds until Mandeep turned around, head and shoulders, to look me in the eye and take my handful of cash. "Good luck, Ms. And do please remember why you came here."

Funny man, Mandeep. Did I look that misguided? I readjusted my red, V-necked sweater, wanting to show a suitable amount of cleavage, made the sign of the cross and walked toward the golden doors.

I smelled the Oak Room before I saw it. Scents like that—oak paneling, men soaked in money, silver polish—dominated my nose, draining to the back of my throat and then leaving my tongue to wrestle with the possibilities. Hope rolled around in my mouth, tasting something like the flinty Sancerre I had bought from LaGuardia Place Wines. (The man behind the counter had convinced me that $35 was a steal of a deal, a price that could be lowered even further if I wrote down my telephone number and e-mailed him pictures of myself on the johnny, not that I did.) My twenty-first-century body still functioned like an animal's, emotions registering in my saliva, my perspiration; somehow this reassured me. I walked in smiling.

"Will you be meeting a friend at the bar, Ms.?" the short, dark-haired maître d' asked with a raised brow and a glance up from his reservation list.

I would never bring one of my newsroom colleagues to a bar, I thought, my smile quickly fading. Lisa was fast approaching friend status, but I didn't quite trust her away from our familiar neighborhood cocktail parties à deux. I imagined her overindulging with the expensive wine and then, when the clock struck midnight, I would have to throw her over my shoulder and hail a hansom cab seventy blocks back to Soho.

At the Plaza, I'm not the new Sullivan Street tenant with the embarrassingly bulky family furniture or the production newbie named Dixie Dorothy who can't operate the equipment. On my own, I can change my posture or my drink order and I'm a different girl for a different man. Reinvention, wasn't that the soul of Manhattan? "I'm young and just pretty enough to believe in everyday miracles," I wanted to tell the maître d'. Even in a bar. *Especially* in a bar.

"No sir, no, no," I stammered, "I'm alone. I'd just like to have a glass of wine and," I paused, holding up my manila envelope as evidence, "I think I'll review some documents." The need to justify and over-explicate is the social cross that Mamma and I have to bear. There's something in our DNA (really, the genetic makeup of most Southerners) that doesn't allow us to shut up and go about our business without openly declaring it for anyone within hollering distance. With a single curt nod, the maître d' pursed his lips and wordlessly returned to his leather-bound book of names, thick as the Old Testament. I looked over his head of monkey grease and found what I needed—a sliver of bar.

The discovery of an empty bar stool in a storied Manhattan bar at 7:30 P.M. on a Friday night! The good Lord was smiling down on me. Even more miraculous, the ghosts of F. Scott Fitzgerald and his wife, Zelda, were probably standing next to me swilling gin. The Montgomery girl had long since given up on her flower staying fresh and her dress staying crisp but she was *there,* right *there.*

I brushed my fingers along the maroon leather and golden grommets trying to figure out how to sit down gracefully. My voluptuous bottom had never seen anything like that diminutive, citified seat, its dimensions shrinking the longer I choreographed my landing. Would my ample behind hang over the sides and create unsightly wings, thus deterring any and all ruby watch–wielding suitors from approaching me? Would it be better to just stand and slenderize, endure the pain of corns and water blisters? "Bartender!" I hurriedly arranged myself on the stool, crossing my legs in hopes of dividing the size of my ass by half, getting its square root, whatever. I needed a drink.

California Syrah—$20. The pretty italics on the drink menu didn't change a thing. "Highway robbery," I said aloud, doing my usual bit of work-to-palate-pleasure ratio. I'd have to work almost two hours recording Arab symbols in the Intake cave to pay for my glass of red.

"Careful sips, honey, that's how you do it," the woman to my left offered through pillowy, frosted pink lips. "You new around here?"

"Pardon me?"

"First time?" she asked, leaning toward me and smiling. Well, she tried to smile but her top and bottom lips were too plump to separate. She fluttered her eyes. A wink? Big, chestnut brown locks of hair danced around her face, making me recall a childhood Easter vacation in the Texas Panhandle.

I paused, not wanting to appear completely out of the loop. "I usually go to . . ." I searched the recesses of my weary brain, trying to remember the name of the hotel on Sixty-first Street. "The Pierre!" I nearly shouted with excitement. "Lovely crowd." I averted my gaze from her carefully shadowed eyes and moved to her enormous breasts, two Georgia watermelons competing for Biggest and Best at the county fair.

"High class," she said, returning the favor and looking me over from stem to stern. "You'll need that tonight—just look at 'em panting, packed in here three deep." She set in again with the indistinct eye movements. I wasn't quite sure what to do with the conspiratorial raise of her eyebrows. Was it the cigarette smoke?

"Tonight's gonna be a long one." She sighed, taking a long, slow sip of her pink wine. For a moment, her smile broke as she became absorbed in the gold rings that wrapped around each of her fingers. Several of the bands boasted diamond chips. "Good thing we have ourselves a free dinner," she finally said, proudly sweeping her arm across the expanse of the bar, a game show hostess presenting our unearned wares.

Chex Mix had been shuffled away to an inferior bar on an inferior block, I supposed. In its place were gorgeous little bowls: hills of fresh pistachios, hand-cut potato chips and cayenne-spiced cashews peaking over silver rims. The bartender prepared a cocktail in front of me, nestling a handsome set of silver tongs deep into an ice bucket. The rumbling sound of the cubes was soothing and expensive. A girl could become addicted to a noise like that.

"Once you've been in one hotel bar, you've been in them all," I said, raising my glass to hers. She was tacky and sweet as hell and I couldn't help but feel a little proud of us sitting up there at the fancy bar, surrounded by men. I recrossed my legs and set the manila envelope by my wineglass.

"Nice touch," she said, nodding toward the bundle of work documents. "You look like a real professional. Well, I guess we *are* professionals." She smiled and I smiled back for reasons I was unaware.

"Revlon," she cooed from behind her raised wineglass. "Ohh, I don't believe it, here comes Revlon." I turned to find her eyeing a short man, bald as a new potato. I had no idea what she meant—he didn't look like he was wearing any makeup. Besides, I was a card-carrying Chanel girl. And the sight of his waxen head wasn't helping to quiet my empty stomach. A plate of Mamma's German potato salad would have tasted real good right about then.

"If I were a nice girl I'd give this one to you," she whispered so quickly it sounded like a hiss, "but I'm not and I can't. Next one's all yours." She hastily ran a pinky finger over her glossed lips. But to her disappointment, it was me he had his eyes on.

"Beautiful," the man said, smiling, "don't I know you from somewhere?"

"I don't believe so," I began, my mouth watering. I could almost taste the small golden tubers, bathed in mustard and olive oil.

He smiled. "Can I get you a drink? Champagne?" The swagger allowed him to substitute ill-fitting Levi's for a suit, sport shoes without laces instead of proper wingtips like Granddaddy's. There was no big gold watch and he certainly wasn't handsome. I had no idea what she was so excited about. And why was he named after a cheap cosmetics brand?

I didn't care to find out. I swiveled on my fanny and turned back to my work.

Now, down to business. One glass of wine had to last me through Guy's memo and the employee handbook. I couldn't afford another glass of anything and such opulence didn't come for free. Guy had thrust the papers in my hand as I left the basement for my one day "weekend." As I thanked him, he muttered something about "dog meat" and the Wallace incident and then the overhead intercom system began cursing at some unfortunate intern so I waved and told him we would speak during my next shift.

And, you know what? There was a glimmer of something in his eyes. I'm here to tell y'all that it just might have been recognition. I do suspect Guy had finally come to his senses. Hear me out. All it took was one long look at my right side—the good one I'd present to cable news land—for him to realize that my features might be close to telegenic. During the toss-off to my coanchor, I'd turn that side to the camera and the people would love it—advertising dollars would soar!

"Out you go!" Excited by the prospect of my imminent career advancement, I upended the envelope, unceremoniously dumping its contents out onto the bar. The bowl of expensively shelled pistachios toppled to its side and the precious green seeds skidded down the polished wood like so many marbles on the school-yard cement. "Please *excuse* me," I said pressing my hand against my chest, looking left and right to see who had witnessed my social faux pas. Revlon shot me a wolfish grin.

"Lord, I'll never be invited back," I whispered.

As I riffled through the pages, I began to formulate Guy's gracious, conciliatory memo in my head. He, along with Wallace, would be the first in a long line of higher-ups to notice me. I took a sip of wine and pondered my Melanie Griffith *Working Girl* existence.

To: Dixie Dorothy
From: Guy
Re: Newsroom Survival

Week One has passed and all ain't peaches and cream, Dixie Dorothy. Your Wallace encounter effectively pissed off half a dozen PA's who have proven themselves and have been angling for placement and recognition in his matrix. Rule #1: Make good with the peons. They will support you when Jack has long since left you behind.

Short and sweet: focus on politics—not the nation's, the newsroom's. It doesn't matter how Holly Hunter did it at her operation. ANC is a beast and you're its bitch. Know the on-air talent, producers, directors, editors and PA's. Start from the bottom and work your way up. Make good with the little ones, know the big ones. And if you really want to move up, strike out on your own. Nothing is nuanced here, only the big guns are recognized.

The newsroom structure is Byzantine. Do your homework. Remember, you look bad, I look worse. So don't fuck up. Please don't fuck up. There. I said it, "please." —Guy

The boy certainly had *not* gone to charm school. (Can you imagine what his thank-you notes looked like?) But at least he had warned me about the rainbow of personalities, scandals and quirks I'd have to deal with. Quickly, I shoved a pile of Oak Room cocktail napkins into my purse. If I were to construct a crib sheet—detailing the sins and relative importance of my coworkers—it'd be done on something suitably dramatic. I tried to picture Mamma back when she was a cub reporter at the *Constitution*. Did she pussyfoot around, creating flow charts of the resident nut cases for the purpose of career advancement?

Goodness, maybe I *did* need Revlon's glass of champagne. Newsroom life up North began to look as complicated as a genealogy chart down South. (Was Uncle Walter Daddy's brother or just Daddy's sister's lover?)

Almost the Plaza Hotel's Cayenne-Spiced Nuts

I didn't suspect the nut jar would be filling up so quickly. Too bad it was chockablock full of my eccentric coworkers instead of the Plaza Hotel's spiced cashews and pecans. I did my best to extract the secret recipe from the bartender (lashes, smiles, bosoms) but to no avail. So I went home, buried myself in the spice cabinet, pulled out the bag of nuts Granddaddy had sent from our pecan groves and vowed to come up with a recipe of my own. A handful of these and a sip of chilled wine in the shade of my patio and I felt as if I could take on anything—even the News Channel.

SERVES A TIPSY COCKTAIL PARTY OF 12.

¾ c. pecans, roasted, unsalted
1¼ c. cashews, roasted, unsalted
¼ tsp. cayenne pepper
2½ tsp. brown sugar
½ tsp. *sriracha*★
Scant 1 Tbsp. kosher salt
1 Tbsp. unsalted butter, melted

Heat oven to 350 degrees. Evenly spread pecans and cashews on a baking sheet. Toast until fragrant and warm, stirring halfway through so nuts will bake evenly, about 5–7 minutes.

In a bowl, mix cayenne, sugar, *sriracha,* salt and melted butter. Pour warm nuts into bowl, add spiced butter and toss. Serve nuts warm.

★*Sriracha* is a Vietnamese hot sauce made from sun-ripened chilis. It is to Vietnamese cuisine what ketchup is to American.

Golden Potato Salad

Food on the brain. It's a condition. And I bet that old, rich man would die if he knew that his waxen, bald head made my belly rumble for a helping of potato salad. Sir, if it's any comfort, three of my all-time favorite ingredients—potatoes, white wine, mayonnaise—are incorporated into this Southern classic. That might just make you the tastiest dish in town.

SERVES 6.

- 3 lbs. red new potatoes
- 1 c. mayonnaise
- 4 Tbsp. white wine
- 3 tsp. Dijon mustard
- ½ tsp. dried oregano
- 1 tsp. kosher salt
- Freshly ground pepper
- 6 Tbsp. chives, finely chopped
- 4 Tbsp. parsley, chopped
- ½ c. celery, finely chopped
- ½ c. yellow onion, very finely chopped

Bring a large pot of water up to a boil. Season generously with salt, as you would season pasta water. Cook potatoes until tender (check doneness with tines of fork; tines should easily cut through to the center of potato), about 18–20 minutes. Remove from heat, drain in a colander and let cool. Cut cooked and cooled potatoes into fourths. Place in a large bowl.

In a small bowl, whisk together mayonnaise, white wine and mustard. Add oregano, salt, pepper and mix well. Stir in chives, parsley, celery and yellow onion. Pour the dressing over the large bowl of potatoes and mix thoroughly.

11

"THE DOOR, PLEASE!" I shouted to a shadowed security guard inside the building, trying to balance Mamma's heavy silver tray and my monogrammed tote bag in the crook of my arm. Lotta good that did. Every glass surface at 1221 was bullet- *and* soundproof, per the facts and minutiae delineated in my employee handbook (*"never* underestimate the Democrats and their desire to rough up GOP broadcasters and executives," the thick, Xeroxed volume had told me). The guard remained motionless on the stool, his back sloped, an italicized parenthesis leaning against the marble wall. The seemingly substantial wooden podium, usually facing forward like the man behind it, was askance, the pin light inside revealing cheap bones of duct tape, bowed plywood and a patchwork quilt of magazine and newspaper clippings. I felt a little ashamed, like I was seeing someone's drawers sunny-side up, so I closed my eyes and tapped the glass door with the toe of my new blue sneaker, hoping that he would hear me. There was no one else around. The revolving doors and entryways, usually clogged by delivery boys and chain-smoking suits, were clear and locked. The darkened lobby shone gold and black and desolate at 10:42 P.M. on a Saturday evening. There was no sense that what lay inside shaped wars and presidents. One last kick and a wave. Aha! The guard pulled back his cap and quickly made his way across the lobby.

"Ain't even late yet," he said, shaking his head, opening the door

for me. "I can't believe I dozed off like that. You haven't been standin'
here long, have ya?" With his hat back, I finally got a good look at his
face. It was the sweet guard from Georgia that had given me directions
the day of my interview. "And what do we have here? Looks mighty
good. Mmmmm, yes, sir, it does." His head circled the round Bundt
cake covered in Saran Wrap.

"I made a pound cake for the peons."

"The cake's for who?" He glanced up at me, brows furrowed, but
then quickly returned to the platter, looking at the tall, golden wonder with a big smile. The height on that sucker *was* impressive. "My
mamma used to make one of them with chocolate chips and raisins.
Then, when someone up and died, she'd pour rum . . ."

Had I just called my coworkers peons? Oh, hell, I couldn't go being
honest like that. Attitude was only allowed by the Yankees if you made
six figures and commanded a staff of Ivy League grads. Having an
apartment high up in the Pierre probably gave you a special behavioral
dispensation as well. And, besides, the whole point of my eight-egg,
two-cups-of-sugar wonder (with accompanying tin foil–covered
ramekin of chocolate buttercream icing) was to make nice. I once read
that Kim Novak took great pains to befriend the lighting technicians
and stagehands before she even shimmied up to her male costar; they
were the ones that would make her look good. Aside from a decent
profile, I needed all the help that I could get.

"I'll slice you up a pretty piece once I get to the Green Room," I
called over my shoulder, pondering the fact that the guard really *was*
shaping up to be my only friend in the building. Why couldn't I social-
ize like any normal twenty-five-year-old? God, I was difficult. I hus-
tled down the escalator, two steps at a time, reminding myself that
there was a shift change in less than fifteen minutes and I had to slice
(the cake) and spray (my hair).

After fifty-odd blocks, would you believe that I had nearly lost it
(the cake, not my mind)? Yes, I have a tendency to misappropriate my
energies and I admit that too much time and focus were folded into
that batter along with the egg whites. There was also the matter of the
spike in my blood pressure while transporting the thing on the sub-

way and that man in the last car advising me to melt down Mamma's wedding silver and use the money to buy dope. The pierced group next to him tossed out some question like, "The hole in that cake gonna be filled with cream by night's end?" What in God's name? My baking wizardry had much more in store for it than any of those carousing delinquents could imagine: *this cake would help me conquer the newsroom*. I was invested in that mass of flour and butter.

With those thoughts swimming around my blond depths, I stepped through the sliding glass doors and promptly tripped over a cardboard box. Then another. And another. "Dag blast it!" Used time cards and steno pads flew out of the boxes just as the cake platter shot out of my hands and I fell to the floor.

"You okay?" a woman's voice called out from behind a computer monitor.

Get your fanny up and come and look! My elbows were throbbing and my tote bag was upturned; a trail of hair products and lip glosses had scattered all the way up to the breaking-news desk. A spray of chocolate buttercream probably reached the tips of her toes.

A slender, pale arm reached down for one of the tubes. "I love Stila glosses. Their nudes do wonders for plumping. Is this from Sephora or Barney's?"

Oh, shut up! Where is my precious cake? "I'm fine, really. Let me just make sure there's no blood."

"Sephora or Barney's? Which did you say? Mind if I give it a little swipe?"

Down on all fours, I looked up at the ceiling and then down the aisle of the newsroom, suddenly realizing that the space was lit like one of the bistros near my apartment—that is to say, not at all. The interminable rows of desks to my right, usually looking like the long, self-important shadows of pecan trees across a sunlit road, were almost indiscernible. Lit computer monitors floated in the near-blackness. The breaking-news studio, situated in the center of the newsroom, served as the only major source of light for a room the size of a football field.

"I'd come and help you but we're just getting a hot one off the wire about a Category Four in Cuba. Just stay right there and don't move. We can't have you suing for damages on my shift." Her tone suggested that this sort of thing happened all the time.

"By any chance do you see a silver platter and cake up there?" I wiped newsroom floor debris—cracker crumbs, city dirt, crushed blue and green M&M's—off the palms of my hands and flipped over. Lying facedown on the curiously scented, stained carpet went against every bone of decorum and politesse in my now bruised body.

"Landfall east of Havana. VO of downed shacks, crying children, irate septuagenarians—preferably holding coconuts, hand-whittled canes, shredded palm fronds." She sounded utterly bored by the work, thoroughly amused by her newfound, nearing-midnight sense of humor and madness. "Everything must shout 'Cuba!' Castro has failed! Cleveland, *naturally,* won't allow anything less dramatic. Keaton, *naturally,* will love the destruction and promptly snap up all waterfront property. Another Grand Bahama at the hands of the gringos."

Such a robust voice coming from that tiny arm. I cleared my throat. "I *do* hate to bother you, but I have to ask if there's a cake by your feet. It's awful hard to see anything in this light." I had landed myself in an awkward pile of horseshit. Again. My life was incapable of running clean and clear and smooth.

"Economizing. Can you believe this no lights business? We're making news in a darkroom. What are we doing, developing X-rated photos of Senator Pelosi? At least we have air-conditioning. Last year they shut off the heat after we lost the November sweeps. Management cited boiler room problems. Christ."

"They should never doubt you," I said, my eyes big, my belief bigger. "You're a member of the nation's number one news channel."

At this, her chair creaked, swiveled and rolled back from her computer station. I heard a deep sigh, the kind of exhale that belongs to the insurer of a sinking house in the Georgia Low Country, the wife of a philandering husband during deer season. I closed my eyes and sighed too, for no reason, really. It just seemed the thing to do, like eating one last tomato and mayonnaise sandwich at afternoon tea. When I opened my eyes, a fine-featured, hazel-eyed pixie hovered above me.

She was freakishly thin, totally devoid of curves. "They really got her," she said quietly, looking directly at me.

I sat there, good and still, and then extended my hand in her direction so she could help me get to my feet. "I'm a little banged up but I'm fine," I said, smiling. She looked at my hand and at me, perplexed. Her men's khaki pants, shrunken red cotton T-shirt and Velcro sneakers didn't quite know what to do with my suggestion of human contact. But I kept my hand out there. *Yes,* she happened to address me in the third person. *Yes,* she looked like a boy wearing his sister's lip gloss. But, she had just gone from mild concern to indifference to professional frustration to pity in sixty seconds flat. For all intents and purposes, she was a Southerner—volatile, fiery, fickle. Thrilling! I considered deferring to her like I would to an older (possibly male) second cousin. Something like that.

Finally she reached out for me. I was careful, though. I didn't need her blowing out anything in her spritelike body.

Blowout: a common phrase back home that describes everything from sudden physical ailments to the malfunctioning of carburetors and washing machines.

A sudden flashback to me in my high chair, Mamma at the stove hollering at my six-year-old sister, Virginia, "Don't go pickin' up the baby! She's too fat. You're gonna blow out that back of yours!" rushed into my mind.

"And my name's Belle," I said, stashing away the ego-crushing, repressed childhood memory.

"Samantha Fisher." She gave me a slight nod. "What was this about a cake? It's not terribly fattening, is it? I do candy, Twizzlers, SweeTarts, PlenTPacks of gum. Concentrated doses of sugar administered at specific times throughout the evening to get me over that four A.M. hump." Her tone and large, carefully lashed eyes made every scenario seem to have dire consequences. It was as if at any moment I would have to force-feed her sticks of Juicy Fruit to prevent twilight hypoglycemic shock. It'd be like in *Steel Magnolias* when Sally Field coaxes orange juice down a diabetic Julia Roberts's throat on her wedding day. Samantha might just fall out of that swivel chair, taking down a stack of newsroom scripts and all that producing knowledge with her. The channel would be forced to call off the subsequent hours of broadcasts and it would be all my fault because I hadn't managed to cram enough sugar into her birdlike body.

"Everyone has their system—you'll have your own soon enough. There's a point of no return that we all hit on this shift and I just happen to screw with my blood sugar level instead of my septum."

At least we had survived. Both the cake and I had been wrapped so tightly (the cake in Saran Wrap, me in my new Joe's blue jeans) that we had managed to stay together.

"Put the cake down and sit at the computer station next to me." Suddenly, she was all business, moving from playtime to work with the cool control of my first-grade teacher, Ms. Walsch. "Guy and a couple of video editors left on a french fry run after the ten-thirty cut-in. We'll shift around when they get back."

"Let me just go set this down in the staff ki—"

"Two questions," she interrupted. "Have you seen the rats that call this place home? And have you had the pleasure of meeting aforementioned editors, the quota hires? They all eat trash. They'll devour this beauty in an instant. Leave it *here*." Her eyes never moved from my face as she arched back in her seat, reaching for an empty chair, quietly commanding me to sit.

I wordlessly unwrapped my creation and set it down between our computers. She patted the seat.

"Here you are. The overnight." Preaching, the primary occupation of Alabama's elderly, is something I can sniff out in an instant. I thrust my hand inside my tote, looking for something to take notes with, and grabbed all that remained after my tumble—Oak Room cocktail napkins and a lip pencil. My steno, along with everything else from my bag, was still splayed across the floor and I was too petrified to ask if I could collect my wares. Samantha seemed more than capable of giving me a lick or two in the corner if I spoke out of turn.

"This shift is a bitch. Guy is a bitch. I can be a bitch. Gina, well, we all know she's a bitch but she was dead-on for putting you here. One day you might be able to work with Fred, Wallace, Chase

Stephens and the others." Her steady voice continued while her fingers flew across her keyboard. The printer began to spit out reams of pages. "This is where you get your television backbone."

Or dorsal fin, I thought.

"This is where you become a television journalist."

Note: Best time to learn job is when rest of female Manhattan is drinking pink cocktails, dancing on banquettes and meeting rich men who will pay downtown rent.

"But you need to be honest with yourself. Are you going to be one of those who is all technique and ambition and you know," she waved her hands over her keyboard, shooing away a swarm of invisible flies, "obsessed with celebrity? A star? Or do you have the guts to be a real journalist who breaks news and puts herself out there for a story?" *Click, click, click* of her mouse. I looked down at her fingernails: shiny, short, functional.

"I want to be a *star journalist*." For once, I enunciated all consonants, speaking, I imagined, like the people of Chicago.

"That's not how it works. You choose." Her eyes furiously scanned the AP copy on the screen while she quietly uttered those words. Samantha had a way of devastating my dreams during her moments of distraction.

"But it's so *easy*," I said, furiously wheeling my chair right up next to hers. "Stick those words together like hot pepper jelly on cream cheese and you've got something special! Throw in someone that gives a damn and teaches me the ropes of writing, filming, editing, speech— and, ta-da, magic! I'm your golden girl."

She glanced at me quickly. "You do look just like her. Well, the *natural* version—before all the surgeries."

"Who?"

"If you didn't have the face, it wouldn't matter how good of a reporter you were."

"Who do I look like?"

"What we need to do is get you some chops, some credentials to compete with the other towheaded wonders around here. That's the secret they don't tell you in J-school—you have to have it all. Of course at ANC that means tits and glossy lips. This industry is so competitive and twisted. I have no idea why you girls do it."

"Who did you say that I looked like?" I chirped, this time sitting up lovely and straight, placing my hands on my knees, hoping she might actually respond to my question.

"Your mind's made up—you want to be talent. No hope of convincing you to become a producer, work behind the scenes? Because after a few months with us learning the ropes, you have to choose sides—are you in front of or behind the camera? And then, of course, there's the matter of moving to a smaller market—Poughkeepsie, Milwaukee—and getting the Q ratings that'll allow you to move back to New Yo—"

"Damnit, Ms. Fisher, *who* on God's green earth is walkin' around with my face?"

"Call me Samantha. And you look just like Paige. Ten years ago." She was quick and quiet about saying it.

"Paige Beaumont, the anchor?" She was the girl from New Orleans—always impeccably dressed—all attitude in heels. The men in the newsroom alternately loved her (flirtatious ways) and loved to hate her (neuroses); with a smirk and a cocked brow, they referred to her as the "Georgia Peach." When they began placing bets what her "crease" was made out of, I stopped listening. The one time I had brushed up against her in the hallway, I immediately ran into a bathroom stall and called home. Mamma swiftly digested the info and, always one step ahead, instructed me to get an autographed head shot for Granddaddy's ninetieth birthday. I said I'd work on it.

"And Wallace likes you, though you don't need to work for him yet. You'll get burned and run scared and I wouldn't blame you."

"You know about my Wallace encounter?"

"Welcome to high school, Ms. Belle. Gossip flies. Just don't set your sights on 'Most Popular' like Paige did in the beginning. She made cupcakes for the staff," Samantha looked down at my cake, "she tried to befriend the *entire,* incestuous Manhattan media circle—especially the bloggers," she continued, rolling her eyes at the absurdity of Paige's desperate quest for attention. "She even went for beers at Langan's, trying to be one of the boys. No one cared. And they wanted to throw that absurd Malti-poo of hers, Snow White, yet another transparent vie for attention—into the path of an oncoming number-five express train. She was just the blonde from the Stix who wanted to be a star. Instead of kissing ass she should have been out nailing stories, practicing her copy, signing on for a double shift. Now, management has relegated her to the thirty-second news cut-ins. They throw her a prime-time news slot every once in a while but it's going to take some time before she can pull herself back up by the bra straps."

Samantha stared me down. "Is that what you'd want after ten years of struggling to get to the belly of American media? A frozen face and the task of delivering sophomoric thirty-second sound bites about Ryan Seacrest and the latest methamphetamine bust in Kansas?"

At least Samantha seemed to care about my future. But I knew better than to respond with an honest answer. Because, quite frankly, thirty seconds of prime-time glory sounded a hell of a lot better than bivalve festivals on the Gulf Coast. And I refused to go to the Panhandle, *again,* to cover the Flora-Bama Bar's Mullet Toss Competition (by now everyone knew to drop the fish in the sand for a little traction). "I've got my cocktail napkins so shoot—I'm ready for anything. You mentioned chops. How do I go about getting those?" I asked, wetting the tip of my lip pencil with my tongue.

"There's no golden ticket, Belle," she said, her tone quickly approaching one of disgust. "No one helped me when I first transferred from CNN."

Sigh. False alarm.

Female mentors—"mammas"—are terribly hard to find.

"Just know the players and get yourself a cause."

A *cause?* Like Daughters of the Confederacy? I wondered.

"What *is* all this shit on the floor?" A herd of men and all the requisite noise and stench that accompanies caged animals burst through the sliding glass doors. If I hadn't spotted their McDonald's bags, I would have thought that we were being robbed by a gang of potbellied, pasty-faced Senator Kerry staffers.

"Eat your artery-clogging trash and hush," Samantha said coolly, swiveling away from me, fixing her gaze above the computer monitor.

Rrrrrring! The kitchen buzzer in my head went off. Time was up. The trajectory of my career had mattered to Samantha for approximately five minutes. But I had exhausted my welcome. Somehow, I had missed my chance to become *her* cause. Now, all eyes were on the outrageous, loud group before us—not the progression of my news career.

"Did the Avon lady *and* a cat's lower intestinal track explode?" Guy asked, emerging from the pack of video editors. "What the fuck?" He stopped just short of the news desk, slapping his hand against his forehead and examining the floor.

"Please get over yourself, princess." Samantha shot him a look of contempt. "We just cut video of decapitated bodies in Darfur and somehow you're more repulsed by a little icing on the floor. Belle, what was that anyway, chocolate buttercream? It really is too bad that you dropped it. The caffeine in chocolate does wonders for me. When we're down to the wire, stumping for Hewitt these next two months before the election, you must bring in more."

"Lord, I'm so sorry. I meant to clean it up but then we got to talkin' . . ." I jumped out of my seat and tucked the cocktail napkins into my back pocket.

"Our new girl." Guy smirked, shoved his right hand into the paper bag and emerged with a fistful of french fries. The oily potatoes, every last one of them, along with his bloated, short fingers, were expertly thrust into his mouth.

So that's how I was supposed to eat during my allotted fifteen-minute dinner "hour."

"It's taken him six years to be able to do that. Something to write home about, hmm?" Samantha looked at me and raised an eyebrow. "Better yet, tell the parents to read about him on About.com. Guy has reached mythic status on the discussion boards." I watched him as he enjoyed his one brief moment of cardiac-arrest-inducing bliss.

"Welcome to the overnight shift, Dixie Dorothy." He wiped the french fry hand on his jeans and then extended it in my direction, some stab at mock formality.

What exactly was posted on that Web site? For Guy, there had to be mention of a physical transformation. At one time, he must have been a handsome thing, five inches taller, toned, with a full head of hair. Then, his body had been forced to slowly adapt to the overnight shift and the lack of sunshine, rest and proper nutrition. Now, squat, balding and irritable, all he knew was the dank newsroom air. Soon, I reckoned, he'd resemble a blind sewer rat, a thin flap of skin covering his small red eyes.

"And you're sportin' some nice hair tonight." He let out a rude little chortle and in the process of stifling his laughter, sprayed a fine mist of potato on my camel-colored twinset.

"The higher the hair, the closer to God," I said, batting my lashes. *Plink, plink.*

Back home after my first midnight shift, I climbed into bed just as the sun rose over Sunday morning in the city. Work time and sleep time had been transposed and so I felt exhausted and hollow in the sunlight. Feelings that were only supposed to come in the safety of night, I now wrestled with during the day. And there was my twenty-first-century bedtime story, waiting on the side table—my laptop. About.com, Google and the sins of my coworkers loomed before me.

Internet research has forever replaced fairy tales.

But there was still time to dig, to strive, to become, I thought, dozing off. Anyway, the truth was much more difficult to defend than ignorance.

Alone, my sleep came with a happy sadness, distant ringing telephones and a Dire Straits tune playing in my head.

> *And here I am again in this mean old town*
> *And you're so far away from me . . .*

Bribe-Your-Coworkers Pound Cake

Down South, pound cake is made on Sundays and is meant to last the entire week, an ever-ready nibble of something sweet for unexpected visitors. Tell that to my coworkers. Once my friendship cake (read: bribe) made landfall in the newsroom, it was devoured within minutes. Am I that good with a whisk or are the news junkies that desperate for something good and honest?

SERVES 8.

- 2 sticks unsalted butter, softened
- 2 c. sifted cake flour
- 4 extra-large eggs, separated
- 1 c. sugar
- 1 tsp. vanilla extract

Preheat oven to 325 degrees. Butter and flour a medium-sized Bundt or tube pan and set aside.

In a medium-sized bowl, cream butter and flour until mixture resembles coarse crumbs. In a separate, large bowl, beat egg yolks, sugar and vanilla until well blended. Add the creamed butter and flour to the egg mixture in three parts, beating well after each addition.

In a separate, small bowl, whip egg whites until stiff peaks form. Add the egg whites to the batter, beating on high speed for 2–3 minutes. Pour into pan.

Bake for 55 minutes, or until top is lightly golden and a toothpick comes out clean. Let cool in pan on rack. Serve with Mamma's chocolate buttercream icing, if desired.

For a "Life's-Too-Short!" nibble with your morning coffee, cut thick slices of pound cake, spread with softened butter and slide under the broiler until toasted. Serve with your favorite, real-fruit preserves.

12

"ROSE, I THINK my most pleasant New York City moments are spent right here," I said, looking out onto our street, patting her white cushion edged in eyelet. I reached for her hand so that she could settle in next to me on the wooden bench outside of Twisted. Feeling sorry for me and my lack of Labor Day plans, Lisa had left me the keys to her store.

"Open shop and play dress-up with the tourists or pull out the bench and watch the world go by. I don't care—I'm off to see Shakespeare!" Lisa twirled from rack to rack in a robin's egg blue, wide-brimmed hat fit for the Kentucky Derby, sick in love with an eighteen-year-old thespian. "He's not *just* an actor—there's a difference!" she chided me. "He's on tour with the Royal Shakespeare Company and is poised to become the next DDL." Daniel Day-Lewis. Dating him, I supposed, was as good an excuse as any to polish her British accent and tour the liberal arts colleges of the Northeast. Anything for the Bard and good sex.

"All right, *cara,* give the old girl a minute." Rose left her walker in the middle of the sidewalk and, taking small steps backward, made her way to the bench. When she could safely feel the wood behind her knees, she'd collapse. I knew this. Rose trusted her surroundings.

"In the neighborhood, late in the afternoon, my mind feels quiet and hopeful," I continued, meaning it but also trying very hard to forget the mass exodus of hip New York to a stretch of Long Island called the Hamptons (you'd think it was Versailles the way they talked about it with such reverence). The last official weekend of summer and I smelled Rose's Aqua Net and Polident instead of coconut lotion and salt water. "Out here on the cement there aren't any egos, just people getting laundry and fresh bread, dodging leaky air conditioners and tryin' to move from one day to the next—we don't know if someone lives in three thousand or three hundred square feet. There's no hierarchy. I like that."

"But I'm the queen," she said, a smile playing across her face.

"Yes, ma'am, you are." Rose was ninety-two years old, and the queen of Sullivan Street. (I do believe the shopkeepers had a T-shirt printed, all uppercase letters, saying just that.) While some neighborhoods have eccentrics, I had her, the sweetest walking, talking memory an out-of-town girl could ask for. If anyone could make me forget about Samantha, Paige and the news "writers" (I recently stumbled across them rearranging the syntax of Reuters news feeds, scanning it into the teleprompter and calling it their own), their weekend wheelie suitcases and talk of clambakes and cocktail parties, it was Rose. Her easy company *almost* stifled the memory of their frank, Yankee-style sex talk and insult-riddled exchanges. Was such openness refreshing or repulsive? I hadn't yet decided because the city, slowly, slowly, was working on me, making me more accepting, indulgent. And I did feel it, like a white wisdom tooth coming in, breaking through the smooth, pink flesh.

"I love the Plaid Pants Set," Paige would begin, gazing into her compact. "They come in under five minutes and then take me shopping in East Hampton." She'd move the mirror closer and began to pull at her cheeks. "I do believe I'll fuck my dermatologist this weekend. Then he can pump more poison into these laugh lines, *gratis.*"

"Aren't you too shallow to ever develop lines?" Samantha would snicker and then swiftly bite the head off her Tootsie Pop. "But you're right, it's time I got laid," she would then declare with the authority she usually reserved for official body counts in Baghdad. "I'm breaking my dry spell this weekend. It's been too long and I'm lonely."

"Don't misunderstand—I'm not talking about *companionship,*

Samantha. If it were up to me, Snow White would lick my Brazilian and then I'd take my postcoital glow for a stroll down Madison and a light lunch at Nello's." They seemed to tolerate each other's company only so they could share in each other's misery.

Suspension of reality. This is what I had with both Granddaddy and Rose that I didn't share with the others. Whether I sat with him on the back porch or held court with her in a plastic fold-up chair outside of Joe's Dairy, I was able to escape. I looked forward to her on my days off. From the single, cement step of the mozzarella store, sloped from decades of wear, she rubbed her smooth, cool palms against my hot cheeks and clenched fists. If Chase Stephens, the resident golden boy and prime-time anchor, called me his "tall drink of water," then Rose was my four-foot-eleven sip of chamomile tea. She was the only one who could calm my anxious mind. It was growing increasingly difficult to convince myself that I was building a solid career and becoming a bona fide journalist when all I did was push Keaton and Cleveland's agenda. In fact, I became a hot mess just remembering my interview with Gina; the channel hadn't lied to me, I had lied to myself. I just didn't want to see them for what they were—a propaganda machine. We "wallpapered" Republican news items while staging blackouts with liberal issues. And now that the elections were only two months away, I presumed things would only get worse.

Rose was my remedy. I'd lean in real close—take in her perfume of talcum and warm milk—and listen to whisperings of old social clubs and the men who played dominoes and how the neighborhood had once been safe with the wave of one man's big pinky. A different world with different rules and an altogether different set of players. Corruption sounded so much more romantic from afar.

"Bella, it's so quiet. Where have they all gone?"

We were two Southern girls—she was from Sicily, you see—with a vast social ignorance between us. We might have both made New York our new home, but I suspected we would never get a handle on the Northerners and their holiday rituals.

"Who knows where these people go. But let's take advantage of these empty sidewalks and go for a spin around the block. Hmmm?"

She pressed her hand into mine and so I left behind Tennessee Williams. I was in the midst of reading *A Streetcar Named Desire* for the fourteenth time. The hushed streets inspired me to read aloud a couple of Blanche's lines. Not a good idea. A girl shouldn't spend her holiday weekend *alone* reading about *loneliness*.

As we walked down the block I began to wonder, would I grow old on Sullivan Street? Could the city take up a place in my soul where the past once resided? The thought of going home again scared me. I didn't want to pass up my fast nights alone for the slow rhythms and crowded dinner tables back home. I wasn't good with complete happiness. Sweet melancholy suited me best.

"That boy is staring at you," Rose said, motioning with her head toward the apron-wrapped cook standing just inside the back door of Ben's Pizza on Thompson Street. He waved with a tut-tut of his first two fingers and cigarette. I smiled at him and thought that *he* would want to go away with me for summer's last weekend. The only ground rules: separate beds and, of equal or greater importance, he would never, *ever* be allowed to call it a "slice"—it was a "piece of pizza," for God's sake.

"No, I think he's admiring *your* new hair color." The Aveda beauty school girls on Spring Street had just dyed Rose's hair the loveliest shade of white; it shone pale blue in the sun.

One block farther and then we turned back, walking the length of the Thompson Street Park. "I call that," I said, pointing toward the tennis backboard, "one of the Lindbergh babylike mysteries of New York City. Why do the teenage boys spend their afternoons beating a tiny blue ball against that wall with their hands instead of using a standard yellow tennis ball and racket like everyone else? Since when have big ol' jeans and T-shirts supplanted tennis whites?" Criticizing others, you see, comes easily when it's just you, the tourists and the pizza makers, the air dense with the smell of coal and yeast and too many ovens going at once. Rose and I clucked and continued down the street.

"It's almost sunset, time for you to get home, Ms. Rose." Though really, I was the one who needed to get inside. I'm no good when the sun dips below the horizon, that time of day when we all have expectations. When twilight burns your eyes, your heart skipping a beat, it makes you wonder why you're not in love or touring the Grand Canal, tasting a gorgeous man's lips or feasting on summer's last peach.

I think: *Something dramatic should be happening to me right now.*

We said our good-byes and I moved the wooden bench inside Lisa's store, stopping for a moment to brush my fingers against the fine, smooth fabrics meant for someone else's back, not mine. Locking the boutique's door, I caught a glimpse of the setting sun. I watched as the New York City day turned to night, the water towers fading into Houston Street's hazy violet sky. I knew that I wanted to go back into my apartment and rig up the piece of screen Mamma had sent from home (she was scared of rabid-mouse bites and thugs) and leave the windows wide so I could stare at the arched windows and pretty cornices just a block away. And with the lamps off and windows open, I could fantasize. Alone in my apartment, I thought about it all—the city, its promise of a future and my place in it—while watching and listening to the elegant shadows, the music and the idling town cars a few hundred feet away. I was Nick Carraway mesmerized by the twinkling lights of the grand party on the adjoining lawn. The bright squares of apartments glowing in the deep midnight sky were a thing of beauty, interchangeable with my memories of shadows of docks jutting out into the warm brown of Mobile Bay at sunset. I would make promises to myself never to trade intelligent loneliness for dull company. (Even though I was a damn fool living out of my league, I knew to give myself over to the city and my dreams instead of to a man.)

But the slam of the apartment door shook me. Once I was back inside, I didn't pull out the piece of screen or pretend to be someone who I wasn't. Instead, I pulled out my laptop and went to the uncomfortable places that I had never wanted to visit.

I needed to know where I was going.

Lemon Chess Squares for the Working (Sulking) Girl

Quick, easy and comforting—this is my chess pie for the working (or sulking) girl. No fiddling with a homemade crust leaves me more time to catch up on world affairs, inter-office affairs and to ponder the crisis that is my nonexistent social and love life. But Mamma's really going to kill me when she finds out that city livin' has turned me on to the white, powdered stuff. Cake mix.

MAKES 15 GENEROUS CHESS SQUARES.

1 box yellow cake mix

1 stick butter

4 eggs

2 tsp. cornmeal

1 8-oz. package cream cheese, softened

1 tsp. vanilla extract

2 Tbsp. lemon juice

2 Tbsp. lemon zest

1 box confectioners' sugar

Preheat oven to 350 degrees. Mix together cake mix, butter and one of the eggs and pat down in a 9x13-inch dish. Mix together cornmeal, cream cheese, eggs, vanilla, lemon juice, lemon zest and confectioners' sugar and pour over the top. Bake for 35–45 minutes. Chess squares should be slightly raised around the edges and light gold in color.

Glam Girl Salad

The glamorous girls in the Hamptons feast on these salads when they're not meeting plaid pants–wearing men at clam bakes. I just know it. Okay, so I've never been . . . but I'm sure East Hampton and Sag Harbor luncheons feature salads chockablock of very precious and unusual things, morsels that you're more inclined to photograph than eat. My greens, however, are as tasty as they are gorgeous.

SERVES 2.

2 Tbsp. slivered almonds
2 Tbsp. Italian flat leaf parsley, chopped
Handful celery leaves (green leaves *and*
    tender yellow leaves from interior)
Handful carrot tops (green leaves), torn
5 sprigs tarragon, freshly picked
2 Tbsp. chives, minced
6 sprigs chervil, freshly picked
1 Tbsp. fresh basil, chiffonade
1–2 tsp. white wine vinegar
2–3 tsp. extra virgin olive oil
Kosher salt
Freshly ground pepper
1 roasted red pepper *or* jarred red pepper
4 oz. mild (not aged or cured in olive oil)
    Manchego cheese★

★Optional special equipment for finely slicing cheese—a vegetable peeler.

Preheat oven to 325 degrees. Spread almond slivers evenly across a baking sheet. Place sheet in oven. Toast almond slivers until colored and fragrant, about 5–7 minutes.

In a large bowl filled with cool water, submerge parsley, celery leaves and carrot tops. Let them chill out and get really nice and clean, all dirt sinking to the bottom of the bowl while leaves float to the top. While greens are soaking, gently clean and dry (on a paper towel) tarragon, chives, chervil and basil.

Transfer greens to a kitchen towel and pat dry. In a medium bowl, combine all greens and herbs. Toss with 1 tsp. white wine vinegar, 2–3 tsp. extra virgin olive oil and salt and pepper to taste.

Arrange the salad by first laying down the strips of roasted red pepper. Nestle a little hill of greens on top of the peppers and sprinkle with 1 Tbsp. almonds. With a vegetable peeler, shave a generous portion of Manchego on top.

13

"DO ME A FAVOR and run these corrections up to Makeup," Samantha said, thrusting a stack of highlighted scripts in my hand. "Paige needs to go over them before she's live in Studio B in twenty. Remind her that the suits on seventeen want Jessica Clayton to come across as a loose-cannon lesbian who, if elected president, will fuck over our national health-care system, subsequently pushing taxes through the roof, putting our personal income and capital gains rates at the same level as those froggies across the pond. Got that? But don't forget to tell her that the Bryn Mawr, carpet-munching college room-mate bit should be the main focus, okay?" She ran her fingers through her short hair, exhaled and returned to her monitor.

I imagined her ideal cold open: "Democrats invest all hopes in Jessica Clayton. Muff-diver for president? Good evening, America, I'm Paige Beaumont."

More lies to contend with. Everyone knew that Jessica Clayton wasn't a lesbian; she was happily married with two children. Maybe broadcasting bold-faced lies was the reason Samantha had been fired from CNN (along with the majority of the present newsroom staff) before being hired by ANC. I supposed the star journalist within me would have to find out through another means of investigation; About.com couldn't be relied on for everything. Really, the site hadn't revealed anything of interest aside from Keaton's political contributions.

"You can't get anyone else to go? Please, Samantha." My dramatic pause and serious gaze would have taken me great places—like not into Paige's hair and makeup room—if only Chase Stephens hadn't barreled past, arms outstretched holding a videocassette, shoving me into Wallace's producing pod. Thank God the gasbag was gone; I didn't know how to politely reject another one of his invitations to the West Indies.

"I've got the new Osama tape! Fuck me! I've got the fucker! Let's roll live in five!" he roared as he ran down the length of the newsroom, back to the video library. Honestly. If he ingested more than Entenmann's cinnamon rolls from the corner deli (labeled the "Hamas Deli" by the rest of the newsroom as a tribute to the surly Middle Eastern owners) and powdered substances from Colombia, he could behave like a civilized human being when there was breaking news. I felt it my express duty to ignore him.

I moved into plea-bargaining mode. "Yesterday, Paige liked to have chewed my head off when the printer went and broke on me. It's not my fault that I couldn't deliver the scripts until four seconds before airtime—I don't repair printers, for Lord's sake. Why don't we get one of the interns to run up there and I'll go buy you some Juicy Fru—"

"You're wrong. Minutiae *is* your job. And I have plenty to chew on to last me through the night, thank you very much." Samantha smiled, handed me another packet of scripts and turned back to her computer.

"Guy, what about—"

"That there printer up and broke on my Dixie ass!" He snorted at his approximation of my accent and sentence structure, waving me away with his hand and a phlegmatic cough. Defeated, I marched toward the sliding doors. Unfortunately, I wasn't quick enough to avoid Guy's parting remarks. "Don't forget—millions of American men would pay to have Paige chew—or suck—on *their* heads!" I spun around to see him pointing at his crotch. "Consider yourself lucky!" Luke, the "crawl guy," gave him a high five. This was the man who made a career out of composing sentence fragments that ran, or "crawled," at the bottom of the screen—and atop the five-story-high

Jumbotron outside the building—during news broadcasts. To think that strip of information used to impress me.

I dragged myself up the back stairwell as quickly as possible though it was hard with my chest puffed out, limbs loose and eyes watery. After yesterday's prime-time shift, I was a weeping willow of a girl.

"What took you so long, idiot?" Paige had hissed at me as I breathlessly handed over her scripts. "We are seconds away from fucking up! Hand me those!"

"Your lip is quivering, Paige," Sam, the director, stated coolly. "Calm down and look at the light. We're going red. Five, four, three," he mouthed the final numbers and swept his index finger from behind his shoulder, toward her, in one graceful scooping motion.

"Iraq bombed. Bad guys dead. Good evening, America, I'm Paige Beaumont." For one minute thirty seconds I watched her perfectly drawn, glossed red lips roll around and push out verbs and proper nouns, making even the most mundane factoid sound sexy, prescient. A raise of the eyebrow on "slaughter," the angling of the chin on "get the bad guys" and a satisfied smile when she told America that she'd return in thirty minutes with breaking news on Britney Spears's C-section scar.

"And we're out. Commercial," Sam called. I slowly released the stale studio air that had been trapped in my lungs throughout her delivery. One single error and I would have been up for dismissal. I didn't know how I would fare with Gina and Human Resources now that I had fallen from Wallace's good graces. Perhaps shredding his little gift—a plane ticket to St. Lucia tucked behind my time card— wasn't the wisest career move. But Wallace and I had been schooled by different mammas. Only one F-word existed in my vocabulary. I knew how to *flirt* and he, well . . . I didn't know what to do with his promises of outdoor showers and sponges in strange places.

Now I was officially no one's darling. That meant I had to keep my head down and run—run scripts, run the Chyron machine, outrun every other production assistant in the building.

Guy and Samantha might have been my generally disinterested, alternately lethargic and spastic leaders; however, they had both given me the tips that I needed: Cleveland didn't respect discretion in his journalists, he respected *balls* and a "cause." And while I confess to having only ovaries, I did possess the savvy to pitch a package on Jessica Clayton, the Democratic presidential hopeful. Everyone else on staff had run scared from the thought of producing a positive piece on the liberal. They must not have had as many sleepless nights as I.

Wrestling with my morals and party affiliation night after night— scouring the Web for clues about the News Channel's past and future— I had come across a report on Keaton and his political contributions. While he might have been Hewitt's most vocal supporter, Keaton was a man who liked to cover his political heinie. It turns out that he had a well-documented past of contributing millions of dollars to *both* parties so as to have a finger in every political pot. Running my package, thus giving Clayton one solid shot of good press, would mean she might consider him in future policy making. And I might be able to finally sleep at night. Piecing together this package was my shot at the big time—and sanity. My conscience (not to mention ego) was just too big for my miniscule studio apartment and even smaller position at the News Channel. I felt it was my destiny to be the bold blonde in the anchor chair. I'd be the Hitchcock ice queen (perhaps melting a bit from my extra fifteen pounds of well-placed padding) delivering objective, intelligent news stories.

But for now, Paige was the towheaded wonder and her delivery was flawless. After the lights had gone down yesterday, she'd simply turned to me and said, "Late scripts will *never* happen again." She had then flipped her blond bob and asked if Sam had picked up her Zone diet meal from the lobby. Poor fella. He was the oldest thing at the News Channel, white-haired, perpetually exhausted, possessing a face that belonged to black-and-white documentary footage of some European war. He had worked with Walter Cronkite back in the Golden Age of the Big Three and now he was fetching dietetic meals for a self-important, sexed-up talking head.

But all that was yesterday. "New day, new me!" I mouthed, trying to crack a smile as I opened the door to the mezzanine-level studios and walked toward the hair and makeup room. One of the girls in my debutante class had told me that the mere act of smiling altered your mental state. I do believe she relayed that nugget of information to me in regard to performing fellatio on her SAE boyfriend; she forced a smile as she made her way down his khaki pants, praying that her gros-grain hair ribbon wouldn't get stuck in his zipper. Apparently flashing those expensively capped pearly whites (thank you, Daddy!) put her in a more amorous, expansive mood.

Just as I began to pull back the blue curtain to the makeup room, I heard Paige's low, heated tone. I gently let the fabric fall and slipped into the adjoining, empty dressing room.

"They've got too much invested to fuck up now, Doreen. The presidency can't land in someone else's lap. Keaton needs the FCC on his side so he can buy Pol24 News—he *needs* Hewitt in office in oh-eight. Remember that guy on the seventeenth floor I used to date, Cleveland's lackey, Christopher Randolph? I swear, their little media monopoly experiment in China has sent him across the Pacific so many times, he has more frequent flier miles than Keaton has dollars in his offshore account."

What? Christopher and Paige had been an item?!

"It's not easy massaging the commies and buying up television rights, is it, boys? But you got your fifty-two percent of the market—*fifty-two percent*! Can you believe that?"

And Keaton supported the commies?! Did that mean the family farm would be turned into some sort of people's commune? I had to hear more but I couldn't just stand in the middle of an empty room while harried PA's and producers rushed past me; idle minds might have populated 1221 but *never* idle bodies. I scanned the dozens of tubes, bottles and brushes that crowded the flat surfaces of the tiny vestibule. Out of the corner of my eye, I spotted a stick of Porcelain Bobby Brown concealer, slapped with a piece of masking tape and labeled "Wallace." A bottle of prescription hair replacement foam sat next to it. I was in Wallace's personal dressing room! Quickly, I grabbed a palette of NARS bronzer, scooted next to the door and began a generous powder application.

"I don't get into any of that business, girl, you know that. Keaton puts food on my table. That's all I care about. Now hush and don't fid-

get," the woman said in a voice as sweet and indulgent as a mother's. "Keep those baby blues closed. Two more minutes and I'll be done with my be-uuu-tee-fee-cation."

"I'm just saying that the dress rehearsal in China better lead up to one hell of an opening night. Cleveland and Christopher promised that once we land Hewitt in office, we'd be able to pay off and control the FCC, buy up Pol24 News, combine the two smaller channels and create a megastation—all Republican agenda, all the time. I'd be back in the head anchor slot. Can you imagine, Doreen? I'd finally be at the top, where I deserve to be. Sometimes I feel like only you and Snow White understand me. . . ."

Doreen clucked; I stifled my gag reflex.

"Why are women so catty?" Paige continued. "They're the ones fucking over my Q ratings. Can't they just accept my jaw-dropping beauty and intellect? I just happen to have it all! I think I'll start a blog, maybe pitch a reality show—the world needs to *see* and *feel* my true depths."

I looked at the clock on the wall—twelve minutes until Paige had to be on air and I *still* held her script in my hand. Shameless propaganda as a means to sway the elections is one thing but doing so to establish a completely illegal media monopoly is another! What happened to the notion of journalistic integrity—everything that Granddaddy and Mamma had ever taught me? The station was a fraud, the men who ran it liars and thieves and the fate of our presidential election—our nation—hung in the balance!

I'd slide the scripts beneath the curtain and run, that's what I'd do. First City Hall, yes, I'd run into the mayor's office and tell him everything! The execs would be arrested and their faces splashed across the tabloids in tomorrow's morning paper. My mind raced with the laundry list of important people to notify and lunch. I spun around, headed for the emergency exit, when I caught a glimpse of myself in the mirror. Oh Lawd! It looked like my body—not my mind—had been running . . . a 20K race . . . in the Georgia cotton fields . . . at high noon. Nervous and distracted from spying on Paige's tirade, I had applied bronzer from my chin clear up to my temples. My face was mottled

orange, brown and pink—every shade in the NARS Bali Bronzed collection. I looked ridiculous. "That's because you are ridiculous," I
muttered to myself, grabbing a tissue.

Keaton owned all the major papers like he owned City Hall, Gra-
cie Mansion, the White House—all of it. He had backed Mayor Clark
in the last election and had supported the current president, innumer-
able senators and lobbyists. To convict these fellas, I thought, you have
to have something big, concrete. The American public has to become
so incensed, they won't allow the media mogul to continue unscathed
in his golden cage above Sixth Avenue.

I had no choice—I had to stick to the course. From the inside, I
could gather evidence, search for more damning clues and *then* present
my case. And I had to get my Clayton package on air. I wanted to win
both ways—nail the suckers *and* invest myself in the political process,
root for change, get my face (the good side, mind you) on camera.
Even if I had to work for horn dogs and thieves (there was more sex,
drugs and rock-and-roll in the basement of 1221 than at a Widespread
Panic concert), I would produce a piece that would get me a job as a
"real" journalist.

I had a prince of a job before me. But first, I had to be a peon.
Script delivery.

"Excuse me, Ms. Beaumont?" I called from outside the curtain.

"Come on in, honey. No time to be shy," replied the other woman.

I pulled back the thin fabric to find Paige reclining in a brown
leather barbershop chair, legs and silk stockings and black heels casually thrown in front of her. Despite her hysterics, she looked serene,
her eyes gently closed. A curvy black woman circled around her with
a sponge and a bottle of liquid foundation. Her movements were as
quick and skilled as a portraitist's.

"Whatcha got there?" she said, not taking her eyes off Paige.

"The producers want Ms. Beaumont to look over a few script corrections. The broadcast needs to focus on, on . . ." I stumbled over several expressions in my mind, vetoing them all as too colorful. From
one Southern belle to another, "muff-diving" might be considered a
touch crass.

"Let me guess, something that will piss off the Clayton camp," Paige said quietly, barely moving a facial muscle.

"According to Samantha," I began, hesitating, "the evening broadcast should focus on Jessica Clayton . . . doing the do-si-do with her roommate at Bryn Mawr." There. I had said it. I had aimed for genteel yet concise.

"This is what I'm talking about, Doreen." Paige recrossed her long, slender legs in frustration. "They dangle *that* carrot I was just telling you about—claim they want me to be more involved, choose stories, write my own scripts, create the lineup, work my way back up to number one—and then they change everything back around. I'm fine with their agenda, but why do they have to be such corporate assholes and make my job impossible?"

"Now, now . . ." Doreen purred.

"I'm telling you, yesterday I gave priority to the Fallujah attacks, putting them at the top of the hour before Bush and his dick played dress-up in a harness and landed on an aircraft carrier, pretending to be Tom Cruise in *Top Gun*. Sure enough, they flipped the lineup a minute before we went live. The president's crotch got prime billing. They said it made him look formidable and tough on terror."

Paige would continue to ignore my presence if I didn't say something, attempt to redeem an IQ point or two after yesterday's printer mishap. And digging up dirt on the station would be a lot easier if I were on speaking terms with at least one of the VIP's.

"How does it go! If it bleeds, it leads? They should know better than to switch your lineup—blood and bodies always lead the hour." I tried hard to affect a face of contempt though I was thrilled to pieces to have successfully delivered a news-jargon-filled sentence. Over the weekend I had rented *Network* and in a matter of one hundred and twenty minutes learned more industry lingo and newsroom psychology than during my five-week gig at ANC.

"You'd think, wouldn't you?" Paige responded, her disgust—gloriously!—directed at the News Channel suits and not at me.

I tried not to blush at my coup, nervously twisting my blond ponytail into a bun. (It had been a bad hair morning, the bobby pins just

sliding right out of my limp locks.) Then, I noticed Paige's chin beginning to quiver, her jawline growing tense. It was as if she was pondering all the great injustices inflicted upon her and her fair beauty by the
suits on seventeen. The last time I had seen her look so concerned was
during the '02 Florida recount. Her emotional, shaky delivery, broadcast live from Palm Beach, hypnotized the male contingent of my
family.

I squeezed the scripts, feeling the papers' edges cut into my palm,
nervous, not knowing if it was my place to console her. I focused on
her now puckered mouth.

"She's a cable news wet dream: blond hair, big lips and tits and a
once-upon-a-time Jewish nose surgically altered to on-camera perfection," Guy had told me two nights ago on the overnight, throwing
back two pills and half a can of Mountain Dew, "that's the reason we
put her on air. She's a nutcase whose Prozac is the camera."

"Don't you think you're being just a little unfair? Samantha met
her when they were both in Atlanta working for CNN and suppos-
edly she was their Golden Girl."

"Hotlanta, capital of the South . . ." He shook his head. "You're
right, I'm forgetting something—those big, blue eyes. They look at
Cleveland and Keaton in their private meetings and they're sure she's
pleading for the big daddies to slip hundies in her thong. Oh, pwetty
pwease, you big news fuckers . . .

"Yeah, she's a bombshell," he said, changing his tone after a brief
pause. "But what do you care about that? Just trust me, don't get close
and you'll be fine. Paige's temper is up and down, moving from pleasant to shit-eating like—"

"—a Naomi Campbell of the Confederacy."

"Do I smell a girl crush?" Guy lifted an arm and smelled one of the
pit stains on his T-shirt.

"All right, one more swipe of eye shadow and you'll be as gorgeous
as they come," Doreen said, mercifully extracting Guy from my mind
and snapping me back to the present.

"I'm fixin' to run out and get dinner so I'll just leave these scripts
by the sink—"

"What'd you just say?" Paige asked.

"I'm going to leave your scripts here so I can run down and get a sandwich before the broadcast."

"Did you say 'fixin' to'?"

"Bad habit, I know." I anxiously reached back for my ponytail and realized that I had already twisted it into a bun. Fantastic. It looked as if I were doing an autistic flamenco move with my right hand.

She gently pushed away Doreen's hand, opened her eyes and sat up in the chair. "You're Southern, aren't you?"

"I'm afraid so."

"Look at you," she bit her plump bottom lip, "of course you are."

Admittedly, we Southerners make quite a sport of checking each other out but this was something altogether different; even if I knew my doubles partner was sporting a new David Yurman, I didn't make it my business whether or not she had invested in a new push-up bra— or new breasts, for that matter. A genteel Dixie lady knows to tease— never taunt—with her eyes. Flutter, bat and wink but *never* stare. If I hadn't been sure, it was growing increasingly obvious that Paige was not 100 percent Dixie.

"Yes, ma'am, fresh off the farm." I looked back at Paige as she knit her smooth brow, making an expression that might accompany, say, an AMBER Alert in Utah.

"Have we met before?"

"Yes, ma'am, we met yesterday, four seconds before airtime. You were quite upset with me."

No point in avoiding it. Granddaddy raised me on the mantra, "In life, do not run away from discomfort." (Well, really, he had said something like, "Life's horseshit is good for you. Deal with it, learn from it." He also told me, "They can stick an umbrella up your ass but they can't open it." You catch his drift.) I just happened to have taken his teaching to the *nth* degree, moved to the hardest, meanest, coldest island on the face of the earth in an attempt to make a name for myself in the dog-eat-dog world of television news. And now, I was going to out the very institution that I had wanted so desperately to belong to. Granddaddy's sentiment, however, was rock solid.

"Really?"

"Yes, it was just me, you and Sam in the breaking-news studio."

"Oh well, forget about me in the chair before broadcasts. I'm so keyed up I can't see straight. It's amazing the teleprompter makes any sense."

"Don't let her give you that! She's at her best in that chair," Doreen said, massaging Paige's temples.

"Where do you live in the city?" She tapped Doreen and motioned for a hand mirror; an errant whitehead had dared to mar the marvelous, angled plane that was her cheekbone. She frowned and examined the little oily beast in the mirror.

"Soho." Living among the downtown bourgeois was my only trump card.

"Daddy's got money, huh?"

"Granddaddy."

"Good for you. You need to be where the action is. Williamsburg is shit, Caryn Gardens—the worst."

"Carroll Gardens, honey," Doreen interrupted. "And that's where I live."

Brash little hussy, that Paige. How had Christopher ever dated *her*? I bowed my head in embarrassment, wishing I could remind her never to cross her hairdresser, colorist, gynecologist or dermatologist. Those are the hands that take us from ordinary to extraordinary. A flick of the eye shadow brush—or forceps—and you've gone from being a broad to a lady (and vice versa). Eyes lowered, I looked over and caught a glimpse of Paige's hands. What?! Her index finger sported a good baker's dozen of long black hairs. Indeed, they were the most masculine hands on a NOLA blonde that I had ever laid eyes on! What would the uncles do if they knew that their conservative goddess had the extremities of a werewolf? I beamed and looked down at my petite, hairless digits.

"You might go out to Caryn Gardens on a lark, spend an afternoon in a dirty little café, but that's it," she said, continuing her antiborough tirade. "We want you at Soho galleries and Chelsea restaurants, Metropolitan benefits and Yoji openings, weekends in Southampton . . ."

"We"—she felt a rapport with me. This was very good indeed. And as she carried on, spouting names of people I didn't know and places that I had yet to see, I nodded my head, wholeheartedly agreeing with her assessment of my ideal social life. Faye Dunaway and Melanie Griffith had taught me that more is accomplished after 8 P.M.—at a cocktail party or on someone else's pillow—than in a board meeting. Up to that point it just so happened that work, or searching for work, had been my entire Manhattan existence.

"I've never been out on the town," I blurted. This was both true *and* pathetic. My only taste of the good life had been Christopher. But, now, just the thought of him made me want to wash my mouth out with Franzia, blight the memory of his finicky taste buds.

"Are you on this Friday?" She riffled through her script, as requested, printed in size 26 font, large enough for Rose to read, and cocked an eyebrow in my direction.

"I just offered to take over someone's midnight shift. I guess that could explain my lack of social—"

"Early Friday night is perfect for Cipriani Downtown. Don't get me wrong, Giuseppe would reserve me a table at any time," she said, speaking more to herself about the dinner and her implied social status than to me, "but this will make for a more intimate affair. I'll have my assistant make a seven P.M. ressy, table for four. How does that sound?"

"Cipriani?" First thought: I wasn't ready to go. Second thought: I didn't deserve to go. Please understand that I wanted nothing more than to get Paige tipsy and pump her for information about the ANC bastards. But, I had *also* just begun to understand a world comprised of only extreme wealth or extreme poverty. New York City presented itself to me as if it were a third-world country complicit in its own military dictatorship. At ANC I worked alongside peons and looked up to titans. In Soho, I lived next to aging Italian pensioners and beneath hedge fund millionaires. While the Sicilians and I were ambitious, we more or less accepted our fate in the hierarchy just so we could watch the truly rich make fools of themselves at Cipriani and *then* make headlines in the morning *Post*. The West Broadway bistro I likened to be their White House, a bonfire of the privileged, political and newly famous.

"I don't know, Paige." Suddenly, I was scared of everything on my plate.

"Come on," she said, standing up from the makeup chair, smoothing down her blazer and what looked to be a tube top masquerading as a skirt, "it'll be fun. I'll invite two hedge funders—they'll foot the bill and make us feel sexy. What more could a girl ask for?"

Indispensable Chicken Salad

An out-of-this-world chicken salad recipe is to a Southern girl what a hedge fund manager is to an upwardly mobile, cash-poor city girl—indispensable. Serve my perfectly calibrated salad—equal parts creamy, crunchy, clean—in lettuce cups, hollowed-out summer tomatoes or between two slices of crustless white bread.

SERVES 6 LUNCHEON-SIZED PORTIONS.

2 tsp. cider vinegar

⅔ c. mayonnaise

3½ c. poached, cubed chicken breast*

1 Tbsp. yellow onion, finely diced

¼ c. celery rib, finely diced

1 Mutsu, Golden Delicious or Granny Smith apple,
    cored, cut into ½-inch cubes

3 Tbsp. fresh basil, chiffonade

½ c. toasted pecans, chopped

⅛ tsp. (pinch) sugar

1 tsp. kosher salt

Freshly ground pepper to taste

In a small bowl, whisk together cider vinegar and mayonnaise until all of the liquid is incorporated and the mixture is smooth.

In a large bowl, pour in all ingredients. Mix with a wooden spoon until well combined.

---

*White meat only. A lady never darkens her chicken salad with flesh from the thigh or drumstick.

14

"WHAT DO YOU think?" I called out to Rose, crossing Sullivan to her perch in front of Joe's Dairy. I twirled around in my new black and white flowered skirt. Two layers of crinoline kept the shape young and full while also ensuring that my waist looked as slender as Delta Burke's (1974 Miss Florida days, before *Designing Women*). The $460 size 6 skirt *also* ensured that a weeklong starvation diet would commence after dinner. Usually, I was a size 8, Filene's Basement kind of girl. But I just couldn't turn down a clever sales pitch.

"With this piece, Oscar de la Renta has masterfully blended the 1950s housewife and bobby-soxer, commingling the ultimate male fantasies of mother and cheerleader into one. Julianne Moore meets Sandra Dee," the Barney's saleswoman had said to her right and then left hand, finally clapping them together. "The skirt with a pair of high heels and red lips—irresistible."

"But can Oscar get me in Cipriani? Did I mention this is a blind date?" I pleaded.

"About five times. Listen, darling," the woman continued, easing me toward the cash register, "it's not a nightclub, it's a *restaurant*. Anyone who's willing to pay forty-five dollars for a bowl of pasta is allowed inside."

"Fine. But I'm not chancing anything," I said, grabbing a slinky strapless top from the rack of black separates in front of me. It was the smallest, most elasticized thing I could find. End-of-summer sales made me giddy. This probably explains why I left Barney's with $32 left in my bank account and an Oscar de la Renta tattoo on the small of my back (the waistband was tight, the tag faulty, I was sweaty—what can I say?). That skirt was gonna get me a man.

I smiled down at Rose and relaxed for a minute as I watched her slice rounds of eggplant into a small sauce pot on her lap. I had to remember that there was more to life than overpriced red sauce joints and size 2 Manhattan fannies.

"I like the flower in your hair," Rose said, looking up. "No one up here does that."

I reached up and carefully felt the velvety petal of the tiger lily, trying to imagine her as a girl, bougainvillea tucked into the long black curls falling down her back.

"Wish me luck." I squeezed her hand.

"*In bocca al lupo, cara.* But why so nervous? You are beautiful and he's just a man. They're powerless, you know."

I was too embarrassed to tell Rose or Lisa—certainly not Paige—it wasn't about the man, it was the restaurant. *A beacon of hope.* I'd gotten into the habit of detouring several blocks south for a five-second sashay past the West Broadway terrace on my way home from work. Depending on my mood, ogling the rich was my wink of wonderment or my taste of *agrodolce.* Sweet and sour. Rose taught me how to make it so I could taste it. And now I could feel it with a stroll past Cipriani.

"You're right," I said, giving her one final squeeze. The unknown was just a man and I didn't need him anyway. "And what are we doing about supper tonight? I'm not leaving until I hear a menu." Sometimes I had to force her to eat. The night before, I had roasted a chicken (Rose allowing me to use only lemon, garlic, thyme and unsalted butter). She had eaten exactly one half of a drumstick and two slices of heirloom tomato. The neighborhood meal rotation fell to Frank on Friday nights. He was the owner of Joe's and could dip into his display case to produce something simple and Italian to suit her very particular tastes.

"*Minestra, puttanesca*—the old girl can't remember. Now go!" She pointed south with her paring knife and pursed her lips like she did when haggling with the fruit vendor on Varick Street. "I want to see you out with a man, behaving like a young *ragazza* should. Too much time in that kitchen. You're not going to find a husband by staring into a pot of boiling water."

Finding a husband, I thought, such an absurd expression. What about a man discovering me?

Final scene. I'm in one of Cipriani's wicker chairs, feeling very Euro Left Bank (at that moment in time, the Left Bank not being the far side of Granddaddy's lake) and a man approaches.

"You have a princess neck," he says, walking toward me, trying to roll his tongue around the *r*'s, soften them up to suit my American ear.

"I do?" I demur, trying for a moment to be the good, ignorant girl of years past. At that moment, I'm very busy being maudlin and analyzing big-city life.

"One meant for a string of diamonds. Pearls on Sundays." A slow sip of his amber-colored drink and he continues staring.

It's a weeknight like any other and I stroke the blond hairs on my neck and the old, tanned man is thankful for the nighttime breeze off the river and his Cuban cigar and the forgiving light cast by Cipriani's awning. The golden hue takes ten years off and he knows it. Without a pause, he asks me to write my phone number on his crisp, linen kerchief.

"Ahh, but you won't answer your phone," he says, suddenly coy.

"Of course I will."

The old man and I continue exchanging lies. Why not? Joan Didion taught me that "I could stay up all night and make mistakes and none of it would count."

A late-summer breeze on Spring Street whipped beneath my skirt and brought me back to reality. Propelled down West Broadway, the *clackety-clack* of my heels kept rhythm with my speeding heart. I realized that I didn't want to lie and I didn't want the man of my dreams to be old.

My mind and its games . . .

Finally I was there, beneath the Cipriani awning, brushing past the seats of my dreams, pushing open the glass doors, entering a world where I could live Ms. Didion's lines instead of just reciting them.

Paige raised her flute of champagne and smiled at me. I saw the back of two men's heads. Chestnut or salt and pepper. Which one was mine? Did it matter? And why was I fraternizing with Paige, my ideological enemy? But before I had time to think, I was whisked away. A white-jacketed waiter extended his arm and paraded me past the millionaires, ushering me to the back table—the good table, I'd learn—beyond the bathrooms and near the finer paintings.

I had arrived.

Eggplant Agrodolce

Agrodolce, an Italian sweet and sour sauce that combines both vine-gar and sugar, is my New York—a wonderful lesson in contrasts. I'll taste now and choose sides later. Pair it with a flaky, meaty white fish or a simple roast chicken.

SERVES 4 AS A SIDE.

2 medium eggplant, diced
¼ c. olive oil
3 garlic cloves, crushed
3 Tbsp. red wine vinegar
2 Tbsp. capers
⅓ c. golden raisins
1 tsp. sugar
Freshly ground black pepper
Kosher salt

Toss the diced eggplant with 1 Tbsp. salt and place in a colander to drain for 20 minutes.

In a medium-sized saucepan over high heat, pour the olive oil and add the garlic cloves. Continue cooking over high heat until aromatic, about 1 minute. Add the eggplant and cook 5 minutes more. Stir in vinegar, capers, raisins, sugar and ½ tsp. fresh pepper. Bring mixture to a boil, reduce to simmer and cook until eggplant is tender and liquid is well reduced. Adjust seasoning with salt, pepper, vinegar and sugar if necessary. There should be a nice balance of sweet and sour. Cool and serve at room temperature.

Rose's Simple Roast Chicken

Chicken not bathed in mayonnaise? Rose was the first person to teach me honest, clean food (well, her and a few choice cookbooks by James Peterson). She sat in one of my kitchen chairs and taught me how to use a sharp knife, a spool of dental floss and a tidy bunch of thyme. Her roast was a revelation. Then again, her herb box did face the church—I bet y'all Saint Anthony had a hand in the special flavor of her thyme. In the winter, you can replace the thyme with rosemary. Rose says that cold weather encourages you to be more bold. (Hmmm . . . that didn't explain my year-round impertinence. . . .)

SERVES 4.

1 4-lb. free-range chicken
Kosher salt
Freshly ground pepper
1 lemon, halved
1 head of garlic, halved
1 bunch fresh thyme
Dental floss or kitchen twine
1 Tbsp. unsalted butter

Preheat oven to 450 degrees.

Place chicken in a roasting pan and generously season with salt and pepper. Stuff the cavity with lemon halves, garlic and thyme.

With your dental floss, tightly tie the drumsticks together (this will trap the juices and ensure a moist chicken). If you're feeling fancy and experienced, wrap the floss around the entire chicken, making sure to tuck in wings for juiciness.

Tear off a sheet of aluminum foil about a foot long and fold it so that it is three sheets thick. Create a snub-nosed triangle shape so that it will adequately cover the breasts. Spread butter on one side of foil and place foil, butter-side down, on the chicken breasts.

Cook chicken for 25 minutes. Remove foil and allow it to continue cooking for 35 minutes longer. Chicken should roast for approximately one hour total, or until skin is perfectly golden and juices run clear when the flesh is pricked between the breast and drumstick.

15

IT WAS EXHILARATING to be normal!

"What'll it be?" the counter boy asked me, peering over the refrigerated deli case.

"I'll have a blueberry bagel, toasted." I smiled and squeezed Fritz's hand so tightly that his grew slick and mine ached.

"Okay, so, wheat bagel with bacon . . ." he said, scribbling on his notepad.

"No, blueberry bagel, toasted."

"Yes, yes . . . José!" he said, turning toward the grill cook. "Lady wants wheat bagel, *no* bacon!"

Fritz chuckled. "Just like two weeks ago at Cipriani, hmmm, darling?" He nuzzled my neck and, for a moment, I considered Kareem's Duane Street Deli & Lotto to be my makeshift heaven. I might never rid myself of my speech impediment (a Southern accent in Manhattan *is* an impediment) but I could fit in and have a boyfriend and lazy Sunday mornings like the rest of the city.

Every once in a while, it feels good to lose yourself to a man; no thinking required.

"Light and sweet; toasted, buttered, scrambled, crisp." He casually rattled off his breakfast order as I pulled him closer; his mock turtleneck smelled like last night's truffle feast at Fiamma. After Fritz paid (he always paid—he said it made him feel virile), we grabbed our white deli bags, a copy of the Sunday *Times* and stepped out into

Tribeca's manicured grunge. But, as we headed back toward his apartment, the crisp fall morning began to feel cloying as I remembered my humiliation that first night at the hands of Paige.

"Parlor game! Parlor game!" she'd squealed, causing a Saudi prince to relocate his bodyguard between his table and ours. "Fritz, Max, you're never going to belieeeeve where our gorge new girl is from. Come on, Belle, say a few words and the boys will guess city, state, depth of Daddy's pockets."

"Ladies and gentlemen," my internal PA system boomed, "welcome to another round of *Snap Judgment!* Your conniving, blond bombshell host, Paige Beaumont, encourages you to make snap judgments about American News Channel peon Belle Lee, based on a few simple facts: hairstyle, accent, sentence structure, expressions.

"Belle, before we begin, take a few seconds to ask Jesus, Mary and Joseph why you've acclimated so poorly to your surroundings. When will you officially be able to declare yourself a naturalized—or newly baptized—New York citizen?

"Audience, if you nail Belle's place of origin, you win the Wallace Fun in the Sun getaway that she so foolishly forfeited. If you lose, Belle gets to dunk herself in the East River or the Jackie Kennedy reservoir in Central Park and become a real New Yorker. Good luck! And remember, never get to know a person when you can make a— audience, will you help me out?"

"Snap Judgment!"

"Really, Fritz, she made me feel like a circus act." We stepped into his keyed elevator and made our way to the sixth floor.

"Oh, come now, darling, it was *droll*. One must liven up dinner conversation so it's not always Page Six and the stock market. And besides, we have Paige to thank for introducing us to each other."

Can a distraction be your soul mate? I wonder.

We stepped into his apartment and I wanted to assault his fuse box. Fritz had decided to invest his considerable wealth in art that required an electrical socket—the pieces reminding me of the Ballantine's French liquor sign hanging in the window of Raoul's.

"Don't you just adore my collection?" he asked as he did every

time we entered his toxic bachelor pad. Next time, we'd just have to go to my place.

Illuminating. "Remind me again," I said, settling in at his dining room table, unfolding the deli wrapper, "how do you know Paige?"

"She was an undergrad at UVA while I was at Darden. *Everyone* knew Paige Beaumont."

"Pretty girls get noticed," I said, chewing on my blueberry bagel . . . with bacon. Damn it.

"No, my darling, pretty girls are a dime a dozen. Everyone knew Paige because of her column in the *Cavalier Daily.*"

"Good writer?" Somehow, I couldn't imagine her investing any time in a project that didn't boast her likeness.

" 'Writer' would be a generous term—author of narcissistic rantings is more like it. She was the *Cavalier*'s first sex columnist. And when she wasn't parsing her erotic exploits for the entire campus to read, she was trying to seduce the political science department, promising she'd be the first female president. You know she's a diagnosed bipolar, right?"

"If I subsisted on champagne and Wheat Thins, I'd be moody too." I considered that Mamma, if given an MD and a pad of paper, would have prescribed Paige *sustenance.* Protein was Mamma's panacea.

"Yes, darling, I suppose meat and potatoes would mollify her in a way, but it wouldn't solve the conundrum of her family tree."

"In English, please?" It was really so unattractive when Fritz complicated his sentences with big words.

"Her mother is a Jewish psychotherapist from Manhasset and her father was Nixon's speechwriter, a good old boy from north Georgia. That's a toxic genetic merger in my book. Maybe that explains the two divorces by age thirty-two."

I knew she was more disturbed than debutante. . . .

"Now come here, you little Jezebel," Fritz said, making his way around the table. "Are you finally going to let me make love to you? What about if I get us a suite at the Delano? . . ."

Fade to black. Literally. Fritz pressed his black mock turtleneck paunch against my face as I tried to finish my breakfast. If I'm not

sleeping with you in Manhattan, I thought, I'm certainly not going to hop a plane with you. What is it with Manhattan men and destination sex?

I turned my head and filed away Paige's flaws, hoping that I could one day use them to great effect.

Cipriani Bolognese on the Cheap

Mr. Salt and Pepper, Fritz, had a thing for Cipriani. Okay, he had a serious thing for me and he knew that I loved the place. Already he called me his girlfriend, so I suppose I had to call him my boyfriend. Wasn't quite married to the idea, I'll confess. Yes, I do believe my taste for him was secondary to my taste for the Cipriani chef's white ragù. The veal, the cream, the sage—I was bound and determined to figure out the proportions of the sucker before the hedge funder and I parted ways. At last, I nailed it (just not Fritz).

SERVES 6.

Extra virgin olive oil
3 cloves garlic, peeled and smashed
1 carrot, finely diced
2 celery ribs, finely diced
1 medium yellow onion, finely diced
½ gallon whole milk
1 c. heavy cream
1½ pork loin end or shoulder★
½ lb. veal leg★
Kosher salt
Freshly ground pepper
3 Tbsp. fresh sage, chopped
½ c. fresh parmigiano reggiano
3 lb. bucatini, ziti or casarecce pasta
Extra parmigiano and pecorino romano
    for garnish

★Have your butcher grind and combine these two meats.

Over medium heat, pour 2 tsp. olive oil in a large skillet and add 3 cloves smashed garlic along with the carrot, celery, onion (this mixture—carrot, onion and celery—is known as *mirepoix*). Slowly cook the *mirepoix* until the onions are translucent, about 12 minutes.

At the same time, in a small saucepan over low heat, bring 8 c. milk and 1 c. heavy cream to a simmer.

Return to large skillet and turn heat to medium high, adding ground meat to the *mirepoix*. Season with 2 tsp. salt and freshly ground pepper, stirring and cooking the meat until no pink remains and all of the meat's rendered liquid has evaporated. Add ⅓ of the milk/cream mixture to the skillet and lower heat to medium. Allow liquid to reduce by half. Add 1½ Tbsp. chopped sage. Repeat process until no more milk/cream mixture remains, making sure to stir mixture as it reduces, not allowing the milk to scorch or meat to stick to bottom. Reduce heat if necessary.

Once the white Bolognese is nice and thick, stir in ½ c. freshly grated parmigiano reggiano. Taste for proper seasoning. Adjust sauce with further salt, pepper, sage and cheese if necessary.

Cook pasta, drain and toss with the sauce immediately. Garnish individual plates with chopped sage and grated pecorino romano.

16

"THROW ME A BONE! Gimme a kidnapping, a boatload of drowning Haitians, a Palestinian suicide bomber—something!" I yelled at the Reuters news feed. I tore Fritz's cashmere scarf from around my neck (the newsroom heat was mysteriously on the blink) and stabbed the "Enter" key with my leaky Bic. Blue ink trickled down the right side of the keyboard. "We need some news here, people—there's a four-thirty A.M. broadcast!"

Blink. Blink. A top line from Paige.

Presents? A spin around Bergdorf's after his signing bonus? Cartier trinkets, Panther Collection?

Paige never ceased to amaze—she had never once sent me a message about a bill passing in the Senate or the war raging in Kenya. The subject was either pricey baubles—paved or pronged—or Botox injections. Our hedge funder beaus were buddies and she seemed very intent on keeping score.

Top-lining, the newsroom version of instant messenger, is definitely fun and useful . . . until it's not. Imagine flashing yellow e-mails marked "URGENT" appearing every thirty seconds at the top of your computer screen. You have no choice but to interrupt your train of thought, click, read and pray that there's a newsworthy nugget being tossed your way by one of the boys on the breaking-news desk. Nine times out of ten, however, it was Paige's neuroses or newsroom gossip.

Our Golden Boy Chase really IS a fucker! And while he's on the clock!
(Condoms found along the baseboards of edit rooms C and D.)

Flat surface residue testing TODAY. Don't sniff where you shit!
(Cocaine residue discovered on the toilet seats in the men's bathroom.)

"It's not HOW you tell the story, it's WHAT news item you tell.
Edit the lineup, you sons of bitches!"
(Cleveland's maxim; means he's about to waddle down to the trenches.)

It was silly and immature and made me feel like I was a sophomore again, passing notes in homeroom at Country Day School. But it lightened the tense mood that weighed on me and our big, nasty twenty-four-hour operation. A moment of levity and then back to top-Nielsen-rated tragedy. You see, I had just been promoted from production assistant to assistant writer on the overnight. It's a toss up as to whether management was tired of my Chyron screwups (I had misidentified the different Hamas leaders on the lower-third of the television screen) or if they really saw a glimmer of Diane Sawyer promise. My bet is that they were simply fed up and didn't want some Muslim extremist group bombing ANC headquarters because I irreverently captioned one of their esteemed, sacred leaders as a mere footman or suicide bomber.

Whatever the reason, I aimed to make the most of my promotion. For two weeks I had been in a constant race, busting my fanny to get a story at the top of every hour so I could have a full thirty minutes to rewrite it and procure the requisite blood and guts B-role. The better I performed now, the more likely it was for Cleveland to run my Clayton package. And I had to get that baby on air. Simple fact: the more I researched Jessica Clayton, the more I adored her (and her strength reminded me of Mamma's). She possessed the spark and the solid political background that would allow her to implement groundbreaking policy, especially in the arena of health care. And she was a woman. God bless her brains and kitten heels, she was a *woman*! I couldn't help but admire her taste in St. John pantsuits. (I knew the chic upstart could bring some desperately needed style to the Beltway.)

Y'all must understand that a young lady's political affiliation down South isn't discussed or debated, it's *assumed*.

From birth, I have been force-fed two things: grits and right-wing politics.

Now, for the first time, I was nourishing myself. I researched and digested the issues, deciding whether I was Republican or Democrat, whether I wanted to help the country continue apace or experience change. And dinner didn't have to be a meat and two sides! (It makes a girl feel independent to order a dirty martini and a plate of fries.)

Perhaps I only had one meaningful job at the station—to invest myself in Clayton's campaign and cause, the belief that every woman and child deserves proper medical attention. She—we—might not win but at least I will have tried. Cleveland's minions had been very careful to clear the company-wide e-mail system of any clues that would disclose his intentions to buy up Pol24 and establish a media monopoly. My one, very slim chance of procuring evidence would be to slip into Guy's computer and access his confidential files. As a producer, he received different correspondence than I; the big boys had dipped their hands in a pot of honey and I bet their fingerprints were all over his top lines, memos and e-mails.

Right then, however, I needed to conjure all my powers of concentration *and* a photogenic tragedy. This was not the time to focus on what Paige deemed to be my "recent acquisitions"—my hedge funder and the gifts he proffered—or fantasize about the fat cats doing their perp walk in orange prison jumpsuits. I had to forget sex and scandal and think *news* (though my inner Brenda Starr acknowledged that the three aforementioned elements were closer than kissing cousins at ANC.)

Okay, fine, one more top line.

No jewelry. Lots of bra & panty sets. Agent Provocateur—you know it? Don't get why Fritz gifts me panties when all he wants to do is take them off. No nooky for now.

I looked over at Guy, bug-eyed and staring at his computer screen, and realized he hadn't blinked—or top-lined—about my outburst. Something was cookin'. Yep, it was my moral obligation to break into his computer first chance I had. Oh, there it went, finger up the

nose—middle-management minutiae had definitely taken a sticky turn. I glanced several desks down and found our front-of-house video editor watching soft-core porn on the jerry-rigged Cinemax connection. Sam, the director, was a chair away, lightly snoring to the audience laughter of *Saturday Night Live.*

Blink. Blink. *Agent Provocateur?! Worth weight in gold. Smart of you to play prudish. Want to double next wknd? I'll take page from yr act, withhold sex 'til receive spensy lingerie.*

4:15 A.M. I shivered and looked back at Guy fingering the stack of memos, exhibiting all possible signs of nonchalance and do-the-broadcast-your-own-damned-self-I've-been-doctored-into-this-institution-you're-still-a-freelancer slouch. Time to pray to the gods of Reuters and the Associated Press. Jesus Christ had taken a backseat as of late. Not that I was some crazed evangelical; I'm Episcopalian, mind you. But it was important at this crucial, three-month stage in the game to pick and choose my supplications to a higher being. At crunch times like this, leaps of faith had to involve sleuthing, producing and the chance that something horrific was taking place on the other side of the globe. Fifteen minutes until the darkened news studio lit up and we went live. What was I going to feed Paige? I needed a fine, headline-grabbing disaster, a menacing graphic and then to slug the sucker with something catchy.

My script last Friday had been flawless. We were down to the wire, ten minutes before air, when I suddenly read a throwaway AP blurb about Bill Clinton visiting tsunami victims. Not exactly a top of the hour headline unless you slug it with an over-the-shoulder "Wet Willie: Ex Prez Clinton Visits Tsunami Victims" and get a freeze frame of the horn-dog-in-chief eyeballing a busty native. *Then,* you've got conservative ratings gold.

"Genius," Samantha had murmured at the end of my news brief. "Don't get me wrong, we're all fucked working here, but her ratings couldn't get any better."

"Dorothy's coming along, isn't she?" Guy had said from behind me. It would have come across as more of a compliment if his tone hadn't been one of disbelief.

"See? Y'all can trust me. I can produce with the best of 'em." The teeny tiny pang of guilt that had arisen from trivializing and politicizing one of the greatest natural disasters in history ever so slowly receded as I considered the political and moral disaster I was trying to prevent come Election Day. As I sat in front of my computer, envisioning my Clayton package airing in a prime-time slot, the big dogs in the newsroom came up to me, one by one, offering nuggets of die-hard conservative newsroom wisdom and congratulations. Even Fred, the infamous executive producer of all-news programming, shook my hand. "We'll be keeping an eye on you. The election is less than a month away and we need talent like yours." I had never seen the man before, unless you count his online mug shot. Gray eyes, gray hair—he was a wolf in pudgy, middle-aged men's clothing. That kiddie porn on his computer during his newspaper days was somethin' else. I tried not to think of his federally confiscated computer hard drive when he shot a wolfish grin and a small, wet hand in my direction.

"Middle America loves infotainment," Guy continued once everyone had retreated back to their darkened basement corners. "They love it like they crave cheap drugs. I like to think we're crystal meth for our viewers out in Kansas. 'You Snort, We Decide.'"

I needed my small triumphs in the newsroom—like I needed a freshly minted Democratic voter registration card—to help Clayton score a victory on November 4. So I stared at my computer, waiting, praying. The orange light! It flashed over and over at the bottom of the monitor. The gods had answered me with a subway bombing in the Eighth Arrondissement I quietly cheered for the dead and injured in Paris.

17

"GET THE STEAK tartare, trust me." Fritz snapped shut the tall, crimson-edged Balthazar menu, readjusted his Vacheron-Constantin watchband and touched his bull and bear cuff links.

"Hmmm, what'd you say, honey? Tartar sauce?" I rubbed his arm in hopes of shutting him up although I wasn't paying attention to him anyway. Couldn't he see that I was utterly absorbed by the menu, attempting to catch up on twenty-five years of lost veloutés, braises and en croutes? I studied my menus like my colleagues studied freshly cut Bin Laden footage—only with more interest. Something as minor as the man sitting across from me was not about to get in the way of my culinary tutelage. "Wait, tartar sauce?" An indignant ponytail swish let him know that I did not appreciate his assumption that all I knew or liked was deep-fried Southern cuisine. "I don't want mayonnaise and pickle relish all over a perfectly good steak!" The waitress hovering next to our table bit the inside of her cheek. Poor thing, such a terribly unattractive facial tic.

"Tartare," he repeated with his approximation of a French accent, a slight gurgle of phlegm in his throat, "means raw, darling. Look at you, so silly and unaffected." Enormously satisfied with his cultural lesson of the day, he brushed the side of my cheek with the back of his hand and gave me that look, the one that's dreamy yet ravenous, as if he wanted to worship me then defile me right there on the distressed-tile floor. He'd toast his unbridled masculinity with a glass of seventeen-year Taylor tawny port and I'd be doomed to taste his musty, saccharine lips for the rest of the night.

But let's not start talking about lips now. I was tired of hearing about mine and all the things he wanted to do to them. Mind you, these aren't the Chanel red lips that I apply in the bathroom mirror. I'm talking about, well . . . Fritz calls it "pussy." It's hard to know what to do with such a word. "Name it," he sputters as I make my way down his unsubstantial penis with my hand, "make it yours" (at this last bit, his eyes have a way of rolling back in his head like a dead man's). I didn't dare do anything more. With Fritz, I didn't yet have a handle on my gag reflex. My throat would close up just talking to him. It must have had something to do with his untidy cuticles (their relative health depended on the Dow) and the two-inch padding of hair—really, a force field of fur—that covered his entire body, sprouting out of his collared shirts, golf socks, ears.

The issue at hand: pussy, talkin' smut. All of his efforts at trying to be dirty and erotic were thoroughly wasted on me. I just got to thinkin' about the animals we have milling around the farmhouse and lake. Pussy calls to mind the sleepy gray cat that prowls around the old dairy and our cocks are nothing but an annoyance, making noise at 5 A.M. from their turf beneath the oak tree by the barn. And I damn sure know who'd win if those two went at it. Cock beats pussy every time. So why did the Wall Street genius continue reinforcing such predatory images? I resolved to keep my distance, unless, of course, we were at the dinner table.

"I think I'll begin with a half dozen oysters," I said, turning toward the waitress. "Do you have any from Apalach—"

"Wonderful choice, darling, and let's get you another flute of champagne with that. But, why don't we consider the Kumamotos from Japan or Bluepoints from the bay? And the Wellfleets and Malpeques would be exceptionally fruity this time of—"

"Do you mind?" I raised an eyebrow, the one that Fritz had just advised me to have threaded by his "Indian girl at Fekkai." "I'd love it if y'all had a few back there from Apalachicola. You think you could do a nice plate of those for me?"

"The Apalachicolas are two seventy-five apiece and a house favorite. Anything else?"

"I am feeling like shells tonight. I think I'll have the escargot for my entrée." Take that, you showboatin' rooster.

"Oysters and escargot? Does this mean that another banker is taking you to La Goulue the nights I play squash with the boys?" His lips spread wide and thin, an expression that was supposed to suggest the outrageously unbelievable nature of his remark. He wanted an answer. Well, he wasn't going to get one.

Trying out a sexy smirk, I leaned forward over the table and whispered, "You don't know anything that I haven't already tasted."

He knew. I knew. Neither of us was going to say it. I had become a bit of a dinner whore, a gal mainly interested in men for the meals they offered. But if I affectionately likened myself to be the young blond girl featured in last week's *New York Post* article, what was I to do with the headline YOUNG GIRLS DINE OUT ON RICH MEN'S FANTASIES? By God, there were two fantasies at stake! For me, it was a taste, a texture, a snap of a freshly ironed napkin (one that I hadn't washed and starched with my own hands), two, sometimes three hours of tangible bliss. Every penniless working girl needs a plate of Chef Daniel Boulud's black sea bass en papillote (something that tastes even better when you're situated at a plush corner banquette) and a glass of Montrachet to revive her spirits. And the man across the table! His escape is utter and complete. The dinner tab is a ticket to big blue eyes, smooth skin and that elusive island in the Gulf Stream—the freshness and unflappability of a young woman. An Eddie Money tune perhaps, but it was the God-honest truth.

"I've gotten fancy on you, haven't I?" I looked at him over my champagne flute and grinned. It was much easier to just hush up and smile, allow him to think that he was educating me about all things sensual and culinary. He didn't realize that as a Southerner, I had been born into the heat, with a hot temper, somewhere in the vicinity of a sizzling-hot frying pan. Fritz merely encouraged my tastes, he didn't inspire them.

And it was too bad for the fellas that I've never been one to underestimate myself. My company more than compensated for my truffle addiction; not to mention his recent membership to a downtown gym and a hair replacement club for men (he had hair everywhere, *except* on his head). Dating a girl half your age plus seven—according to the girl in the *Post,* this was the perfect mathematical formula for acquiring a trophy date—required upkeep. And a Black American Express Card.

"Do you remember that first night as vividly as I do?" Whenever we were on the cusp of an argument, he placated himself with memories of our first date, a time when I had been impressed by his offers of Caspian Sea caviar and pan-fried veal sweetbreads.

I closed my eyes for a beat. "At Cipriani with Paige?" I kept them closed but not in an effort to conjure up another evening of his domineering personality and babblings of energy stock. It was the bubbles! Such divine little bubbles! I took another sip from my flute.

Nothing in the world like vintage Veuve on a Tuesday night.

"No. Our first date alone."

I opened my eyes and looked at Fritz, a man that I sometimes called "Mister" in the morning before my two cups of coffee. Of course I remembered that night—it was my first taste of the *really* good life. Actually, it was a sensation. That night felt like the aforementioned bubbles exploding in my mind instead of my mouth; such a feeling makes a girl vow never to go back. Fritz had won me over with the appetizer—*foie gras au torchon* with "trois"-berry gastrique. Don't ask me right now what all of that means, just know that it did not taste like a meal of Zeola's fried chicken gizzards followed by lattice-top blueberry pie.

"Delicious."

"*You* were delicious."

"A half dozen Apalachicolas for the lady," the waitress said, presenting me with a plate adorned with more seaweed, crushed ice and lemon wedges than could be found in all the Red Lobsters in the state of Alabama. "And for you, sir, the foie gras and liver mousse with brioche toasts and pickled onions."

Fritz greedily snapped open his napkin and tucked it between the top buttons of his shirt like a toddler at a crawfish boil. If it weren't for your hyper taste buds, Belle, you could be having a fine time with a twenty-six-year-old real estate broker in an innocuous Irish pub on Second Avenue. Pitcher beer, chicken wings, passable blue cheese dressing. You could do *something* age appropriate. I looked across the table at forty-eight-year-old Fritz, my first Manhattan boyfriend. He was handsome enough. I liked salt-and-pepper hair (tufts), and psoriasis and penile malfunctions didn't bother me all that much. They all made for easy, early nights. *A girl must always hold beauty rest at a premium.*

But something was off. The smell was so bad it couldn't be ignored. I looked down at the shells, little pools of ocean, my food, my home shipped so many thousands of miles.

"Mmmmm, an aphrodisiac for my Belle." He cocked an eyebrow and followed my gaze to the oysters, purring then snarling, finally cramming a liver-laden toast point in his mouth. A blob of mousse dangled from his lower lip. "Listen, I think it's time," he said, grabbing my hands, brown cream rolling around in his half-opened mouth, "I think it's time we finally spent the night together. The entire night. And we make this thing legitimate. Penetration, orgasm, the whole deal." To him, sex was a macrofinance deal in the global market.

I removed my hands from his. Sniffed. "It's passed."

"What?"

"They've passed."

"Who's passed? We have? No, baby, don't say that. We've hit a few bumps here and there but, but . . . It's that goddamned job of yours! How can I be relaxed and how can you feel sexy when—"

"I'm telling you it's spoiled—"

"Nothing is spoiled. And I've been good. So good, haven't I?" His questioning brow, the wrinkled one, the one with the deep line through it like a scar—quickly turned into one of conviction. "No, damnit, I've been superb. I've been treating you like Class A stock and you've yet to yield any sort of return. How much patience can a man have? We're at the one-month mark, for Christ's sake! By now, we should at least be engaging in oral sex!" He beat his fist on the table, surely scuffing his bull (or bear, I couldn't remember which cuff link was where), perhaps even setting back his watch a few time zones to the opening bell in Bangkok.

"I'm talking about the oysters, Fritz." I paused, leaned toward him and the plate and smelled again. "My oysters have gone bad." I might have been blonde with a funny way of talking, but I knew my bivalves. "Vibrio vulnificus." And I was getting to know my men. The rotten oyster smelled like my rotten egg of a boyfriend. It was time to leave behind pussy talk and market minutiae.

For a moment he was stunned into silence, mouth open, the globule of brown mousse wiggling, attempting to free itself from his thin bottom lip and make it onto the thick, white rim of his plate. Unfortunately, I didn't see its liberating fall.

I left him at the table and walked north, back to my apartment, staring at the sky above the riverbed, the white and silver scales atop the Chrysler Building. Alone and heading home.

It reminded me of my first weeks in the city, walking from Union Square down Broadway after going to the movies—always alone—past Grace Church and Amalgamated Insurance. The education of a girl and her sensibilities. Then it came to me, *finally,* "alone" and "lonely" were very different. I was by myself yet felt a part of those around me, Broadway, a river of souls, the echo of heavy heels, sneezes, monologues of crazy street poets. I considered all of my romances—the city, my job, the men. Manhattan was real and the only thing that had grabbed a hold of me, never once letting go.

So I had that.

I'd always have that.

Breathe.

Modern Girl Make-at-Home Tuna Tartare

Dinner dates come with a big 'ol price tag. There's the expensive food, the emotional duress of fiddling with your wallet when the bill comes and, of course, there's <u>him</u>. If he weren't paying for my champagne and allowing me to nibble his tartare, would I actually be spending time with him? I've cut out the middle man and learned how to chop, toss and arrange ruby-colored morsels (tuna—instead of steak—for the waistline) at home. No more excruciating free meals . . . well, maybe just a few.

SERVES 2.

1 Tbsp. plum vinegar

½ tsp. sesame oil

2 Tbsp. fresh lemon juice

3 tsp. extra virgin olive oil

Kosher salt

Freshly ground black pepper

10 oz. sashimi-grade ahi-tuna loin,
    cut into ⅓-inch cubes

1 Tbsp. chopped seedless cucumber

1 tsp. finely chopped green onion

2½ tsp. finely chopped fresh chives

1 medium ripe avocado, peeled, pit removed

Mâche or any microgreen to garnish tartare

In a medium-sized bowl, whisk together plum vinegar, sesame oil, 1 Tbsp. freshly squeezed lemon juice, 2 tsp. olive oil with salt and pepper to taste.

Add tuna, chopped cucumber, green onion and chives and gently combine.

In a separate bowl, mash avocado with 1 Tbsp. lemon juice, 1 tsp. olive oil and salt and pepper to taste.

With your ring mold placed in the middle of a large, white plate, spoon half of avocado mixture, pressing firmly with back of spoon. Follow by adding half of tuna mixture on top. Remove ring mold and garnish with mâche or microgreens. Serve immediately.

Oyster Stew

If you're uncertain as to the origin of your oyster, don't consume it in one hurried gulp. Look at it. Smell it. Know that if you cook him slowly, letting him stew long enough, simmering him until his juices run clear, you'll get rid of the unsavory stuff. Make him sweat it out. There. You just got a recipe intro and top-notch, twenty-first-century dating advice.

SERVES 2, GENEROUSLY.

2 pints oysters, preferably Apalachicola
2 Tbsp. unsalted butter
2 c. whole milk
1 tsp. (or 1 cube) chicken bouillon granules
2 oz. sherry
Kosher salt, to taste
White pepper, to taste

Heat oven to 375 degrees. In a colander, drain oysters, retaining the juice for later use. Melt butter in a 9x13 baking pan and add drained oysters. Bake oysters for approximately five minutes. Remove oysters from oven.

In a medium-sized pot, heat milk over a low flame. Once milk is warm, add cooked oysters, butter, chicken bouillon seasoning, oyster juice, sherry and salt and pepper to taste. Stir and serve immediately.

Zeola's Lattice-Top Blueberry Pie

Because a girl can't live on "trois"-berry gastrique alone.

SERVES 6–8.

For crust
> ½ tsp. salt
> 2 c. all-purpose flour
> ⅔ c. chilled unsalted butter,
>   cut into small pieces
> ⅓ c. ice water

For blueberry filling
> 2½ c. blueberries, rinsed and
>   picked over
> ¾ c. sugar
> 2 heaping tsp. flour
> ⅛ tsp. salt
> 2 tsp. finely grated lemon zest
> 2 Tbsp. fresh lemon juice
> 2 Tbsp. chilled unsalted butter,
>   cut into small bits

Preheat oven to 375 degrees.

In a medium-sized bowl, combine salt and flour. Add butter and mix well with your fingers until dough has reached crumblike texture. Moisten the dough with the ice water, working with your fingers or a pastry cutter, until ingredients are well incorporated. Divide the dough into two balls. Wrap one ball in plastic wrap and place in refrigerator. Roll out the other ball on a lightly floured work surface. Place the pie dough in a nine-inch buttered pie pan and prick with a fork.

Carefully toss together blueberries, sugar, flour, salt, lemon zest and lemon juice. Mound blueberry mixture atop pie crust.

Remove dough from refrigerator, roll out on a lightly floured work surface and cut into ½-inch-wide strips. Weave strips on top of pie. Dot top of pie with butter bits.

Place pie dish on a baking sheet. Bake for 10 minutes. Reduce oven heat to 325 degrees and bake another 45 minutes or until crust is golden.

Allow pie to partially cool on a wire rack. Serve warm.

18

"NOPE, NO INTERMISSION. We've got to get you back out there." Paige had thrust her crimson-colored Birkin bag into my arms already loaded with her enormous three-ring binders. I scurried after her to the curb.

"I can't do it. I'm telling you, these Yankee men leave me cold. All this dating nonsense is a waste of time." My fingertips grazed the surely scandalous memos tucked inside her notebooks. My mouth began to water as I considered the confidential information that I held between my hands. For Paige to take work home, it *had* to be important. The stacks of papers probably delineated her stock options and enormous raise if Hewitt was elected to the presidency and the Pol24 hostile takeover was accomplished. Vanity and vainglory always seemed to win on the island.

I watched as she shimmied her midnight blue Narciso Rodriguez evening gown to its proper place. She reached inside the dress, cupped one bosom and then another, adjusting them to great effect, not even considering the fact that we were standing on Sixth Avenue in full view of her driver—and rush-hour Manhattan.

"Listen to me, you're warmed up, you're loose—Well, okay, unfortunately we know you're not loose. . . ." she muttered, sounding deeply disappointed that I was not, in fact, a harlot. "You've got to get back out there while your mind's a little numb but your body knows what to do. I want you on a date your first free night, understood?"

"But, coach . . ." I looked for some sort of acknowledgment that she knew I was kidding but she gave me nothing save a fine mist of Tresemmé hair spray from her travel-sized atomizer. Paige continued spraying her halo of blonde until she wheezed from the fumes.

"How," she began, coughing, "does freezing your eggs on a Friday night and then going home alone to watch TBS's *Dinner and a Movie* sound, hmmm? Pad thai, aching ovaries and *Sixteen Candles*." My Lord, she certainly had her details down pat. "Because, in the end, that's what it comes down to. You're twenty-five today, thirty-five tomorrow. Remember, an egg dies every month and so does your chance of landing a hedge fund manager or venture capitalist." She peered into her Chanel compact and practiced her pout, thrust out her hip.

The National Academy of Television Arts and Sciences' award show had begun a half hour ago and yet Paige still had time to lecture me on her favorite subjects—dating, crow's feet and my potentially shriveled eggs. Then again, if she missed the awards portion of the evening it didn't matter. The News Channel had never won a single honor or decoration from the "commies on Fifty-second Street" (descriptor directly pulled from Cleveland's company-wide e-mail disregarding the evening's pomp and circumstance) and my guess was that they weren't about to decorate Paige with the Journalist of the Year award. Samantha and I had placed bets that she was just attending the ceremony so afterward she could run next door to the "21" Club and pick up a thrice-divorced, blue pill–popping captain of industry. For months, Paige had been eyeing a "Classic Six"—an elegantly proportioned, six-room apartment—on Park Avenue. She was determined to find a man to fork over the 50 percent down payment. (And, yes, it says something about the kind of life I was leading—one that Mamma would say was "hedgin' on the vulgar"—that "Classic Six," Cialis, jihad and dirty bomb had become a part of my everyday lexicon.)

"But I don't *know* anyone." I hoped to put the matter to rest immediately—a chilled bottle of Pinot Gris and freshly laundered sheets were the only things on my agenda for the evening. That and writing copy on Clayton. Only ten days remained before the election and the News Channel's right-wing stumping had reached a fevered pitch. Live interviews, rallies and packages of Hewitt crowded our prime-time lineup while Clayton and her platform—namely, universal health care—languished in obscurity. Not one of the producers would touch her for fear of losing their jobs. Did a package by lil' ol' me have a chance to air, considering the stakes? Even *my* optimism had its limits—and the dating scene was definitely not helping matters.

"You know how it goes, Paige. At work, I'm stuck with the likes of Wallace and his producers, men with wedding bands and roving eyes. I have them *or* the fratastic production boys fresh off their last bender from Langan's."

Paige poured herself into the car, showing off her long, slender legs to great effect. "I know there's someone for you down in Soho. Listen, you find one guy and I'll match you. Yes!" she said, clapping her hands together. Her fingers looked a touch red and irritated. She must have had her digits waxed for her evening with the liberal elite. If Barbara Walters saw her hairy paws reaching for the crudité platter or a mini crab cake, she'd run a special on *The View* about female hormone imbalance and its proliferation in red-state America. "That's what you'll do. You'll have your first doubleheader."

"I absolutely refuse to go to a baseball game." I didn't mind a soft pretzel now and again but, my Lord, I wasn't about to make a habit out of it.

"Haven't I taught you a thing? A doubleheader is two dates in one night," she said, brushing the half-moons of her exposed bosoms with sparkly bronzed powder. Somehow, I couldn't picture Diane Sawyer preparing for her Excellence in Journalism award in the same manner. "You meet one date for an aperitif at, say, sixish, and then another at eight-thirty for dinner."

And that was how this evening had been set in motion. Paige's Shock and Awe/Wrinkles and Sterility campaign was the reason that, on my one scheduled night off for the next fourteen days, I had climbed out of bed, put down the hunk of Roquefort and bag of California apricots and tucked away my Julia Child *Mastering the Art of*

French Cooking DVD collection. I slipped into a silk handkerchief dress with plunging neckline and wore Ferragamo strappy heels that pinched my pinky toes to the point of possible amputation.

"I *do* want children eventually," I conceded aloud, peeking through the gates into the back garden of Barolo Restaurant. The white tablecloths and tea lights, the lithe, naked tree limbs, the humming of wine-warm voices. If only my evening hadn't included Andrew, the *commercial-real-estate-developer-cum-art-collector-and-Ducati-racer* (all Paige's male friends were hyphenated), I could have enjoyed the crisp October night.

"You look fucking fantastic!" he said by way of greeting.

"Nice to meet you too." Now please, sir, I'm going to have to ask you to clean out that filthy mouth of yours, tuck away your penis and order me an Italian Super Tuscan—pronto. I'll sip it, giving you more time than you deserve, then hit the streets running and hunt down Paige at the "21" Club.

"So how does it feel knowing that you can fuck anyone you want to?" Andrew began, before the wine list had arrived.

"Excuse me?" I nervously fingered the *grissini,* plotting my silent revenge. Perhaps Mace instead of hair spray in Paige's travel-sized atomizer. And why had I trusted her in the first place? Someone so self-involved could never play cupid.

"Come on, don't be modest. A woman like you can have *whatever, whenever.* So what do you dream about? What is your biggest sexual fantasy?"

"You Yankees are inquisitive beasts, aren't you?" But I bet he was full of it. He probably liked missionary with the lights off. I whistled down the waiter (protocol having already flown out the window) and pointed to a glass of $26 Podere Luigi '97. Imported elixir would sustain me.

"Beasts? Mmmm, I like the sound of that. If I tell you my erotic fantasy, maybe you'll tell me yours," he said, visibly readjusting himself at the table and leaning back in his chair to more comfortably spread his legs. "I saw this porn flick a few weeks ago—you watch a lotta porn? Bet you do, you sexy thing." He ran his fingers through his dark, greased waves, momentarily getting his gold signet pinky ring stuck in the tangle. "The blonde in the flick—who looked a hell of a lot like you, by the way—wore a black leather catsuit and heels. First thing, she walks into the bedroom and straps on a huge black dildo—"

Back out on the sidewalk, I considered the perversions and persuasions of all my dates. I also considered what it meant to be twenty-five and single in the city. So many excruciating moments, expectations invested and brightness lost. My New York was downtown and moody and persistent. Nothing came to me in a flash of brilliance—including the men, *especially* the men. My needs were simple enough, right?

All I wanted was an apartment in the sky with enough room for me, my husband, our love, his ego and my ambition.

I checked my makeup in the rearview mirror of a silver convertible Benz and pondered the law of averages. Date number two *had* to run more smoothly. Besides, I had orchestrated this one. Octavio was a restaurateur extraordinaire *and* my neighbor. Since I had canceled my single girl buffet of imported nibbles in bed, I decided to spend the evening with a man who at least understood appetites. And Octavio was safe, right? Ever since we had met by accident as only a twenty-five-year-old aspiring journalist and a fifty-five-year-old Soho personality can—at the bar of a swanky restaurant—we'd been sidewalk friends, all smiles and nods and talk of city headlines.

"I m finally going to step inside an honest-to-goodness *real* New York City apartment," I mused aloud. It would have multiple rooms and maybe even a washer and dryer, an ice maker if we're talkin' crazy. My new ritual under fall's Spanish blue skies was to walk down Bedford, Charles, West Tenth and all the rest of the nice streets just so I could spy real people in real homes. The fact that these homes cost upward of ten million dollars didn't deter me from imagining that I'd eventually live in one. I looked through the panes of the brownstones to the earnest shadows of cooks and nannies standing over sinks, wiping the noses of young children. I knew that the mamma was upstairs sliding bangles onto her thin, tanned wrists and Daddy would eventually come home to a roasted piece of meat, scotch and a family that smells of lilac and vanilla. A doll's house for millionaires. The scenes seemed much more real than what took place in my box, the one room forced to accommodate my moods and half meals and sighs.

I quickened my pace; the little bit of grape running through my veins pushed me along Spring Street, toward Octavio's apartment on the Hudson. By the time I stepped inside the elevator, on my way up to his triplex penthouse in the clouds, I had near forgotten about Andrew, the walking, smirking, readjusting 1–900 number. All I considered was the opulent normalcy that awaited me.

And then the doors opened.

Candles burning.

Sinatra crooning.

Dom chilling on ice.

"There's my girl," Octavio said in a soft, intimate tone, descending the floating staircase. I moved my eyes from his, around his contemporary apartment—all angles, charcoals and grays—finally resting them on the long dining room table. I immediately recognized the pink and black Agent Provocateur lingerie bag.

Air kiss. Air kiss.

"How are you, doll?" I tried out my most platonic voice. He stared back at me with his tight, gray curls and shrunken black T-shirt, standing in the middle of his very industrial loft. He looked like a little boy lost in the screwdriver aisle of Home Depot.

"I got a little something for you," he said, reaching for the bag. His expectations were tangible, making me flush despite the chill of the apartment.

"What in the world?" I tried out one of Mamma's rhetoricals while I pondered my role as the indulgent mother to every Manhattan male; I lectured Guy on cirrhosis of the liver, Wallace on the sanctity of marriage, Golden Boy Chase on the truly delicate construction of his septum. Boys.

"Go on, open it."

Composure, girl. Nothing could be as bad as stumbling across one of the suits in edit room C, riding a J-school intern in nothing more than a Paul Smith taupe-colored tie. I had quietly closed the door and never breathed a word of it to my coworkers, hoping my prudence would result in a hefty hourly pay increase.

Access deep reserves of calm and Southern class.

I plunged my hand inside the bag and pulled out a very large box. Quickly, I shrugged off the satin ribbon. Inside, waiting for me, was a black silk bed coat lined with brown mink (very Brigitte Bardot) and a pair of black, lace panties with satin ties at the hips (very Carmen Electra).

My year's salary in lingerie. "Octavio, I don't know what to say." Was this what rich, *much* older men did on first dates? I imagined the two of us in bed, me discreetly brushing off a silver hair atop my right breast, a souvenir of his good intentions.

"Wait, I have something else," he said, reaching into his jeans pocket, pulling out a slender, midnight blue velvet box.

"Go on." He extended it in my direction.

With shaking hands, I took the box. Was this my answered prayer? Was Octavio my ruby watch–wielding suitor, the man of my dreams having always lived just a few penthouses away? Yes, admittedly, the panty gift was inappropriate and made me feel like a tart-for-hire but jewelry meant that he was *serious.* Paige had taught me that precious stones were the real deal. He had *profound* intentions. I swiftly considered how I would finally leap from producing to on-air reporting in the coming weeks, all the while orchestrating a too-chic downtown wedding and preparing my body for motherhood. Lots of folic acid and lean protein. A baby boy. We'd alternate days of dressing him in cowboy boots and mini Gucci loafers. It would all be difficult but doable with my gray-haired, worldly husband by my side.

Before prying open the tiny hinges I stopped and grabbed Octavio's hand. "I just want you to know that I've always felt something for you. But I was confused, I thought it was friendship, our love of imported food products. We both order the same cuts of meat from Pino the butcher, requesting our chicken to be scaloppine and our prosciutto tissue-thin. You like the small, salted mozzarella at Joe's and so do I. We both eat olive oil–packed Sicilian anchovies out of the jar for a quick lunch on the run. I just never thought it could lead anywhere because of, you know," I hesitated, feeling silly to even mention something so minor, "our thirty-year age difference." I gazed into his black eyes (goodness, his pupils were large!) and considered how life could turn on a nickel.

"I've had my eye on you for some time," he said, his nostrils twitching, running his tongue across his teeth and then his lips. "Your phone call clued me in. We want the same thing. Now, open it, baby. You're going to love what Daddy's given you." He leaned toward me and I waited for his kiss. But before our lips could touch, his tiny pink tongue shot out, jabbing at the general vicinity of my mouth until my lips parted and he gained access to my two front teeth.

Unusual.

And he was so jumpy.

But I could adjust. Maybe that was the way of Old New York.

After he put his tongue away, I gently closed my eyes and opened the box, marking the moment in my mind with something akin to the red silk ribbon that holds my place in my old debutante diary.

"What?" I stared down at the open box, at the bed of blue velvet that held two tiny black cones studded with diamonds, shreds of leather dangling from their tips.

"Fucking sexy, aren't they?"

"I don't understand."

"Pasties, baby—pasties! Now go put everything on. I can't wait to see those big titties of yours topped off with my black leather and diamonds."

Jewelry for my bosoms? For once in my life, I couldn't speak.

"I *said,* go put everything on." He forced a smile and pointed up the stairs.

Practical matters first. Could I form a sentence? I flexed my lips. "I'm not trying this on." My tone was steady.

"When I spend fifteen fucking grand, you'll do whatever I tell you to do." Spit began collecting at the corners of his mouth. His leg twitched. Of course, he'd been doing lines. I knew the signs because of all my overnights with Guy and prime-time shifts with Chase. A week ago, I had pointed out the powdered sugar around Guy's nose. "Blow," he sputtered, once he had finally stopped laughing and could stand up straight. "Blow, my dear Dorothy, is what keeps me—and this station—alive."

"I didn't ask for any of this. I'm *not* trying it on," I said, backing away from him, trying to move toward the elevator.

"Then you can't have any of it—you can't take them home with you." He stuffed everything back into the gift bag and grabbed me by the arm, pulling me across the dining and living rooms, toward the French doors that opened onto his terrace. "Stay there," he commanded, forcing me outside, slamming and locking the doors behind him.

I considered the fire escape. Fourteen floors down to street level. Across the street, in an apartment of a new high-rise building, a cocktail party was in full swing. Their fun looked simple enough. Martini glasses, a tight cocktail dress with panty lines, stories being told that made everyone's eyes crinkle. A guest pointed to me, lit up on the patio in the otherwise perfect October night. Everyone turned and waved. They thought I was lucky. The host, a husband, I presumed, raised a glass in my direction and politely nodded.

Yeah, cheers. Cheers to powdered sugar and porn and pasties and the long fall back to earth. Was this New York mine? Because it didn't seem real. Someone, somewhere was about to yell "Cut!" and the joke and the chaos would be over.

Who's the belle now, baby? What do you think?"

I slowly turned toward Octavio's voice. Starting at the feet and working my way up, I looked at him posing in the doorway.

Four-inch Lucite heels.

Black fishnet stockings.

My black panties.

My mink-lined bed coat.

A studded dog collar wrapped around his neck.

"You're not the only hot number around here. And look at my stems," he said, angling one leg in my direction and then another, an absurd grin on his face. "So, whaddya think?"

"I think you're stretching out my panties." A wiggle of his narrow hips and he slipped them off to reveal some sort of medieval torture device around his penis.

"It's a cock ring, baby, keeps me hard for young girls like you."

The door was parted, begging me to slip through so I could make my escape. I strode toward him, stopping long enough to say the first words that came to mind.

"I've seen bigger balls on a poodle."

I had nerves to last me a lifetime, but, somehow, my memory had grown short. My romantic and culinary escapades had made me forget why I had made the big trip North. It was high time for me to make a name for myself and nothing—not even a cock ring—was going to get in my way.

Single-Girl Sustenance

I love my single nights staying in. I can forget about his ego and taste buds and focus on the flavors, colors and textures that make me happy. And I'm not talking about preparing full, hot meals here. Think petite, potent tastes of cheese, really good bread, cured meats and fish, seasonal fruits with nuts. Cancel a date and treat yourself to a solitary bite. Because sometimes, when you're alone, the wine is like rubies and the small plates, little pieces of heaven.

- Five-minute organic, farmhouse-fresh egg served over steamed asparagus spears or spicy Italian arugula.

- Zucchini ribbons tossed with olive oil, lemon juice and fresh oregano topped with a generous spoonful of fresh ricotta and a sprinkle of kosher salt.

- Raw sea scallops sliced horizontally, sprinkled with fresh lime juice, olive oil, sea salt, dried chilis and coriander, topped with sliced picholine or taggiasca olives.

- Dried California apricots spread with Gorgonzola or a good domestic blue cheese (i.e., Maytag).

- Anchovies (bottled in olive oil, not vegetable oil) on a simple white cracker spread with Dijon mustard.

- Manchego cheese topped with thinly sliced roasted red peppers, speared with a rosemary sprig.

- A slice of thick-cut country bread, lightly toasted, rubbed with olive oil and halved raw garlic clove, crowned with a nest of caramelized onions and a dollop of fresh ricotta cheese.

- Sliced Golden Delicious or Jonah apple topped with smoked trout (canned, good quality) and a dot of Dijon mustard.

- A square pallet of Bulgarian feta, fan of sliced avocado, thinly sliced red onion rings, a shower of dried oregano, drizzle of olive oil and lemon juice.

- Thinly cut dried chorizo sausage paired with sliced cucumber.

- Wild Atlantic salmon, thinly sliced along the grain, sprinkled with lemon juice, olive oil, sea salt and thin shavings of fennel.

- Four fresh figs, scored (cut an X through the stem toward the bottom, making sure not to cut all the way through), sprinkled with chopped, fresh rosemary, drizzle of honey.

- Saltine cracker capped with a square of guava paste, a slice of cream cheese.

- Finest-quality dark chocolate square topped with a sliver of triple-cream Brie.

Buttermilk and Raspberry "Morning After" Muffins

These muffins should be thrown together after a lazy morning in bed. They're easy, decadent and tangy, thanks to the buttermilk. If you have more luck than I on the dating scene, you can enjoy them back in a warm bed with last night's honey.

MAKES 9.

- 1½ c. whole wheat flour
- ¼ c. wheat germ
- ⅓ c. white granulated sugar
- ⅓ c. light brown sugar
- ½ tsp. baking powder
- ½ tsp. baking soda
- ¼ tsp. salt
- ½ c. vegetable oil
- 1 c. buttermilk
- 1 tsp. fresh lemon juice
- ¼ c. slivered, blanched almonds
- 1 c. raspberries

Preheat oven to 350 degrees. In a large bowl, sift together flour, wheat germ, sugars, baking powder, baking soda and salt. Put aside. In a separate bowl, combine oil, buttermilk and lemon juice. Gently stir almonds and raspberries into flour mixture. Make a well in center and pour in buttermilk mixture. Stir until just blended. Spoon into greased muffin tins. Bake for 20 minutes. Allow muffins to cool on a baking rack for 10 minutes.

19

NEED SPRING ROLLS and happy ending. Off to Little Korea. You cover broadcasts?

I glanced over at Guy, sitting just five feet away, as he rattled off another message to me. He was juiced, sweating through his "Moody Blues Tour of '89" T-shirt and furiously stabbing at the keyboard.

32nd Street is the only stretch of land . . .

". . . that Korea has ever invaded," I mouthed, finishing off his racist yarn.

Off-color jokes are merely Guy's stab at charm, I thought. And Little Korea, a maze of Asian barbecue joints, rub-and-tugs and karaoke bars near Herald Square, was an endless source of wonderment for him. He stopped there during dinner breaks or after doing a double shift and called it decompressing. I called it soliciting prostitution.

I wished he would get out of here already and leave me alone. I had too much on my mind to let myself think about the consequences of his drug habit and his predilection for seedy Asian massage joints. Topping off my list of pending crises:

1. Guy must not encourage walls of heart to explode in Herald Square brothel.
2. If he does exit for a "tug," hack into his computer, make copies of confidential correspondence regarding Hewitt and media monopoly; immediately sanitize hands.

3. Write sexy yet tragic news blurb about troop of kidnapped Florida Girl Scouts for upcoming broadcast.

"We have ten more broadcasts before the dayside shift begins and we're relieved. Are you sure now is the time to skip out for dinner and entertainment?" I had to protest a *little,* right? Now that I was an official writer/producer—capable of editing footage with the Avid machine and transitioning my copy from breaking news in the Middle East to coverage of the party candidates—I had to at least *appear* responsible.

This surge of intelligence, extreme handiness and maturity shocked even me. Admittedly, I knew it had a little something to do with priority alignment; I had shifted my focus from sex-crazed, worthless dates back to my career—and it seemed to have worked. (A city of four million men and countless gourmet dining opportunities present quite a distraction to a curious girl from L.A.—Lower Alabama.) And all the major time suckage that was office gossip had come to an abrupt halt when Samantha and Paige were promoted to dayside, though Paige still bombarded me with matchmaking e-mails. I ignored them; I had been pricked in the fanny, not the heart, by her cupid's arrow one too many times.

"Belle, what can I do?" he whined. "I gotta have a little fun. You know this place busts my balls."

"Why don't you ask to be transferred to dayside? You've been on this shift too long, Guy, the hours are killing you. No one can live like this year after year." I tried to write a few lines about the Girl Scout uniforms (could I describe their sleeves as "blouson," the skirts more beige than khaki?) but I was worried—the sweating and the dilated pupils scared me. He'd made five trips to the bathroom in the past two hours.

I turned to watch him shove his hand into his pocket. I knew that the right side was where he kept it. He would finger the small blue plastic bag in his jeans pocket and then take it out, play with it when he thought no one was looking. He was like a damned five-year-old boy who had just discovered something hanging between his legs; he touched it just enough to reassure himself that it was still there.

"Fuck me if we caught Osama before daylight! Hell, I don't care— throw a dead Nancy Reagan my way and I'd be thrilled!"

The shouting and hysterics? All drugs. But the little-known fact about Guy was that he was a genius at getting the scoop, spinning stories. He didn't need a disaster. In fact, the more I worked with him, the more I realized that he was a highly skilled raconteur with a keyboard, a press badge and a right-wing political ax to grind. It was easy to joke about him, but he knew his stuff (and he knew how to twist it). He was the spitball-throwing class cutup who just so happened to crack straight A's every semester. The strange thing was, no matter how much brilliance or ignorance he showed, he couldn't get promoted or fired. I smelled a scandal of a backstory.

"Go on then," I said, shooing him away, "just don't fall in love and make sure to bring me back *chap chae* and *galbi gue.*" During my Date Embargo, I had also mastered the complexities of local takeout menus. And then there was my platinum membership to Babes in Toyland. I took to the den of sin like a crawdaddy to a dirty puddle in a Louisiana ditch. The salesgirls knew me by name and we all agreed—a battery (not a banker) is one of life's greatest pleasures.

"Three marriages in nine years," he blurted out, apropos of nothing. He was high out of his mind.

I needed to be Nancy Drew (sans the blue Mustang; I couldn't afford parking) and get into his computer—not Freud, exploring his neuroses. I sat back in my swivel chair and began rocking, slow and steady. Back and forth, back and forth . . . I had to make hard copies of any evidence I found. "I think you'll feel a lot better if you get a little Korean barbecue in your stomach—"

"Did you hear me? I'm averaging a wife every three years. And I'm supposed to be on top of my game? Give a shit about producing ninety-second news cut-ins?" He spun around but I could hear him mutter, "This shit better get wrapped up soon. I want my cut and then I'm out." He turned back toward me just as I shifted my gaze to the small blue Ziploc bag next to his computer. A single wrinkle cut into the otherwise taut plastic surface.

"What? We've got shit for coffee in the Green Room. You think that's the same shit they pour Kissinger and Morris? Fuck no." He stood up and began pacing between a row of deserted workstations and the War Room. He was acting more anxious and crazed than I had ever seen him.

"You're right, you deserve time off." I stood up, and in a bold move akin to saving Tara from the Yankees, voluntarily *touched* Guy, putting my arm (halfway) around his burly shoulders. "Go enjoy a nice long midnight *snack* on Thirty-second Street," I said with Wallace's signature lascivious wink, "and don't think about work, your wives—any of it." We must have been standing under the motion detector, because the sliding glass doors of "The Nation's #1 News Channel!" continued opening and closing at a rapid clip. "I've got everything covered."

"You do?" For the first time he stopped fidgeting, muttering, cursing, and looked me directly in the eye. "You really think you could carry these broadcasts all on your own?"

"Of course. I've been trained by the best, haven't I?" He shrugged, high and confused, stepped through the doors and disappeared.

Move those thighs, girl—go!

I careened through the reception area—knocking over a life-sized cardboard likeness of Wallace wearing a three-cornered hat, holding a "Patriot Act" scroll—past the main desk and Gina's office, through Wallace's producing pod and finally threw myself into Guy's swivel chair. Was he still logged in? Yes! With one eye on the clock—fifteen minutes until the Girl Scout breaking-news broadcast—I quickly scanned the left hand-side toolbar of his computer screen, looking for folders that might be slugged with something belying the confidential information inside. A handful of porn videos, *One Night in Paris, Driving Into Miss Daisy*; the usual sports gambling, "Giants Betting Pool" . . . Aha! One of his folders had been very cleverly titled, "Secrets." Just as I double-clicked on the icon, Christopher, whom I hadn't seen in months, walked through the sliding doors.

"I thought I'd find you down here," he said, making his way around the news desk, a manila envelope tucked beneath his arm. Working as Cleveland's and Keaton's henchman in China, brokering satellite television deals with the commies, suited him. He looked gorgeous as ever in his charcoal gray, three-button blazer and slacks.

"Christopher—mercy me!" I couldn't let him see that I was root-
ing around Guy's computer. I furiously clicked on the mouse, trying
to minimize the file. As my luck, and Guy's pervy mind would have
it, a Condoleezza Rice screensaver—her head airbrushed onto the latest cover of *JUGS*—filled the screen. I quickly stood up, trying to
block the monitor.

"It's been too long, hasn't it? So much has changed since we met
up just a few short months ago," Christopher began, his head bowed
in earnestness. I was repulsed by his dirty politics but he was a fine-
lookin' specimen. Sigh. Another attractive man with whom I would
not be having babies. "I understand you want to run a sympathetic
piece on Jessica Clayton."

"I think it's important for me to uphold the 'fair' end of the journalism bargain, don't you?"

"What would your grandfather think, Belle? Have you considered
that?" He continued pacing, taking slow, deliberate steps toward the
War Room and away from the desk.

"I finally believe in something bigger than myself," I said, keeping
an eye on him, feeling for the mouse. There was no telling when Guy
would be back and I had to get a look at the documents. "And after
the election, I'm going to follow your advice and move on. I've got
my chops. I'm ready for another channel."

Click, click.

"But when all is said and done, there might not be anywhere else
to work." He opened the door to the War Room and sauntered inside.

I watched him through the glass walls as he circled the conference
room table, seemingly lost in thought. Quickly, I sat back down in
Guy's chair and scanned the screen.

Confidential e-mails and top lines—hundreds of them—unfurled
as I clicked on the mouse and scrolled down. Pages of correspondence
had been exchanged among everyone in my direct orbit, leading all the
way up to Cleveland. They confirmed my greatest fears about defeating
Jessica Clayton, getting Hewitt in office, controlling the FCC to create
a Keaton-owned media monopoly and . . . *me*? What? That thread of

correspondence began the exact week when I rejected Wallace and his efforts to whisk me away for a XXX holiday under the sun (and him).

Guy—*"I told Dorothy to keep her distance from Wallace, not push him away. If she's stupid enough to reject him and think she'll advance at this station, then we have a naive little instrument on our hands. . . ."*

Christopher—*"Leave her alone. She's practically a child."*

Cleveland—*"Nothing wrong with child labor."*

Gina—*"She already knows too much. If we fire her, she'll run to Cindy Adams with the Wallace sexual harassment bit. She's all yours, Guy. While I'm in the Middle East, figure out how we can use her."*

Samantha—*"She's turning Dem on us . . . pushing a Clayton package around the office. . . ."*

Guy—*"That shit will never make it—no matter how much Keaton likes political favors."*

Samantha—*"Or could we air it? With her inexperience . . ."*

Paige—*", , , she'll screw up and forward our agenda."*

Cleveland—*"How do you know Dixie won't pull through?"*

Paige—*"I'll distract her with the usual—sex and the city. She won't survive. Just make sure that anchor slot is mine."*

Guy—*"Here it is: eleventh hour we'll kill the package and make her go live. Dixie Dorothy, Jessica Clayton, 15 million Americans and me in her earpiece. Hewitt's in!"*

Cleveland—*"We'll definitely make her go live."*

I minimized the files, pulled up the ANC homepage and stood just as Christopher walked back to the desk.

"I was a child with the right and now I've become an adult with the left, Christopher. I'm a different girl than the one you used to know." I was amazed at how easily the words came tumbling out. Maybe that's why a wave of cold or nausea didn't overcome me after reading about my conspiring coworkers and the News Channel—the most corrupt organization in the world. They had all shaped me, forcing me to become a different—better—person.

"Be careful what you say," he said, brushing past me. "No one's going to save you now—least of all your grandfather." I watched him as he walked out of the newsroom, and my life, as quickly as he had entered.

I knew that I was powerful and my voice would be heard. I was the intangible, the swing vote, the young, blue-state urban professional with an old-fashioned, red-state rural upbringing. I was the MTV, Facebook Generation plagued by issues like health care, a woman's right to choose, the Patriot Act versus First Amendment rights. And I just happened to believe in silly things like truth and integrity and a woman in the White House. No matter what Christopher or the others thought, that broadcast was going to be a showdown, a day of reckoning that would forever shape me—maybe even the future of my country.

My voice would help decide the election.

With Christopher out of my hair, I needed to print out the most damning documents in Guy's files; there had to be enough evidence to lock up the big boys for at least fifty years after my journalistic debut on prime-time television. I glanced at the clock—only six minutes before the next broadcast. Was there time? *Go, girl, go!* No telling who would be milling around the print station as night approached dawn. I furiously scanned the screen, checked off the most outrageous subject lines and hit "Print," praying once and for all that I had done something right.

Just as I tucked the last printout into my purse, Guy came cruising through the sliding doors.

"I forgot my credit card. And what I want costs a lot more than twenty-five dollars." He smirked.

"Mmm-hmmm," I said, collapsing into my chair.

"What's wrong with you? You always this pale in the morning before you spackle on your makeup?"

I looked beyond Guy, over at the string of clocks hanging on the far wall: London, Paris, Moscow, Baghdad, Kabul, Beijing . . .

"We're so proud of you workin' up at that station in New York City—you're at the center of the thinkin,' conservative world," Mamma had said at the end of our Sunday phone conversation. I liked the way she pronounced "Nuwah Yawk"—all breathy and earnest. Her accent imparted the city with an exoticism that otherwise belonged to those distant time zones on the wall.

"To think they trust you to make all that news. And I just can't imagine the wondrous things you see. . . ."

Plunk.

Guy dropped his bag of cocaine onto my keyboard: it sat upright, a stubborn, blue beast on the keys. Letters danced across the screen, punctuating my 3 A.M. news script.

"This might do you some good," he said, smirking, nodding toward the bag. "You gotta wake up, kid, this is the big time."

I needed to clear my head, eat a hot meal, formulate a plan. I needed my mamma.

Fudge/Mocha-Frosted Brownies

Courtesy of *Some Like It South!*
a Cookbook by the Junior League of Pensacola

When the goin' gets tough, there's always chocolate.

MAKES 3 DOZEN.

Brownies
- 1 cup butter
- 2 cups sugar
- 4 eggs
- 4 ounces unsweetened chocolate, melted
- 2 teaspoons vanilla
- 1 cup flour
- 1 cup nuts

Preheat oven to 325 degrees. With an electric mixer, cream butter and sugar. Add eggs, beating well. Blend in melted chocolate and vanilla. Stir in flour and nuts. Bake in a 13x9x2-inch greased baking pan for 30 minutes. Spread with frosting of your choice.

Fudge Frosting
- 3 cups confectioners' sugar, sifted
- 6 tablespoons half and half
- 3 tablespoons butter
- 3 tablespoons cocoa

Combine ingredients in a saucepan in the order listed. Cook over medium heat, stirring constantly, until mixture boils. Remove from heat and beat until of spreading consistency. Frost brownies.

Mocha Frosting
    4 tablespoons butter
    4 tablespoons milk
    2 tablespoons coffee granules
    2 teaspoons vanilla
    Confectioners' sugar

Heat butter and milk in a saucepan. Add coffee and stir to dissolve. Add vanilla; then add enough confectioners' sugar to make a thin icing. Spread over hot brownies. Cool before cutting.

20

"YOU EVER GONNA have one of these up in the city?" my sister, Virginia, seven months pregnant, asked me as she lounged in Mother's four-poster bed. Dozens of paper white pillows were stacked behind her, arranged to the side of her, on top of her.

I'd even been looking forward to my sister's inane questions as I cashed in my frequent flier miles for my trip down South. I knew that the family, in their own strange way, would help me figure out what to do. Unfortunately, I had a short turnaround. Five o'clock tomorrow morning and I was off, flying back to the city for the ANC *mandatory attendance* holiday party. "Day of Giving Thanks to Red State America" was HR's brainchild of a celebration—a combination of Halloween, Thanksgiving, Hanukkah, Christmas and Cleveland's "State of the Network" address wrapped up in one sure-to-be-tasteless package. Don't even ask me how I was supposed to select a party dress for such an affair. After that, I had the weekend to prep my skin, hair and composure for Monday night, Election Eve 2008. I would settle for nothing less than my interview ensuring Jessica Clayton a place in the Oval Office (according to Mamma, the "Oval Orifice" during Bill Clinton's tenure as president).

"Oh, come on," she continued, "*la vie métropolitaine* and a baby of your own . . . you could teach it all those languages you hear on the subway."

She made a grand gesture, mocking me. Her arm gently descended on the pillow as her voice faded. Slowly, slowly . . . she almost fell into a quiet slumber before I had crossed the room. Pregnancy kept her eyelids perpetually swollen. Mamma had warned me that Virginia's blue irises were always searching for the next nap behind padded lids and now I knew that she was telling me the truth. Lying in that cavernous bedroom strewn with mismatched teacups and saucers, floral sheets twisted and discarded miles from the bed, yellowed book jackets waving like daisies under the fan's breeze, she looked like a round nymph in our mother's overgrown garden. I pried open the three windows that Zeola had been so careful to close and felt the winter chill. The lifeless azalea bushes that surrounded the house and lake were still, waiting. "One day," I said quietly, looking at them. Five hundred acres of tawny, overgrown grasses stretched before me. I wanted to cry and curse and laugh all at the same time. The News Channel was a fraud, my eggs were shriveling and the mattress atop the family's fabled bed was fifty years old and full of dust mites.

"Do you think Mamma minds that I'm laid up like this?" Virginia asked, her eyes still closed.

"She likes having people dependent on her—hell, look at Daddy. You don't worry about a thing, all right?" I was the one that needed to worry. How was I going to explain my lying, cheating, stealing employer to the family? Was I even capable of interviewing a woman—a force—as important as Jessica Clayton? Producing a package was one thing, but *live* television? And did leaving the News Channel mean I would have to abandon New York? Would D'Artagnan and Dean & DeLuca ship below the Mason-Dixon? I suddenly looked like a fool, a failure and a dinner whore: I was a Southern upstart who had made all the wrong decisions and acquired nothing but a very expensive palate along the way. The circumstances couldn't have been worse for my first trip back home.

"As a matter of fact, I know she's real happy you're here." The bed that Virginia lay in was one of the family's prized antiques, a golden creation of polished oak, delicately carved pinecones gracing each of its four posts. After having learned of Virginia's pregnancy, Mamma decided that Virginia had to rest in that particular bed throughout the entire gestation period.

"Pinecones are powerful symbols of hospitality and warm reception. As such, we welcome this first, unborn grandchild into our family," Mamma had said, tucking Virginia and the fetus under the covers.

I felt responsible for livening up her goosedown-and-lace confinement.

I had to rouse her; I had to play my role no matter how preoccupied I was with my big-city fiascos. The familiar pattern of our conversation would reassure me. Her brow did look smoother and her expression was more relaxed, even playful. The thought of leaving her like that, just so, crept into my mind. But instead, I walked over and pressed my palms against the slant of the roof above the dormer window. I stared out the glass panes and squinted.

"What does today's sunlight remind you of? Can I tell you what I think of?"

"Tell me, lil' one," she said, her voice assuring me that things were good this morning. Virginia had moments of ease, days of madness. Mamma called it an imbalance of humors ("too much damn Tabasco sauce when I was pregnant with your sister"). She and I were as different as they come and we rarely got along. But, slowly, my sister smiled and tilted her head to the side. A hand rested on her large belly and she submitted to the morning light, allowing its warm rays to rest on her broad, ivory cheeks.

"Duh duh duh da!" I held up my arms and turned my torso toward the window, to the door and finally to my sister in bed, like a gymnast saluting the Olympic committee. "For my very privileged audience of one, in list fashion, I give you 'Morning Light'! Chicken feathers, fresh laundry, Mamma's golden arm hair, the sheen of a fresh catch of grouper, the reflection pools outside the courthouse and, last but not least, the glow of my lovely sister's smile after giving birth to a beautiful baby girl!"

She gave me a smile, broad and lazy. She was good, I was good— we were trying very hard to be good together in the white sunshine. I stepped toward the window again and looked out.

Decaying grandeur. I expected Miss Havisham to walk up the flagstone.

"Mamma hired a chef to cook tonight's supper, did she tell you?"

"What'd she go do that for?" I asked, keeping my eyes on the property. Mamma was matchless.

"She's afraid to cook for you now, thinks your taste buds have gone and gotten too refined. The guy's coming down from some fancy restaurant in Birmingham."

In the distance, I saw a blue pickup coming down the winding dirt road. "This must be him. . . ."

Virginia continued speaking and sighing, as was her habit, but I wasn't listening. I was too busy watching the truck, waiting to see the stranger who would cook my one meal down South. My one taste of the South had better be damned good, I thought, hurrying down the staircase to find Mamma poised on the divan by the picture window, silverware spread around her on a white sheet.

"Why the fuss, Mamma? It's just me." It looked as if she had polished every fork, sugar bowl and platter in the house.

"Well, who knows when you're coming home next? You never call, never write, never tell us what you're up to. And when you *do* call, it's during my REM cycle, leavin' me with a set of luggage under my eyes more expensive than a showroom full of Vuitton. Do you know how much eye cream I had to apply this morning just to look decent?"

She sat there in her Alexandra mauve living room, utterly furious with me and my whims. Our decorator had gone to great pains to duplicate the czarina's wall color for her—the last Russian czar, Nicholas II, and his wife, Alexandra, were her obsession. Something about their tragic demise enthralled her. Really, the fall of anything captivated Mamma's imagination—I assumed it was her Confederate Complex. As a member of the landed, Southern bourgeoisie, Mamma used to cite the War of Northern Aggression (never, *ever* referred to as the Civil War) as the most disastrous moment in our nation's history. Then, along came Clinton. I didn't even want to think of how she would respond to my new political affiliation and my personal mission to place a Democrat in office.

"It was last minute, I know—"

"What *are* you doin' home?" she asked, fighting to keep a smile on her face. "We still have no idea what prompted this visit, why you deigned to come back to your home, to—what do you call it? Oh yes, the Redneck Riviera." Her vein, our vein—from brow to hairline, smack in the middle of the forehead—pulsated quick and blue, the one feature we shared. We were going to be in a race to the finish, blue blood pounding away.

Normally I had an arsenal of clever, hurtful things to throw back her way. And this time, I could go even further with the bombshell about the News Channel and the plotting of her political party. But when I opened my mouth to shout something childish and cruel, I whispered instead, "I love you." Jessica Clayton and her politics might have changed me, but Mamma had raised me. And she had dared to let me come into my own. We were three strong women who, in our own unique ways, would change the world.

She looked over at me, silver cake knife in hand, and stared, motionless. Mamma was predisposed to hyperbole, dramatics—outlandish thoughts—all the while sitting perfectly still, a serene air about her. Such theatrics didn't make her disingenuous, quite the contrary. She was the most honest fifty-five-year-old child I had ever known.

She touched her neck, her gold earrings, and cleared her throat. "I think I heard the cook drive up. Why don't you go see if he needs some help, darlin'."

I walked out onto the porch and vowed to tend to my Northern mess on my own. Wouldn't even tell Granddaddy. I'd sit next to him, though, and listen to his stories and eat the food off his table and Mamma's china and I'd feel whole again. That's all that I needed to help me fight my New York City battles. "You want some help out there?" I called to the chef. His back was toward me as he unloaded copper pots and Le Creuset pieces, setting them in a neat row on the lawn. I didn't know what looked better, his tight little bottom encased in Levi's and his broad shoulders in a white chef's jacket or the kitchenware. Poppy-colored Le Creuset was my new obsession.

Stilettos are dispensable but Le Creuset is forever.

"What about taking these stockpots?" he said, turning around, smiling.

Too busy reading *The Economist* and skimming *The Nation,* I must have missed the *Gourmet* and *Cosmo* features on chefs becoming tall, chiseled and supremely sexy. What happened to soft bodies and faces like a pot of polenta? My knees buckled at the sight of his brown, tousled hair and heavily lashed, dark eyes flecked with gold.

"And that voice!" Mamma made her grand entrance onto the porch with an exclamation and a slam of the screen door. ESP again. Difference was, she said what I thought. Zero filter. "Has anyone told you that your voice is simply mellifluous? Like *honey,*" she hollered, wiping her hand on a dish cloth. "Have y'all introduced yourselves yet?"

I made my way down to the truck, afraid of what else Mamma might say if she was directing the conversation. It'd be like a beauty pageant announcer gone wrong: "Belle proudly sports a D cup and is most limber from a childhood of gymnastics and tennis. She is handy with a rolling pin and a hunting rifle and strives for world peace and the control of greenhouse gas emissions in the developed world. If given the chance, she will give you the world and three babies. I present to you—Miss Alabama."

"I'm sorry, I don't even know your name," I said, extending my hand. "I'm Belle."

"A pleasure." He smiled. "And I'm Jeffrey, Jeff, Chef—take your pick."

"Chef will do just fine." Hmmmm . . . I immediately imagined Chef in New York.

In my bed

Breakfast.

After nibbling on him for a good hour or two, we'd move on to something that could fit on a plate. . . . Lawd! What an affection-starved little harlot I had become! What had happened to my old deep reserves of cool and calm? My hormones were boiling, that's what had happened; having simmered for three months on the back burner, they had suddenly spilled out of their very-well seasoned skillet. "Come inside and we'll show you the kitchen."

I'll save the bedroom for later.

"Jeffrey, did you know that our Belle works at American News Channel up in New York City?" Mamma exclaimed in the kitchen like an excited cotillion chaperone.

"You're a fan, I assume?"

"Yes, ma'am, I watch the News Channel on occasion. And I bet if you give me a few more hours, I'll be a fan of your daughter's as well. But the real question, can the city girl cook?"

"Can I cook? Can I *cook*? I'll show the boy from Alabama what I can do." Hand me an apron and I'm yours.

We were easy company, working our way around the marble island in the middle of the kitchen, moving from sink to cutting board to stovetop, talking about different lives in different cities that, somehow, made perfect sense together. That Thursday we belonged to each other.

But I'll admit—supper took an *exceptionally* long time to prepare. When I should have been washing the collards, my eyes were busy stroking his chest and the backs of his (hopefully) skinny knees. I wanted to live in the hidden places; I wanted to take in his skin. And when he should have been rolling out biscuits, he was tying my apron, allowing his big, rough hands to linger on the small of my back.

"Your mother said that it's your one day home so I shouldn't stray too far from your favorites—collard greens, chicken, ham and biscuits, macaroni and cheese, sweet potato pie," he called out from the pantry. "You gotta realize, though," he said, walking toward me, "it's my job to reinvent what you already know."

I assumed that dinner would mean awkward fussing over Virginia's belly and joking and asking for second helpings that I didn't need. But Chef changed the chemistry. Simple, good men do that. They rearrange the molecules in the air and on our plates so we can know contentment again. I had tasted money at the Plaza. But at the table, with him, I tasted happiness.

"What *gorgeous* grandbabies they'd be . . ." Grandmother said after dinner with a flutter of her eyes toward the high heavens.

Granddaddy followed her toward the front door. "Some things

happen in an instant," he whispered in my ear. "When you know, you know."

I knew to come home more often and call Mamma just because, not waiting until I was frantic and needed her voice. I knew that Virginia and her baby, my niece, would need so much of my love. I'd be the strong one for all of us. I knew that Chef was someone whom I was meant to keep for a good long while, to listen to, to surrender to. He was a man to soften me to the idea of love. I knew that once I had a purpose in my profession, I could turn to my sentimental life with honest eyes. Ruby watch–wielding suitors no longer held the importance they once did.

"You don't mention the News Channel much," Chef said, sitting with me on the back porch swing after we had washed the dishes. "Just tired of talking about it? I'm sure everyone wants to know what it feels like to be so important."

"Being home, I feel like I don't really need to talk about that stuff, or I can't talk about it. I don't know, it's hard. When I'm here, life in New York feels like lies and livin' too fast. My life on the family farm is honest and real. The two worlds don't meet. I need to change that, but I just don't know how yet—" I stopped, suddenly embarrassed. "I'm sorry, I know I'm not makin' much sense. I spend too much time in my head and then when I go to speak—"

"I think it says a lot that you can move between both places. You're comfortable here, you're succeeding in New York. My only advice, if you don't mind," he said, bowing his head, brushing his fingertips over my mine, "is to watch out when one of those worlds compromises who you really are. And nobody will know when that happens except for you." I looked into his dark brown eyes, slowly making my way into the flecks of light. "Me? I'm ready for a change and no one seems to understand. The guys in Birmingham call me crazy—"

"That's because they have jobs and we have *careers,* a *calling.* It chooses you—it chose *us.* I'm in the newsroom, you're in the kitchen, and we're touching more lives than we ever could have imagined. You nourish, I inform, but we're the same; we both feed the soul."

"You're right," he smiled, "we *are* the same." He stopped and looked out to the shadowed pines and silver lake. "And so why not be one of the greats? I want to cook with genius like Boulud, Keller, Robuchon, Gagnaire. . . ."

"That means New York and black sea bass en papillote. . . ." I said dreamily, drifting in and out of sleep as the night ended and morning began.

"Or Paris and buying the day's food on Rue Mouffetard, a little apartment by the Seine . . ."

"Come here, Chef." For once, I spoke for all my appetites. "I'm going to lean in," I whispered, "and you're going to sit very still and I'll make a memory of your skin." Oranges and yellows and blues rose over the lake as I pressed my cheek to his, breathed in, moved down his neck. His lips finally made their way to my mine. Musk. He was meat and earth, honesty and promise. Funny thing, that promise. It fills you up, swears you eternal to the unknown.

"Tomorrow—today—I'm going to feel empty flying back to New York. I want you to know that."

"Don't worry, I'm coming," he said, gently kissing me again and again. "I'll come for you."

Chicken and Collard Greens with BB's Homemade Hot Sauce

Granddaddy, BB, carries a bottle of vinegar hot sauce wherever he goes. It pokes out of his blazer pocket like a proud Cuban cigar. During our Sunday in the kitchen, Chef and I developed this dish for him and his love of heat and greens. I show off by sometimes calling it a "roulade," but I know Granddaddy approves of the down-home ingredients. Peanuts make him smile.

SERVES 4.

Roulade
- 1 bunch collard greens
- Extra virgin olive oil
- 1 medium yellow onion, roughly chopped
- Kosher salt
- 1 clove garlic, crushed/flattened
- Red pepper flakes (optional)
- ½ c. salted peanuts
- 2 chicken breasts, split and pounded thinly, Milanese-style
- Freshly ground pepper

BB's Vinegar Hot Sauce
- ½ c. white wine vinegar
- 1 Tbsp. sugar
- 1 tsp. iodized salt
- 1½ red Fresno peppers, thinly sliced into rounds

Remove collard leaves from their thick, tough stems with a sharp knife (this will reduce cooking time). Chiffonade (roll the leaves into a cigar shape and cut crosswise) the leaves and submerge them in a large bowl filled with water, rinsing them thoroughly.

Place a large pot over high heat, adding just enough oil to coat the bottom, approximately 1 Tbsp. Add chopped onion, reduce heat to medium and add 1 tsp. kosher salt. Allow onions to slightly color and add clove of garlic and a pinch of crushed red pepper. Continue cooking garlic and onions until fragrant.

Lift collards from rinsing bowl—shaking off excess water—and add to the pot of onions. Combine well, coating the collard leaves with oil. Add 1 tsp. kosher salt and continue to cook for approx 3–5 more minutes. Add 2 c. of water to the greens—or just enough to cover them—bring to a boil and then immediately reduce to a simmer.

Pull out a bottle of crisp white wine and go out onto the porch (or fire escape) for 25 minutes or just until the greens are tender. Pour in a heaping ½ c. of peanuts and cook over high heat. Stir. Taste for seasoning and tenderness and adjust. Remove greens to a plate to cool.

Season both sides of thinly pounded chicken breast with salt and freshly ground pepper. Spoon 1 Tbsp. of greens on one side of cutlet and firmly roll. Secure with 2–3 toothpicks. Place skillet over high heat, adding 1 Tbsp. olive oil. Add chicken and brown on all sides. Lower heat after all sides of the chicken have been browned. Cover skillet with a plate and continue cooking for 7–10 minutes, until chicken is firm to the touch.

For Vinegar Hot Sauce: Bring vinegar to a boil, allowing sugar and salt to dissolve. Place sliced Fresno pepper rounds in a shallow dish or bowl. Pour boiling vinegar mixture over peppers and set aside to pickle. Ta da! Your very own homemade hot sauce!

Serving suggestion: Slice chicken into rounds and serve over a bed of fluffy, white rice. The rice not only frames the gorgeous roulade (who knew peanuts were so darned attractive when cut in cross section?) but serves as a method of soaking up all that wonderful hot sauce and getting it back up to your lips.

Shrimp and Crab Gumbo

Mamma made gumbo—not chicken noodle soup—to soothe my soul. She packed a thermos full of the shrimp and crab confection for my plane ride back to New York. I've never come across a recipe that equals ours for rich, soul-satisfying goodness. This is a bubbling, brewing, all-day affair so make sure to cook it for those you love.

SERVES 8.

1 stalk celery, chopped

1 green bell pepper, seeds removed, chopped

1 large yellow onion, finely chopped

2 tsp. crab boil,* measured into small
    tea ball or a small square of cheesecloth
    tied with kitchen twine

½ lb. baby okra

2 lb. raw, peeled, deveined shrimp

1 lb. fresh crabmeat

1 15-oz. can chopped tomatoes

1 package white rice

Roux†

4 Tbsp. bacon grease

4 Tbsp. flour

---

*I love Zatarain's crab boil, a brand that's very easy to find if you live in the vicinity of New Orleans. But if you can't find crab or seafood boil, it's a snap to make your own. In a small bowl, combine 3 Tbsp. yellow mustard seeds, 2 Tbsp. coriander, 2 Tbsp. allspice, 1 Tbsp. dill seeds, 1 tsp. whole cloves, 1 Tbsp. crushed red pepper and 7 bay leaves. Place mixture in square of cheesecloth and tie with butcher's twine.

†The secret of the perfect roux is to make one that is very dark. Cook the flour mixture past golden to a nutty, dark brown—almost black.

1¾ c. water
Kosher salt
Freshly ground black pepper

In an eight-gallon pot over medium heat, start the roux by melting the bacon grease and slowly working in the flour. Continue stirring the mixture until very dark like a rich, Thanksgiving Day gravy. Add the celery, bell pepper, onion and baby okra. Stir well. Add water, crab boil, salt and pepper to taste. Bring to a boil, turn down heat immediately and simmer, covered, for two and a half hours.

Add shrimp, crabmeat and tomatoes and cook for twenty more minutes or until shrimp have turned pink.

Serve gumbo atop white rice in a shallow bowl or cup.

21

I FLEW BACK to a Northern morning that was bitter cold, not possessing the gentle rhythm of my new love. When would I see Chef again? I unlocked the deadbolts and walked into my dark apartment.

At the kitchen table with my computer open, I was back to being List Girl, one of those who feels as if she hasn't accomplished anything until a big black Sharpie line slashes through the belly of each of her tasks.

1. Outline talking points for Jessica Clayton interview.
2. Review printouts of Guy's confidential files; statements in memos must ensure Keaton and Cleveland spend lives bending over to pick up prison soap.
3. ★★URGENT★★ Put together sexy yet socially aware ensemble reminiscent of ancient pilgrims for tonight's ANC holiday party.

But I no longer enjoyed listing my life in a steno pad, as if every action had to be cataloged as a challenge or a chore with a number beside it. That's just it—I didn't want to fight anything anymore. I wanted to lie under warm, white sheets with that gorgeous man next to me and then maybe spend a day at a long table under the pine trees, Mamma's white tablecloth set with mismatched plates, wedding silver and casserole dishes.

Instead, I stood at my back window, looking out onto the frozen ground, heart beating in my head, thinking of all that I had to accomplish and unearth, pick apart and then piece back together, for a life that was beginning to scare me.

"Always bury the lead. Always have an agenda. And, for Christ's sake," Cleveland bellowed, thrusting his plastic cup of Yellowtail Shiraz in the air, "remember that a real journalist considers Nielsen before Pulitzer!" A chorus of voices joined his as the War Room erupted in applause and cheers. Everyone seemed to know his lines except for me (was that his typical office party toast?). But I suppose that had become the story of my life.

I had tucked myself away in the far corner of the room, next to an enormous satellite image of the Afghan desert bearing the headline WEAPONS OF MASS DESTRUCTION FOUND HERE! SHAME ON YOU KOFI ANNAN! The map was riddled with red thumbtacks like the face of a thirteen-year-old boy plagued by acne. I had hoped to sport the most clever and culturally sensitive holiday party costume—not the *only* costume. Apparently, up North, a large gathering with booze isn't an excuse to play dress-up like it is down in Alabama. There was nary a Native American loincloth, Santa Suit or life-sized dreidel in the mix. When I made my War Room entrance as Sassy Pilgrim #1—brown felt mini, white DKNY bodysuit with detachable white organza square collar, Jimmy Choo ankle boots—Paige, Samantha and the rest of the female staff couldn't stifle their laughter. I supposed there would be no more pretenses made about friendship now that the election, and Paige's anchor position, was spitting distance away. Wallace, Chase Stephens, the directors, gaffers and video editors however, shot me approving grins.

"No, no, seriously, folks," Cleveland continued, chuckling, "quiet down. I have some very important things to say today." He clasped his hands behind his back and paced in the narrow space that had been left him beneath the wall of clocks. I wasn't nearly important enough to have ever attended one of his 2:30 P.M. story meetings but it was known that he never tired of hearing his own voice. Then again, the sound of his crisp consonants was preferable to looking at his rotund body and fleshy, red face—his second chin quite possibly larger than the first. He looked like the newsman with his hand up the skirt of America.

"Our nation is at a critical juncture. We have an election on our soil next week, a war on somebody else's for years to come and the eyes of God upon us—always. As a company, as a news force, as a family, we are the underdogs, a specially selected group of Americans," he said, pointing toward the high heavens, "that will steer our country in the holiest and mightiest of directions." Had I missed something? I didn't know about the rest of the folks in the room, but Gina had been the one to interview me—not Jesus. And Sandra in HR had printed out my contract and W-2's. White smoke didn't waft out of a chimney once contract negotiations were settled.

A quiet buzz spread through our party as the War Room's glass door opened and Keaton and Christopher slipped inside. Christopher looked dapper as ever in a blue pinstriped suit and red tie. But the turncoat didn't make my heart race anymore. A principled man like Chef was far sexier than a spineless corporate sellout. Keaton cut a more demure figure than I would have imagined. He was a good six inches shorter than Christopher with several wisps of gray hair combed over his otherwise bald head, wide-set, watery blue eyes magnified by thick glasses. They looked straight ahead, silently commanding all of us to return our attention to the speech. Cleveland gave a quick nod in their direction and continued.

"Monday, twenty-four hours before the polls open, we show red-state, blue-state America, hell—the whole damn world—that only American News Channel is dedicated to fair and balanced journalism. We've examined Hewitt's and Clayton's lives as public servants, we've spoken with family members, political colleagues, checked their speeches and promises against their accomplishments—all of this is part of our Election Eve 2008 coverage. Most importantly, for the first time in ANC's history, I am proud to announce that we are running a live debate featuring the platforms of both candidates."

A collective gasp rippled through the crowd. I followed suit, choking on my wine (then again, that could have been a knee-jerk reaction to the horrendously overripe raspberry notes of the $6 jeroboam of Shiraz). From Guy's memos, my interview with Jessica Clayton was scheduled as the *only* live segment. Had the old man gone crazy? Swing votes—swing states—could hang on this broadcast. How many more wild cards did he want to throw into Monday night?

"We've done well for ourselves these past ten years but we cannot rest on our laurels. This is the year that we make ourselves the dominant news source in the world!" He had rallied the troops; the cheers were deafening. There looked to be no stopping the monopolistic moguls.

"And without further adieu, our fearless leader, Mr. Dax Keaton, would like to announce the two reporters who will be featured with the presidential nominees. Dax, the floor is yours."

Keaton knew drama; our broadcasts reflected this with their menacing graphics and booming voice-overs. He had revolutionized the patina of news. And then there was his timing—as perfectly calibrated in our business as it was in the corporate and political spheres. Many called him a visionary. His slow, deliberate walk to the front of the room was fitting, eye contact made with no one until he abruptly twisted on his heel and stared us down.

"We are not part of the Establishment," he annunciated. "We are outside of it and therefore above it." I stopped dabbing seltzer water on my Shiraz stain. "I founded this station to give a voice to the silenced. Yes, angry middle-aged white men happen to love us," he digressed, "but so do tens of millions of marginalized others. We are the American conscience. And so it is very important that we help our nation choose fairly and wisely come Tuesday. Our live debate will be a rare, unscripted opportunity to see these individuals for who and what they really are. My decision has been made."

Then again, maybe he was a touch *too* dramatic, having watched one too many hours of his network's reality programming. I was waiting for him to tell the rest of us to pack our bags and meet the stretch Hummer outside on Sixth Avenue.

"Our esteemed and highest Nielsen-ranked ego, Jack Wallace, has the formidable task of representing Senator Hewitt from Texas. Congratulations, Jack, make us proud." While others clapped, Chase Stephens looked utterly devastated, his stare as cold and dejected as it had been a few weeks ago when we got word off the AP wire that Scores, Manhattan's finest strip joint, would be closed for a month due to an outbreak of herpes.

Did that mean Wallace and Hewitt would be on air—*on the same set*—with me and Clayton? A Boys vs. Girls Election Eve debate? I continued stabbing at my wine stain with the shredded, soaked cocktail napkin; my Fashion 911 had deteriorated beyond repair. What had started off as a smallish red dot (unfortunately located over my left nipple) had morphed into a giant pink amoeba that now covered both breasts. It looked as if I had bought my top at the Museum of Modern Art gift shop.

Suddenly, I noticed that the room was silent, Keaton had stopped talking and all eyes were on me. I crossed my arms over my chest. "I swear, I bought this on West Broadwa—"

"Belle Lee, the torch of truth burns brightly within these hallowed walls." He extended his hands to the cheap popcorn siding like a Messiah, motioning to the very same walls that had once housed the sacred establishment of Tower Records before the News Channel was founded. "You will carry that torch on Election Eve 2008 when you enlighten us as to the political platform of Jessica Clayton, asking the tough questions and proclaiming a truth that will affect your generation and generations to come. But it is not just one honor we bestow on you. That same evening you will become the youngest on-air reporter in the history of American News Channel." He paused, narrowing his eyes. "Expect the unexpected and surprise us with your poise and, and—" He broke off, looking flummoxed by his inability to pinpoint my "otherness." "Surprise us, Belle, with your poise and Southern charm."

Jessica Clayton and I were two girls who were about to make history.

Shrimp and Scallop Gratin with Champagne Velouté

This is my career girl favorite. Even Jessica Clayton could find the time to make this glorified Southern casserole, a dish that can be made in fifteen minutes flat. Gussying up shrimp and bay scallops with cream and a touch of bubbly is easy, just a matter of adding New York gloss to flavors I've known all my life. I think I could even impress Chef with this easy, elegant dinner, one I would serve by the lake under the shade of the pines.

SERVES 2.

½ lb. shrimp (peeled and deveined, 16/20 count)★
¼ lb. large scallops (30/40 count)★
Kosher salt, to taste
Freshly ground pepper, to taste
2–3 tsp. vegetable oil
1 very small onion, sliced
1 c. champagne or prosecco
2 Tbsp. heavy whipping cream
2 slices of bread torn into pieces, pulsed in
    a food processor or blender†

On a plate, sprinkle the shrimp and scallops with salt and pepper. Place a stainless frying pan on the stove over high heat. Add about 2 tsp. of vegetable oil, just enough to cover the bottom of the pan. When oil

---

★This means that it takes 16–20 shrimp to make 1 lb.; 30–40 scallops make 1 lb.

†If you don't want to make bread crumbs, buy Panko, a coarse, Japanese-style bread crumb. Do not use "Italian-style" bread crumbs.

begins to shimmer, place the scallops in the pan, flat side down. Sear until golden on one side (about 1 minute). Flip and cook on the other side for 30 seconds. Remove to a clean plate. Turn the heat down to medium-high, add the sliced onions to the empty pan and cook for 2 minutes. (You may need a little more oil.)

When the onions begin to soften, add the shrimp and cook for 2 minutes on each side. The shrimp will begin to turn opaque; at this point pour in the champagne, just over one cup. Simmer until reduced to 2 Tbsp. Add the heavy cream and reduce until thickened. Taste and season with salt and pepper. Add another little splash of champagne (you can't have too much!).

Divide the shrimp, scallops, and sauce between two gratin dishes (in a pinch, you can use shallow bowls) and top with the bread crumbs. Slide into the oven under the broiler until well browned and bubbly on the sides. Carefully remove from the oven and enjoy by a lake under the pines.

22

WHILE SOHO WAS sleeping in, its inhabitants recovering from borrowed money spent—and lies ingested—at the swanky restaurants and lounges that line the cobble-stoned streets of Mercer and Grand, I had to wake up for the two people who would change my life.

"Who is this? I can't understand," I screamed into the intercom after hopscotching over the Post-its, printouts and steno pads that covered the apartment. Attempting to memorize Jessica Clayton's past decade of policy making as well as her entire presidential platform in the span of forty-eight hours was like trying to wrestle nonstick tape away from a Delta beauty queen. Impossible. I had woken up at dawn to apply a calming algae mask and to review my notes when I must have dozed off on the white tiled kitchen floor. The buzzer startled me out of sleep.

"Who?" The indiscernible gurgle of my apartment building's intercom system absolutely *prevented* identifying potential thieves and intruders. Absentmindedly, I popped the first and then the second of the cucumber rounds into my mouth. The little buggers weren't worth a damn unless infused in a martini; my eyes still looked puffy and sleep-deprived. And now my face was an algae-cracked mess. I was like an episode of the *Golden Girls* at Bliss Spa gone terribly wrong.

Enough! I had zero time for such disturbances with the fate of the free world resting in my hands. And Clayton would expect nothing less than an exacting, concise interview from me. She would be whisked onto our set for thirty minutes and then most certainly expected at Pol24 and CNN for final stumping before the polls went live on the fourth. I belted my Burberry trench around my skivvies and ran out to meet my intruder face-to-face. Out in the hallway, I was immediately assaulted: the super had forgotten to take out the trash, *again*. What smelled like Limburger and apple cider cleared my sinuses and brought tears to my eyes, making it very difficult to decipher the tall figure standing outside the pane-glass doors.

Chef!

One glimpse of him and an enormous grin cracked through the last of my mask. He waved and pointed toward his duffel bag.

"One minute!" I mouthed, leaving him standing in the snow as I ran back into the apartment, splashed warm water on my face, Kiehl's musk on my body and twisted my hair into an elegant-yet-Sunday-morning-relaxed chignon.

"I missed my Belle. I couldn't stay away," he said, folding me into his arms once he was inside the building. I pressed up against his chest and breathed, trying to take in the man that I had missed so much.

"But how'd you get the address?" I asked, pulling him into the apartment. "How'd you get time off from the restaurant? Wha, why? New York? You're in New York!" Brenda Starr came out with a vengeance.

"Slow down, honey, one at a time." He scanned the mess, looking for a way to traverse the piles of paper and make it over to the couch.

"I have an interview tomorrow," I said, trying to justify my apartment-cum-producing pod. "We'll call it 'A Night to Remember'— like a Kappa Delta formal. A woman by the name of Jessica Clayton and I have a little date set up," I said, tilting my head back so he could kiss me. "Care to join? Eight P.M., twelve twenty-one Avenue of the Americas, Studio B. There'll be bad coffee, even worse crudités, and if we're lucky, a bowl of stale M&M's. My entrance will be grand, my exit unforgettable."

He dropped his bag to the floor. "*You're* interviewing the Democratic presidential nominee tomorrow night? I couldn't have chosen a worse time for a surprise visit, could I?" His eyebrows—the hairs chestnut, honey and blond from his Mondays surfing the Gulf— formed two intense slashes, making him look very worried.

The logical answer should be yes, I thought. You have the timing of the life insurance salesman who came callin' two weeks *after* Aunt Maybel's death. I should be gathering my loins for the Clayton interview, not fantasizing about all the things I want to do with yours.

"Your timing is perfect."

"Are you sure?"

The more I thought about it, the more certain I became. I considered my decision to fly back home after hacking into Guy's computer. Completely irrational. But I had followed my belly and, in the end, that trip had given me the courage to follow my convictions (Willie Morris would have told me that by spending time on my native soil, I had gathered the strength of the Confederate dead, thrown them into cargo and flown Delta with them back to New York). I had not backed down from the prospect of the live Clayton broadcast. Instead, I welcomed the challenge, knowing that whatever the outcome, I'd always have a place on the swing and a warm kitchen to return to. Oh, and I just might have found love.

"Let's try to sit down," he said, tiptoeing back to the kitchen, "and then you tell me your plan. I want to help."

"Oh, honey, it's too hard, there's so much—"

He drew my face to his and gently kissed me. "We're going to do this together."

I sat on the countertop and let him settle in my only kitchen chair. I exhaled, ridding myself of opening night anxieties and fear. It felt wonderful and strange to have someone by my side. "Are you ready? And I'm not just going to tell you about Jessica Clayton—I'm going to tell you *everything*." I thought about the New York that I had known alone and the secrets that I had kept as I watched him shrug off his brown leather motorcycle jacket and pull his hair back with the rubber band that had been wrapped around the morning's `Times.`

"I'm ready for it all."

"I know too much. I'm involved in a scandal that goes all the way up to the office of the president of the United States. But if I say all the right things tomorrow on television—move forward with my heart and my head—we'll be fine. Jessica Clayton is our girl, maybe the underdog for now, but I suspect she's going to win Florida and Ohio in the eleventh hour and save . . ."

He listened patiently as I rattled off the basics, thought through my interview and slowly shaped its progression in my head. And then we began our kitchen dance, the rhythm slow, changing places as he pulled out the sauté pan, sliced and sweated the onions. Bacon sizzled and he simplified my talking points. I worked on the tomatoes as he worked on me.

"So the first thing we're going to do," he said, brushing his lips against my neck, "is buy you a decent set of chef's knives when I move to New York City."

"What? You're moving? To be with me?"

"I'm moving to live my dream, and you're part of it. I'll try to live only a few blocks away, but I want you to have your own set of knives for all the big Sunday suppers we're going to enjoy in your garden. And, *and,* my little Diane Sawyer, I want you to be able to protect yourself against any disgruntled Republicans. From what I can see, you're gonna knock 'em dead tomorrow."

Fancy Shrimp and Grits

*Chef created this sexy, Southern brunch to satisfy everyone. It's a deli-
cious, lusty little plate that demands seconds.*

SERVES 6.

1 recipe stone-ground grits, prepared
½ lb. thinly sliced bacon, about
    2 slices per person
2 shallots, minced
2 cloves garlic, crushed
1 Tbsp. olive oil
2 Tbsp. red wine vinegar
3 medium red tomatoes, chopped
1 Tbsp. butter
2 lbs. 26/30 or smaller fresh shrimp,
    peeled and deveined
Mixture of chopped herbs—parsley,
    chives, chervil (optional)
½ lemon

Preheat oven to 350 degrees.

Prepare the grits following the directions on the package. Keep grits
tightly covered in a warm place. Cook the bacon in the oven until very
crisp and set aside on towels to drain.

In a heavy-bottomed saucepan over medium heat, sweat half of the
shallots and the garlic in a bit of olive oil until well softened, but not
browned. Add 1 Tbsp. of the red wine vinegar and reduce slightly.
Scrape the chopped tomatoes and all their juices off the cutting board

and into the pot. Simmer for about 20 minutes at medium-high heat, not letting it reach a full boil. After 20 minutes, take the pan off the heat, throw the whole thing in the blender—make sure you put the lid on tight—and flip it on high. When it starts running smoothly, open the top and slowly drizzle in olive oil. When the oil is fully incorporated, add the remaining Tbsp. of the red wine vinegar.

Place a large sauté pan over medium-high heat and add a Tbsp. of butter. Let it get a little foamy and toss in the shallots; cook about 2 minutes, until just softened (again, no color!). Add the shrimp, season well with salt and pepper and continue cooking over medium-high heat until the shrimp is bright pink, very firm and no translucence remains in the center. Stir in the herbs and squeeze half a lemon over the pan.

To assemble, place a heaping spoonful of the grits in the center of the plate and pour a generous amount of the tomato sauce over them. Top with the bacon arranged in an X and divide the shrimp between the plates.

23

"THIS," GUY SAID, holding up my earpiece "is your savior. You got that? With a projected audience of sixteen and a half million viewers, you'll need a god," he grunted.

"The worries of the world do not rest on your shoulders, my sweet Belle. Do you understand?" Chef had kissed my forehead as I shivered outside of headquarters in the black November chill. "And Clayton can debate circles around Wallace and Hewitt. You're the one who told *me* she's one of the finest speakers in the Senate. You have absolutely nothing to worry about." For closure, I had insisted on wearing the same navy blue interview suit of months past. I would exit the doors of American News Channel exactly as I had entered—just with a different party affiliation.

He wrapped his jacket around both of us and I looked up to the stars. Aquarius, the Little Dipper? Fat chance—this was Manhattan. Instead, Paige looked down on me from the fifth-story television screen, her beautiful, hard face unchanged since that first day in August. I wondered if her conscience remained unaffected by her conniving and scheming. (The minute they could Botox the heart and the soul, she'd invest.)

"Mamma and Granddaddy are underneath this same sky." Taxi horns blared and trucks rumbled past as I imagined the quiet back home. I'd soon change that. "They're going to kill me, aren't they? Granddaddy gave me money and an interview. And what did I do with it?"

"You came into your own. That's all. And I'm here for you, honey. Just look for me on the sidelines."

"Light check!" one of the directors yelled at the back of the studio. Suddenly the entire lighting grid flashed, blinding me as I tried to search for Chef in the darkness offstage.

"Dixie!" Guy waved his bloated fingers in my face. "Snap out of it! Look at me—I'm your producer tonight. I'll feed you lines and talking points throughout the broadcast. Just listen to this puppy," he said, tapping the earpiece; "if you forget a question, can't read the teleprompter, need commentary to accompany the images we're running—whatever."

"But where are the hard copies of my script? I want to hold on to—I just want to hold something."

"Beats the hell out of me where your scripts are. Some PA probably fucked up and can't get the printer to work. You know how that goes, don't you?" Just as he stepped away, fiddling with mike wires, Doreen and three assistants from Hair and Makeup descended, circling me with an arsenal of products and brushes. Suddenly I realized that from the moment I had stepped through the News Channel doors that night, I had been surrounded by people and chatter, no one giving me a moment to breathe or a chance to ask questions. I hadn't even gotten a good look at the set. As the girls shellacked, painted and prodded every square inch of my torso, I glanced over their shoulders at the two-camera setup. Odd—I knew that Sam preferred at least three cameras for group interviews.

"I want fire-engine red on these lips, Doreen," I said, eyeing the tube of frosted pink lipstick she had just pulled from her tray. "And please, make the hair *high*." Mamma really would kill me if I sported iridescent lips and limp hair on national television while *also* declaring myself a Democrat. She'd be happy with nothing less than Grace Kelly with a little Dolly Parton "oomph."

"Well, well, if it isn't our Belle." Jack Wallace threw down a stack of scripts on the anchor desk and hovered above me. A swarm of producers and writers followed in his wake, murmuring into headpieces and studying clipboards. "Such an amazing opportunity for you, isn't it? To think you landed this plumb debate whilst dressed as a sexed-up colonial." He licked his lips. "If you ask me, that's false advertising."

"It's a pleasure to see you professional as always, Jack. Now where's your man Hewitt, caught up having a martini with the FCC, hmmm?"

I felt the color rise in my cheeks as I shifted uncomfortably in the anchor chair. *You gotta calm down, girl. He doesn't have a clue as to how much you know, and the good stuff has to be banked until Clayton is here and America is watching. And why does everyone keep calling it a debate when it's really a four-person interview?*

"I don't know what you're talking about," he said, pointing his finger inches from my face, "but if you're smart, you'll shut up! Just shut up, you Dixie punk!"

I wondered if Daddy would at least give me permission to call him a turd.

"Ten minutes and we're live," one of the grips shouted. "Ten minutes!"

Where in the hell was Clayton? I was moments away from quite possibly the bravest—or worst—performance of my life and I needed my cast. Where *was* she? Hewitt?

"Belle? Can you hear me? Sound check, count to ten for me." The tiny earpiece was a technological marvel. I could hear everything crystal clear.

"One, two, three—"

"Fine, fine, okay. Listen. Mr. Keaton and Mr. Cleveland are in the booth with me. We're all miked."

"Good evening, Belle," Cleveland greeted me, sounding like the host of *Masterpiece Theatre*.

"All eyes on you, Ms. Lee," Keaton added with a moneyed, Eton rumble.

"If Mr. Cleveland or Mr. Keaton call out a talking point, you go with it. Do you understand?" Guy fired away. I could hear fabric or a hand pressed against Cleveland's mike, his booming voice stifled to a mumble. He was staring at me through the director's lens, I could feel it, making comments to the others.

I knew that darkened space inside and out; I had spent countless

Saturday nights in that very same producing booth with Guy and Samantha. You get some sort of badge for working seventy-hour weeks, right? I knew that four large monitors mounted high on the wall were, at that very moment, scrutinizing my every flinch and freckle. A dozen smaller screens rendered wide shots, extreme close-ups and more obscure angles. The producer in the booth would insert these for variety. A sound table with hundreds of buttons, dials and knobs could enhance the faintest sound, or silence even Wallace's ramblings. A flick of the switch. Live broadcasts might be wild cards but the deck was much more manageable when you were the dealer.

"This is not your show. This is *our* show. Nonetheless, sixteen and a half million sets of eyes and ears are on *you* and tomorrow is Election Day. Your performance with Wallace will be scrutinized and votes cast. Do. You. Understand. What. Tonight. Means? But don't worry—no one has actually ever died of embarrassment," Guy cracked. "Break a leg." The microphone clicked off.

"Two minutes!"

Distant eyes are watching, Belle. Breathe. I slowly rose out of my seat and raised my hand to my brow, trying to shield my eyes from the blinding studio lights.

Clayton and Hewitt would not be joining us.

The realization hit me in the gut like a bad batch of mayonnaise. It was so obvious. Why had it taken me that long to piece together? VIP's and presidential nominees require a bomb squad sweep, guard dogs, the ATF and an accompanying private unit of bodyguards. Hell, even Dick Norris, the toe-sucking wonder, was assigned a special protection unit when he visited us every Wednesday. There had been none of that in the past two hours. I had been played; I was the naive fool yet again. Keaton and Cleveland would never hand Clayton an open mike mere hours before the polls opened. As far as Hewitt, he was borderline mentally challenged, almost incapable of stringing together a cohesive speech. If the two went head-to-head, Clayton would be the uncontested victor. I thought back to the War Room speeches. *We are running a live debate featuring the platforms of both candidates. . . . Jack Wallace has the formidable task of representing Senator*

Hewitt. . . . Suddenly I was calm. I was no longer their fool. Their hands might have been up the skirts of America but *I,* for one, was wearing a pantsuit.

"In your seat, Ms. Lee!" Keaton's voice boomed both over the studio's PA system and in my earpiece.

"We're going live in thirty," Sam called out.

"I guess our candidates got caught in traffic," Wallace said, looking straight ahead, concentrating on the teleprompter and his cold open. "Looks like it's just you and me."

One last time, I looked into the darkness, searching for Chef. This time, I spotted him, hands clasped behind his back, waiting patiently for me and my victory. Even if things didn't turn out as my overly optimistic imagination planned, he'd still be there to scrape me up off Sixth Avenue. After talking health care, dirty politics and media monopolies, Cleveland and Keaton—and *their* bodyguards—might just pick me up by my French twist and toss me under the front wheels of a Yellow Cab.

"That's right, Jack. It's showtime."

"Belle, Jack, look at me. And five, four . . ." Sam waited three beats more and then nodded his head.

The red light flashed.

"Election Eve 2008. Who's it going to be, America?" Wallace boomed. "On the right, we have Senator Thomas Hewitt from Texas, a man who stands for individual freedoms like the right to bear arms and the Patriot Act. On the left stands Jessica Clayton, a communist liberal dedicated to importing boatloads of AIDS babies, destroying the national health care system and raising income taxes by twenty percent. Where's your vote, America?"

I glanced at the monitors, and realized they were a split screen, Hewitt on the right-hand side, Clayton on the left. While the Texas senator was afforded a very flattering montage of shots—striding through his ranch in chaps, speaking to an audience of thousands at West Point, taking communion with his wife—Clayton wasn't even pictured. Instead they showed Haitian day boats, teeming with bodies, and an exterior shot of the IRS headquarters.

"Today I'm running a little experiment on the *Republican Revival!* Joining me is Belle Lee, a twenty-five-year-old Southerner living in New York City who fashions herself a young Democrat and supporter of Jessica Clayton. Does she really speak for America's youth?"

"Thank you, Wi—"

"Let's go to the viewer e-mails and see what America has to say about our two candidates!"

I was on Wallace's turf and he wasn't going to let me forget it. I had to force my way in.

"Mark in Missouri writes, 'Jessica Clayton has—*beeped!*—over our state so damn good by sending all my money to education. Education? That's what Mamma and I and the church are here for,'" Jack intoned, trying out his most scholarly tone despite the e-mail's questionable sentence structure. "'I don't need my state senator pushing for no more schools. She's going to bankrupt us if she lands in that Oval Office.'"

"I couldn't agree with you more, Mark," Wallace said, cocking his eyebrow. "And you brought up something that I want to drive home to my loyal viewing audience—Senator Clayton's policy-making and voting record. Shocking, America, shocking."

"I'd also like to touch on Senator Clayton's policy making, Jack. Let's start with health care."

"This isn't your show!" Guy screamed into my earpiece. "Twenty fucking seconds and then you pass the baton to Wallace. You got that?" Conducting a live interview with a coked-out voice in your ear and nagging fears of a Princess Diana–like untimely death is not ideal, I pondered. I still had so many hairstyles to try out. And now I had love in my life. I wanted to live in Paris with Chef for at least a year before I died. Was that too much to ask?

I forged on, ignoring the voice in my ear, the devil on my shoulder. "Despite twenty years in politics, Senator Clayton's focus on health care has remained consistent. And she came by it honestly. Her father was a surgeon who loved his work but loathed the medical system. Time and again he was told to turn away patients because they didn't have proper coverage. And this is a man who made house calls to save destitute, dying grandmothers. The testimonials I read about Dr. Clayton were amazing, heartwarming."

"Fine, Ms. Lee, have it your way," Keaton growled into my earpiece.

I glanced over at the monitor. Shots of a needle exchange program for drug addicts at Bellevue flashed on the screen.

"Are you sure your candidate's been called a 'health-care visionary' and not something else?" Wallace chuckled, stacking and restacking the scripts on the desk.

The monitor's image quickly changed to one of Clayton at Bryn Mawr, her arm around her roommate in their dorm room. They slugged it "Women Who Love Women." The crawl at the bottom of the screen began quoting statistics of lesbianism and mental health. Next up, the Pussycat Lounge, a lesbian club on the Lower East Side. Two women in spiked collars were humping on the dance floor.

This was it. Now or never. "Meaningful female friendships—female mentors—are what make us extraordinary. If I had been given an ounce of female guidance at American News Channel—instead of fending off your unwanted sexual advances and wading through the double-crossings of Paige Beaumont—I might not be in the situation I'm in right now."

"Liar! You're a liar! America, do you know what a liar and a liberal look like? This woman!"

"What was that plane ticket to St. Lucia, Jack? Hmmm? Tell America about the outdoor showers you want to take and where you'll hide the sponge."

"I was doing an investigative piece on the disappearance of teens on spring break!"

"Wrong island."

"Commercial in ninety seconds," Cleveland barked in my ear. "Then, your ass is on the pavement and your name is dirt! Shut your mouth now or we're going to eviscerate you in the tabloids! I'll make your name shit! You'll never work in this town again, do you hear me? You're going to wish you never set foot into twelve twenty-one Avenue of the Americas!"

Perfect segue. Thank you, earpiece. "I almost regret the day that I walked into this building. *Almost,*" I said, looking dead center at the camera, at America. "But working here has opened my eyes, even if that has been to the detriment of my health, causing my blood pressure to spike to one forty over eighty."

"Cut the crap. This isn't about your health—this is about the election!" Wallace roared. "Now let's go back to our viewer e-mail—"

"You're wrong, health care is the election!" I interrupted. "This is an important issue for me and young America." I glanced at the digital clock by the teleprompter—fifty-five seconds. "I don't have health coverage, Jack, and neither do they. Does that bother you? Even though I work seventy-hour weeks at this right-wing propaganda network, I'm still classified as a freelancer."

Be quick about this, I thought, touching my pearls. You've got to move from health care to exposing the dirty media monopoly before the segment is over and America ruined.

"Why have the bottom-feeding heads of industry decided that I don't deserve to see the age of sixty-five?"

"I think you're being glib and I think you need to leave." He motioned for his ever-present security detail. He collected death threats like Justin Timberlake did fan mail. There was always a bodyguard hovering in Wallace's shadow. "My show exists as an alternative to the lying liberal media community. And I refuse to pander to liars like you in my studio."

"Ah, yes, you're an alternative voice, Jack. Good thing the FCC exists to allow such variety in our media outlets. For the young folks out there, I'll define the FCC." I touched the heights of my sprayed blond locks and felt a surge of confidence.

"The FCC is a watchdog agency that protects the public's interests and ensures that no single individual or organization controls the dissemination of information. They play an extremely important role in our lives. So it'd be a real travesty for one individual, say, Dax Keaton, to get a certain candidate in office, say, Senator Hewitt, who would then convince this watchdog agency to allow Keaton to buy rival news station Pol24. Then, one single organization—one single man!—

would reach forty percent of the viewing public. That'd be illegal and a real shame, wouldn't it?" Wallace slammed his fist on the desk as I ticked off all the facts, secrets and crimes that I had held in for so long.

"But still, this very powerful, *very rich* man won't help pay for a teeth cleaning and a Pap smear. Can you imagine what would happen if I broke a bone, or God forbid, was diagnosed with cancer? Forget it! My family and I would be unceremoniously dumped into the poorhouse. So *that*," I said, sweetly dabbing at my sweat mustache, "is just one of the issues that Jessica Clayton and I had wanted to address today. The FCC bit is just the cherry on top for your devoted audience. My viewers, the young voters, however," I said, leaning down, reaching into my purse, "are really going to take issue with the media monopoly bit. Senator Hewitt couldn't possibly be their president if he was conspiring with Dax Keaton to control the news we watch and the papers we read. We're the crazy kids who believe in freedom." *Plop.* I dropped copies of Guy's confidential memos describing the FCC and Pol24 takeover in front of Wallace's stunned face. "You and the bosses might want to reconsider your plans. And leave your schedule open tomorrow, I think you have a luncheon with the federal prosecutors."

My earpiece emitted a steady stream of "fuck's," one pressed right up against the other, while two young production assistants did a little jig of happiness. One clap, then two. I stood up, yanking my microphone off my blouse, and followed the noise. It was Chef, my one fan, trying to give me a standing ovation. I might not yet be the most popular media personality in Manhattan but I had become my own woman. And, hopefully, I had helped a woman into the White House. I grabbed Chef's hand and we ran out into the Midtown night, counting down the hours until we could hit the polls.

ELECTION NIGHT BITES

Dixie Hummus

Let them eat butter beans! I'm egalitarian and nonpartisan when it comes to legumes. I love all my beans and peas. We Southerners begin the New Year with black-eyed peas, herald the coming of spring with sugar snap peas and mourn the passing of a crazy uncle with a pinto bean casserole. But I just can't get into chickpeas. You have to mix in a gut-busting amount of tahini or other liquid fat to make them passable. Butter beans are a whole different ball game; they're crazy creamy and have a decadent mouth-feel. Deelish!

SERVES 8, 3 CROSTINI PER PERSON.

- 1 baguette, sliced into rounds
- ½ c. extra virgin olive oil
- 2 15.5-oz. cans unsalted butter beans or *habas grandes**
- 2 medium shallots, chopped
- 1 clove garlic, minced
- 1¼ tsp. kosher salt
- Freshly ground pepper
- 1½ tsp. fresh rosemary, roughly chopped
- 4 tsp. Italian parsley, roughly chopped
- 1 lemon, juiced
- 3 oz. parmigiano reggiano, finely grated

---

*If your canned butter beans come salted, modify the amount of kosher salt you add to the heated bean mixture.

Preheat oven to 300 degrees. Slice baguette horizontally into ¼-inch-thick rounds (do not angle knife when cutting) and place on cookie sheet. Drizzle with olive oil. Toast until crisp, 12–15 minutes.

Open cans of butter beans and strain liquid into a bowl. Reserve the liquid. In a medium-sized skillet over medium heat, pour 4 Tbsp. olive oil and add chopped shallots and minced garlic. Cook until aromatic but no color. Add beans and warm through. Continue by adding 4 Tbsp. of reserved liquid and allow mixture to slightly reduce. Season with salt and pepper to taste. If mixture reduces too much and there is no excess liquid, add one more Tbsp. reserved liquid. Remove from heat.

Transfer all but a half dozen beans to food processor (you will use the reserved beans for garnish). Next, add rosemary, flat leaf parsley, lemon juice and cheese to food processor. Puree beans while pouring the last of the olive oil—approximately 3 Tbsp.—into the blender. Continue to puree until mixture is creamy and smooth. Remove beans to a bowl.

On a large plate, fan toasted baguette rounds around the bowl of Dixie Hummus. Garnish hummus with reserved butter beans and a sprinkling of chopped rosemary and flat leaf parsley. Enjoy the gorgeous and good-for-you nibble!

ELECTION NIGHT BITES

Macaroni & Cheese Arancini

Chef went glam <u>and</u> international with this Election Night Bite. Consider his to be an elegant take on mac & cheese—comfort food at its best.

MAKES 4 DOZEN ARANCINI.

1 16-oz. box small elbow macaroni (size "81")
2 c. heavy whipping cream
8 oz. Cheddar cheese, grated
4 oz. Parmesan cheese, grated
1 tsp. cayenne pepper
1 tsp. paprika
1½ tsp. garlic powder
Kosher salt
Freshly ground black pepper to taste
4 Tbsp. (½ stick) butter
4 c. bread crumbs
½ c. flour
2 eggs
2 Tbsp. water

Bring a large pot of water to a boil. Line two baking sheets with parchment paper. Add the pasta and cook until very tender, about 5–6 minutes. Remove the pasta to a colander and drain. Add the heavy cream to the empty pasta pot and simmer. Whisk in the grated cheeses and cook 5 minutes, until well thickened. Return the cooked pasta to the pot along with the cayenne, paprika and garlic powder. Stir until well combined and cook 3 minutes more, stirring occasionally to ensure nothing sticks. Season to taste with salt and pepper. Spread the mixture into a thin layer on a lined baking sheet and refrigerate for approximately 3 hours, or until thoroughly chilled.

Remove the chilled pasta from the fridge. Scoop large tablespoons of the mixture and, using your hands, roll macaroni into a tight ball. Place macaroni balls, or *arancini,* on another lined baking tray until all of the mixture is rolled and formed. Return to the fridge.

Melt the butter in a large skillet and add the bread crumbs. Cook over medium heat until the bread crumbs are well toasted and golden brown. Transfer immediately to a large bowl. Add flour to another bowl, crack the eggs into a third bowl, whisking them with 2 Tbsp. water.

Arrange the bowls in this order: flour, eggs, bread crumbs.

Working in line, roll the mac and cheese balls in the flour and pat off all of the excess. Next, dip the floured balls into the eggs, remove with a slotted spoon and toss with the bread crumbs. Make sure they are well coated with the bread crumbs and arrange on a baking sheet, making sure they do not touch one another. Bake at 350 for 12 minutes or until heated through. Rest 3 minutes before serving.

Garnish with finely grated Parmesan cheese and a dusting of paprika.

24

"ALL I COULD think about was Paris. . . ."

"Let me get this straight," Lisa said, taking a sip of her morning cappuccino and cognac, "you were being eaten alive by that gasbag on national television and all you could think about was runny Brie and the Pont Neuf?"

Six-thirty A.M. and I had barely been able to pull myself out of Chef's arms (men can be clingy too, you know) and walk next door to Lisa's store. We had promised we'd read the papers together, finding out both the election results and the trash that had been written about me in the conservative rags. I wanted to be done with it and move on.

"I obviously don't fit into the Manhattan media puzzle. Why shouldn't I try across the pond? I want cosmopolitan but I want a slower pace. And it's always better when I don't understand what people are saying."

"Are you sure you don't fit in, honey?" Chef opened the door to Lisa's store and helped Rose up the two steps. His arms were stacked with dozens of newspapers while she carried a bowl covered in plastic wrap. Something delicious was inside, I knew it. My belly rumbled. Now that I didn't have to face the misery of the News Channel, my appetite was back in fine form. Really, all I could think of was food.

"*Cara, piccola* Diane Sawyer," Rose said, kissing my cheeks and settling in next to me.

I turned to Chef. "Did you bribe her with homemade *panettone* to say that?" He shrugged and then smiled, fanning out the papers.

The Prison Cats & The Presidency

Dixie Democrat with the Heart of Gold
Scores For Clayton

Red-State Gasbags Doomed to Orange

Blue-State Belle Saves Election

"What do you think now, hmmm? You're on fire! New York loves you and the country wants to know more about you."

First things first—I grabbed the *Post*. I had to read Cindy Adams's reaction to my broadcast. But it took me a good minute or two to get past the cover shot: Keaton, Cleveland, Wallace, Chase Stephens, Christopher Randolph, Guy, Samantha, Paige and dozens of other ANC employees were in handcuffs, lined up on the front steps of 1221 Avenue of the Americas, "guilty" stamped over their faces.

I flipped to Cindy and feverishly scanned her wit and brilliance. "Lord have mercy!" I jumped up from my seat and almost began doing a jig. "Cindy Adams has extended an open invitation to me to do luncheon at Le Cirque! She wants to write a column on me and Jessica Clayton—the two most influential ladies of 2008!" I just had to make sure I stayed the same girl, none of it rushing to my head like that other Mobile native, Christopher Randolph.

"See? You can't leave us for Paris."

"But I want to cook, I want to clear my head. . . ." I looked to Chef for some sort of support.

"The home cook who becomes a real chef."

"I could go to the Cordon Bleu."

"My Belle at the Cordon Bleu. I like that . . . Belle at the Bleu. . . . We could work side by side."

"Go on, you two," Rose said, unwrapping the bowl and setting out forks, "try the ambrosia—food of the gods."

I bit into the fruit and savored the sweetness. For once, there was no bitter.

And then something, someone whispered in my ear, "Paris . . ."

Ambrosia

Let the sweetness speak to you. . . .

SERVES 4.

 3 navel oranges
 2 c. fresh pineapple chunks
 1 crisp, slightly tart apple, cored, peeled, cubed
 ⅓ c. sweetened coconut flakes
 1 banana
 ½ c. maraschino cherries, drained well

Peel the oranges, being sure to remove all of the bitter, white pith. Section the oranges or slice them horizontally into a medium-sized bowl, retaining all juice. Add pineapple, cubed apple and coconut flakes. Slice the banana and add cherries last.

LIST OF RECIPES

ACKNOWLEDGMENTS

A first book is a very sentimental affair—just like my first years in New York City. I want to thank the people who made these pages, and those years, just a little bit better.

To my mother, who has always given me the unconditional love and support to make my dreams come true. Mom, everything always has been—and always will be—for you. Bill Contardi, my agent, is a man of never-ending patience, sensitivity and joy. One breakfast at Balthazar and I was hooked on you, Bill. You're more than this girl could ever hope or want for in an agent.

My editor, Beth Wareham, is a blessing from above. We came together in a roundabout way and she's kept me laughing ever since. Thank you, my delicious, blond Texan, for allowing me to dream *and* for keeping it real. And Ms. Whitney Frick, second-in-command, you were a delight to work with and an invaluable source of feedback. Thank you for the tough edits and the sweet words.

And I am very grateful to my Thompson and Sullivan Street neighbors for welcoming me, the strange Southern soul, into their world. Susan Saraf, you were my across-the-hall neighbor, my first city friend *and* my first reader. Because of you, wine time on my patio and pages slipped beneath the door became a book! Ellen Loyd De Benedittis, you're a partner-in-crime and a cherished friend. Thank you for bringing so much joy into my life when I was writing this book. And to the rest of the neighborhood (my de facto Yankee family)—Linda Pagan, Peter Mercurio, Mike Robinson, Pino Cinquemani, Rob Kaufelt, Frank, Ro, Robin—I thank you for the mornings, afternoons and cocktail hours of love and amazing fun.